Nightingale Girl

Sparrow Man Series
Book Two

M. R. Pritchard

Nightingale Girl is a work of fiction. Names, characters, places, and incidents either are the product of the author's imagination or are used fictitiously. Any resemblance to actual persons, living or dead; events; or locales is entirely coincidental.

Copyright © 2022, 2023 M. R. Pritchard

All rights reserved. No part of this book may be reproduced or transmitted in any form or by any means whatsoever without express written permission from the author, except in the case of brief quotations embodied in critical articles and reviews. Please refer all pertinent questions to the publisher. All rights reserved. No part of this book may be reproduced or transmitted in any form or by any means, electronic or mechanical, including photocopying, recording, or by an information storage and retrieval system—except by a reviewer who may quote brief passages in a review to be printed in a magazine or newspaper— without permission in writing from the publisher.

Second Edition 2022/2023
Paperback ISBN:978-1-957709-31-4

Sometimes following your heart
means losing your mind.
—Anonymous

Twisted Paradise

Restlessness prickles under my skin. It feels like one of those never-ending winter days when breathing kerosene heater fumes for hours on end starts getting on your last nerve. It's sad, really; all it took was one week for me to go trailer park crazy. I'm edgy and antsy. And to make it worse, Sparrow vowed to respect King Gabriel's wishes regarding sins of the flesh. That's what I get for swearing never to leave the Seven Kingdoms of Heaven.

"You know, if you focused on other things instead of what Sparrow's got hiding in his pants, you'd be doing this better." Teari's chipper voice breaks my concentration.

The gentle brush of her fingers flutters across the skin of my shoulders. I turn quick to face her. "Don't touch me," I warn.

She holds her hands out as though she were thinking about doing it again. "Wouldn't dream of it." She smiles sweetly.

"You're not supposed to be able to lie." I glare.

"I didn't lie, Meg. I just said I wouldn't dream of it. Because I wouldn't. You rarely enter my dreams."

I run to the mirror on the far end of the dining room to see what she did.

"Teari!" I yell when I see that my hair is three inches longer.

"What?" She shrugs and sits on a velvet-upholstered club chair, crosses her long legs, and admires her fingernails.

"I told you to stop doing that!" I pull my shirt up and check my skin. The tattoos are still there. The spattering of stars is still across my left shoulder, the anchor still on my rib cage. I pull out the waistband of my pants and check the heart—it's still there. Thank God. I pull the shoulder of my shirt down and check the tattoo of the black quill across my right collarbone. Disappointment hits me hard. It's faded.

"That is his favorite one!" I turn to Teari and clench my hands into fists. "You know how Sparrow likes feathers."

Teari stands quickly, her skin blanching when she gets a good look at how angry I am. "You're supposed to look like a princess."

"I don't give a crap what your fluttery Angel princesses are supposed to look like. Stop trying to change me." I grit my teeth and hold in a long stream of curse words. I don't care if the Archangel Gabriel is my father. I'm not going to pretend to be one of their princesses. He said he liked my spunk. It reminded him of my mother.

"I can't get this fixed up here in *Angel-land*. And I promised on Sparrow's life not to leave."

I would love to strangle Teari right now. I don't care if she towers a foot above my head. I think my hands would wrap nicely around her neck.

Teari fidgets with the waistband of her slacks. She looks like a damn supermodel standing in front of me. I want to claw her eyes out.

"It's fine," she says.

"It's not fine. It's faded!" I walk toward her, ready to attack. I point to my shoulder where the quill tattoo is. "And it's his favorite."

Teari steps back, her eyes widening. "I helped you," she reminds me. "When you were in Hell, I healed you. I made you whole again." Her perfect face begins to look worried.

True, she did heal me. Teari came to help me and Sparrow when we were trapped together in Hell. She healed my wounds after my a-hole of an ex strung me up like a turkey and stabbed me in the chest with a knife.

While strangling Teari might help me feel better, it would leave my father without his personal healer. I cross the room to get away from her.

"Stop screwing with my tattoos and hair," I warn her.

A few moments pass before I come to the conclusion that causing Teari physical harm is unladylike—something Sparrow's always nagging me about. I weave around her and leave the room, slamming the door closed behind me.

They want me to be on my best behavior here, but Teari is making it awfully difficult.

I walk down lengthy hallways with towering windows that let in the bright, heavenly light of this place. Shielding my eyes, I wish I had brought my sunglasses with me. I avoid the sunlit expanses and walk in the shadows along the wall. It's not long before I'm standing at the door to my room.

There's a plush mattress on a frame, a bathroom with a tub and shower, fluffy towels, clean sheets, fresh pillows, a balcony, and a closet full of clothing. None of this ever existed in the single-wide trailer I grew up in. I came close when I spent my inheritance on that little house with a white picket fence. Tried to pull my roots out of the North Country gutter, but while it seemed money could buy me a home, it couldn't hide me from my demons.

I open my door and step into my room. A warm breeze billows the curtains of the floor-to-ceiling windows. The golden linens on the giant four-poster are not the crumpled mess that I had left them in earlier. I look around and notice that my towel is no longer on the floor by the bathroom, either. Teari must've sent someone in here to clean up.

I walk past the bed and grab my sunglasses off the table in the sitting area. It's so bright here that it hurts my eyes, gives me a headache. Trying to control the darkness within me is hard enough; I can't stand constantly being illuminated by the sunshine of Heaven, as well. Even if it does sparkle prettily. Daylight hurts Hell-dark adjusted eyes.

I reach for the small machete-style weapon on my nightstand. Forged in the fires of Hell, it only cuts if I'm the one holding it. Lucifer gifted it to me after I delivered him the bag of bones that was my mother. He also promised me one favor that I have yet to use.

My thoughts turn to Sparrow and our time together down there.

Sparrow's an Angel, tall and handsome and a little peculiar. He's better than he used to be. When we were trapped in Hell, he was batshit crazy. The poor guy was nothing but a cracked nut when we found each other. We can blame my father for that, though. He banished Sparrow, stripping his wings and taking his memories, leaving him to wander the zombie-strewn wasteland of Hell. As fate would have it, that's where we found each other.

Sometimes I think that Sparrow is the best thing that's ever happened to me. Better than finding out what I truly was: more than North Country trash, the daughter of an Archangel, the child of forbidden love.

I secure the weapon in the thigh holster Sparrow made for me and put my sunglasses on. Leaving my room, I make my way to the door leading to the courtyard at the end of the hall. As soon as I step outside, my skin sizzles. It's bearable, almost.

I wonder if the sun is like this in the other Kingdoms of Heaven? Teari is supposed to teach me about them, but she's too busy working with the Legion, being my father's personal healer, and trying her damnedest to turn me into a princess. I've learned a few things, though: The earthen plane is God's land. The Seven Kingdoms of Heaven are ruled over by the Council of Seven Archangels. Hell has Lucifer.

I make my way past the sparkling stone fountain and down the marble steps set into the hillside. I stroll past the barracks where the Legion trains; the grounds are empty. They must be on break, which means Sparrow will be home. Good, I haven't gotten him alone in a few days. I pick up speed and head for the trail behind the barracks.

Thick forest shades the winding path to Sparrow's house. Having finally escaped the sun, I take off my sunglasses and hang them on the front of my shirt. Windows and doors close at the houses as I pass. There are some inhabitants of this place who are not happy about my presence here. They don't like the idea of me tainting their *goodness*. I am the blackened stain of my father's Kingdom.

My mother birthed me on the earthen plane. I am half darkness and half light; my soul doesn't know where it belongs, and because of this I can *poof* between realms at will. All I have to do is whisper the words *"Angele Dei, illumina, custodi, rege et guberna,"* and I'm gone, traveling faster than you can blink. Everyone else has to use the governed portals.

People here don't like that. They don't like my darkness, my foul mouth, or the fact that I'm with Sparrow. There are whispers and disapproving stares. It's like I'm back in my tiny hometown of Gouverneur, New York. Everyone watching. Nobody saying a word.

Screw them, I tell myself. They don't know the literal hell we went through.

I step up onto Sparrow's stoop, my hand hovering over the doorknob. I lean closer and listen. "Livin' on a Prayer" is blaring. I smile. Sparrow loves Bon Jovi. I turn the knob and inch the door open until I can squeeze inside without making a sound. The music is so loud that when I close the door I can't even hear the lock click into place. I move toward the living room and find Sparrow rocking out.

Sparrow is standing in front of the stereo. He turns the music louder, his head bobbing to the beat, his shoulders ticking along, as well. His entire body is in motion. And just as the chorus starts, he spins and rips his shirt off.

I freeze, taking in the scene of Sparrow in full Bon Jovi impersonation mode. It's a beautiful sight. His white wings are tucked tight against his back, and the muscles of his broad shoulders tense as he dances and sings. His narrow hips thrust from side to side with the beat. He kicks his boots off, sends them flying across the room, and then runs to collect them like it was choreographed, bellowing out lyrics the entire time. Sparrow sets the boots side by side near the back door of his house. Next, his socks come off, followed by his Legion-issued black cargo pants, leaving him in nothing but a pair of boxer briefs.

My jaw drops, and my trailer park roots quiver. This is better than the strip club I went to in college. The Thunder from Down Under has got nothing on Sparrow.

Sparrow spins, stomps his feet, then looks up. His eyes lock with mine, and a wide grin spreads across his handsome face. He spins again and turns the music down.

"You didn't have to do that," I say. "I was enjoying myself."

"Bet you were." Sparrow's brown hair is tousled, and dimples appear in each of his cheeks as he smiles. Bright green eyes take me in. "What's different about you?" he asks, taking a step toward me.

"Nothing," I lie.

"Something." He reaches out and touches my hair. "It's longer."

"Teari was getting a little handsy." I shake my head, and my hair tickles my shoulders. It used to be long; trouble changed that. Remembering what happened last time I had long hair makes my stomach churn.

Sparrow frowns, like he's read my mind. He knows I don't like being touched—suffered far too much pain at the hands of others. Now I trust no one and allow even fewer to touch my skin. I trust Sparrow enough, though. Trust him with my life. He's saved it enough times.

"Can you fix it?" I ask.

Sparrow's fingers linger in my dark hair for just a moment too long. No doubt he's remembering the haircut he gave me with his machete.

"Just let me jump in the shower quick, and then I'll do it."

I look up at him. "No."

He presses his lips together. "You can't join me." His fingers leave my hair and trail down the side of my neck. I tilt my head and give him access to the collar of my shirt, knowing that he's going for that quill tattoo on my collarbone.

Sparrow frowns. "It's pale."

"Teari did it." I pull away from him and walk across the room. "I'm going to punch her in the throat one of these days. And since I am forbidden from going to the earthen plane, I can't even get this fixed." I motion to the tattoo. "Pisses me off to no end."

Sparrow puts his hands on his hips and watches me. "It's going to be okay," he says.

I begin to pace. "I'm going stir-crazy here."

"It's only been a few weeks."

"I know. I just . . . I just feel . . ." I look at Sparrow and find him watching me intently. I can't tell him what I feel. Darkness. My grandfather's darkness is threatening to overtake me. I can't tell Sparrow my soul is about to burst, the dark wanting out. When I was a kid, I could burn it off by doing bad shit like stealing, drinking, partying, et cetera. I'm not allowed to do any of that here.

I try to shake it off.

"Just go shower," I tell Sparrow. "I need you to take care of this for me." I motion to the mess Teari created on my head.

He collects his clothes and heads for the bathroom.

Damn, I wish he had finished his striptease.

I cross my arms and turn away from the hall he just walked down. Controlling the urge to follow him is hard. I guess I'll have to entertain myself.

I've never been alone in Sparrow's house before. I snoop around a bit. The place is small but tidy, with stone walls, large windows, and dark leather furniture. There's a deck attached to the back of the house with an amazing view of the sloping forest.

I make my way to the bookshelf behind the couch. The shelves are lined with leather-bound hardbacks. I tilt my head to the side and read the titles on the spines: *Birds of Paradise*, *Birds of the Arctic*, *Birds of the Northern Plains*, *Birds of the Pacific Northwest*. They go on and on, rows and rows of books about birds.

This doesn't surprise me much. I mean, when we were in Hell, Sparrow got a hard-on over every feather we came across—dragged me all over the place collecting hundreds of them. But he never mentioned being infatuated with them before becoming a fallen Angel.

I select *Birds of Paradise* and begin flipping through. There are a hundred different species in here highlighted with full-color pictures. I recognize a few of the parrots we saw at the zoo. Images of their limp bodies on the ground and Sparrow crouching down to pull out their feathers flood my mind. One memory leads to the next, and soon I am staring off into space, remembering the first time I saw him dressed in an old trench coat in Noah's cellar. Sparrow was taller than any man I'd ever met, and his eyes were so green and intense.

Suddenly Sparrow is standing next to me. He's dressed, hair damp, smelling fresh from the shower.

"What are you doing?" he asks as I flip the book closed.

"Just looking." I run my fingers over the textured spine of *Birds of Paradise*.

Sparrow takes the book out of my hand and flips a few pages. "That bird." He points to a smooth brown bird with a sharp pointed beak. "It's my favorite. This week."

"Why that one?"

"The beak reminds me of a macadamia nut shell. The smoothness and angles."

He sounds like a hippie artist from New York City. I have no idea how to respond to that.

"Why do you have all these books?" I ask.

"I like birds."

"You like feathers."

Sparrow smiles as he returns *Birds of Paradise* to the shelf. He runs his finger down the spine, ensuring that it is in the exact place it was before I touched it.

I want him to touch me like that. Now. Courting phase be damned. I'm tired of following the rules up here. I want to do what I want just for once. I want—

Sparrow turns to face me, gripping his machete in his left hand. "Haircut?"

Well, there go those feelings.

We step out to his back deck. I turn around, and Sparrow collects my hair in his fist. I feel the cool, dull edge of his machete against the back of my neck right before he swipes and cuts.

I turn. He's holding my black hair in his fist, looking indecisive.

"You going to give it to the birds?" I ask.

Sparrow smiles quick before arching his arm over the deck and throwing the handful of hair into the branches of a nearby tree. Then he just stands there, watching me.

I take a step closer to him. Then another. And another.

"I want you," Sparrow whispers. "It's killing me."

Yes. I'll teach him to be bad to the bone in no time at all. I run a few quick steps and launch myself into his arms. Sparrow's hands catch my ass, and my arms wrap around his neck, and then we're kissing like two high schoolers under the bleachers on a Friday night.

He sets me down on the railing of the deck so his hands are free to roam. In the weeks we've been here, this is the most he's touched me. I've missed it. I've missed all the time we had to ourselves in Hell, even if we were being chased by the dead.

The minutes that pass are not long enough before Sparrow pulls away. He's out of breath.

"I promised your father." Sparrow backs away from me, as though I'm poisonous. "Gabriel can see everything in his Kingdom," he reminds me.

I frown and slide off the deck railing so I'm standing in front of him.

"We need to work off this angst." Sparrow runs his hands through his hair. "Want me to teach you how to fight?"

"I can fight. I took on Jim and seven Hellions when they invaded my house on the earthen plane," I remind him.

In the end they put me in a coma, but that didn't stop me from filling their bodies full of bullets. Unbeknownst to me at the time, I was engaged to the son of a powerful Demon. Jim and his Hellions killed my unborn baby and tried to kill me for a boatload of cash.

Sparrow's face blanches. "I don't like it when you talk about that."

Sparrow feels guilty. He thinks it's his fault. If he hadn't lost me, none of that would have happened. If Sparrow had kept his post all those years ago, my mother wouldn't have been killed, and a very bad man wouldn't have raised me. Sparrow couldn't help it; he had his reasons, no matter how fucked up they seem.

I should apologize for bringing it up. But I rarely apologize, unless it's for something really, really bad.

"Fight with your hands." Sparrow's holding his palms up.

I guess he's stuck on this. I'll humor him.

"Usually I pull their hair and scratch their face. That's how chicks fight," I reply.

Not that I was in many fights. John Lewis was too busy knocking me around for me to get into a fight with someone else. He killed my mother for her money, but the money was wrapped up in a trust fund. All he got was me in return, and he made me pay for it every day of my life.

Sparrow nods to the machete strapped to my thigh. "Let me show you how to use that."

I know how to use the weapon. Heck, it pretty much does everything itself. All I have to do is touch it, and the piece of metal comes alive in my hand.

"Don't you have to go back and train with the Legion?" I ask.

Sparrow shakes his head, and his body stiffens. "Done for today."

I touch the weapon on my thigh. "I know how to use it," I assure him.

"Let me see it, Meg." Sparrow holds his hand out. This isn't the first time he's asked to touch it. I'm starting to think he's a little obsessed.

I shake my head. I know what he wants. I know what I want. I decide to toy with him a bit. I like to watch him get frustrated.

"What do you want?" I ask, reaching for the hem of my shirt. It's printed with swirls and petals, pink and soft and flouncy. Teari picked it out for me when she overhauled my wardrobe. She said there was too much black in there and too much skin showing. Now everything is loose and long, real princesslike. I hate it all. I'd much rather have jeans or shorts and a drawerful of T-shirts.

"Come on," Sparrow urges. "I want to see it again."

I pull my shirt up, flashing my midriff; then ever so slowly, I drag the shirt higher.

"No. Not that." His eyes are glued to the weapon strapped to my thigh. "The blade."

I make a noise of disgust in my throat and say, "Seriously? This is worse than you and those damn feathers." I drop my shirt and let it cover me again.

"Come on, Meg. Please?" As he steps toward me, I straighten my back, trying to seem taller. Sparrow measures in at six and a half feet. Gabriel at seven. Angels are giants.

"Okay," I say, trying to force my lips to stop grinning.

"Okay?" His eyes open wider with anticipation.

He used to make expressions like this all the time. Thinking about those moments makes me a bit sad. He's different now, a lot less crazy but still a little quirky. At times the old Sparrow shines through, like when he asks to see my weapon, and it's a total turn on. That's the Sparrow I fell in love with. That's the Sparrow who saved my life a bunch of times. The Sparrow I never want to forget.

"Now?" he asks.

"Sure." I close the space between us, reach up on my toes, snake my hand up his chest and across the back of his neck so I can pull him closer and whisper in his ear. "After you do one thing." I flick my tongue across his earlobe and feel every muscle in his body stiffen. "Take me to your bedroom and let's do some dirty, dirty things together for a few hours. And then I'll let you touch my blade all you want." I step away.

Sparrow's eyes reveal a mischievous glint. He lunges for me, but I'm quick to move and duck out of his way. I spin and run, then leap off his deck and round the side of his house, laughing.

Sparrow follows. I hear his footsteps behind me, and I'm surprised he hasn't caught me yet; his legs are longer than mine. He's holding back—must be enjoying the chase.

I round the front corner of his house, looking back for just a split second to make sure he's there. He is. When I look forward again, there is a large object in my path. I slam right into it, full force.

Large hands grip my arms and lift my feet off the ground.

"Sparrow!" King Gabriel shouts. "What in the grace of God are you doing?"

I am set on my feet.

"We were just running," I say, out of breath and nervous. I wonder what my father is doing here.

Looking up, I notice Sparrow standing stiffly behind me.

"You were supposed to come see me," Gabriel bellows. "Mother of God, boy! This is what I'm talking about." He steps forward and grips Sparrow's shoulder with his giant hand. "Come with me now. Let's go."

With the powerful thrust of their downy white wings, King Gabriel and Sparrow take off into the sky, leaving me alone.

I hate it when they fly. Especially since I can't. I don't have wings. Gabriel says they will come when I'm ready—that I lack faith in God and in myself.

He's right, though; I don't believe in a God who would allow the horrible things that happened to me. If there's anything I have faith in, it's how bad shit can get. I hold the most faith in Hell.

...

"The Legion won't take him back." Gabriel shakes his head and looks away.

Sparrow left hours ago and never came to find me afterward. I came to the king to find out what happened between the two of them. Sparrow never mentioned any problems, but something is definitely going on.

"What the hell do you mean they won't take him back?" I ask Gabriel. "You're the king. Tell them to take him back."

"Can't just toss him back to being Legion Commander." Gabriel throws his hands in the air in frustration. "Fucking figures. Was probably those asshole Council members."

Gabriel and I resemble each other. We have blue eyes, black hair, and filthy mouths. The only difference is he can get away with all the cussing.

The Council holds every curse word against me. They hate my guts. Gabriel warned me when I first came here. He said, *"Been watching you for a while now. You'll do good here. Don't think the Council will like your attitude, though."*

Boy, was he right.

"Bet they planned this," Gabriel continues. "Always had a problem with me taking in their strays."

"Their strays?" I ask. "What's that mean?"

Gabriel's mouth snaps shut, and his eyes level on me. "He's not like we remember."

"He's more put together than when I ran into him in the bowels of Hell. He was flat out nuts when I met him."

"You didn't know him before." Teari appears in the room. I didn't even hear her come in. "He's very different from what he used to be. I've seen him in training. It's not safe. He could hurt himself or the others. There's something wrong that we can't fix here. Believe me, I've tried."

She's tried? The thought of Teari alone with Sparrow makes my blood boil. I caught her with her lips on him when I first arrived in Gabriel's Kingdom. And while she apologized, I still don't trust her. My father forbade her from going near Sparrow with romantic intentions ever again.

"What's wrong with him?" I ask.

Gabriel and Teari look at each other, avoiding the answer.

They're hiding something.

"Tell me!"

"Go ask him." Gabriel waves toward the door. "He needs to tell you. The Council forbids *me* from revealing some things. I can't say it, but he can. Go."

I look at both of them with disgust before turning and running out of the room. The Council forbids it? Bullshit.

I search everywhere for Sparrow: his house, my room, the pool, the closets, the kitchen—because he's always shoving his face full of food. I walk my father's land until my feet hurt. If I had wings, I could just fly everywhere real quick, but I have to walk, and traipsing across Gabriel's Kingdom is a royal pain in my ass.

It's night by the time I finally find Sparrow. He's sitting in the middle of the barracks alone. I move toward him, wanting to take him in my arms and figure out what the heck is going on. I've never wanted to do that before. I was never touchy-feely, but something about Sparrow draws it out of me.

"What happened?" I ask.

Sparrow wraps his arms tight around my middle and buries his face in my abdomen.

I push my fingers into his silky hair.

"Gabriel says I can't do it."

My clothing muffles his words.

"Why?" I ask.

"Seems he scrambled my brains a bit beyond repair."

"But he fixed you."

Gabriel gifted Sparrow back his memories when Sparrow found me in Hell. He brought him back to life. Gave his soul back to his body. Gave him back his house and belongings in Heaven. Sparrow paid his dues; he was *forgiven*.

"He can't fix me all the way. They said something isn't right. It's . . ." His voice trails.

I don't like seeing him like this. I want to fix him, fix this, *poof* him away from here, and make it all better.

I swore to Gabriel on Sparrow's life that I wouldn't leave. But I'm developing the strong urge to pack my shit and run away, just like I did when I finally got the nerve to ditch my small town and head off to college.

My head is spinning. Deciding between what's right and wrong in this moment is frustratingly hard. I made a promise to an Archangel, to my father, but I'd break it in a heartbeat to help Sparrow.

One thing worries me, though. My mother, Clea. She gifted us a feather. And her feathers revealed a dire future after we left Hell: *Wars. Blood and death. Good and Evil. A dead Sparrow. A motherless child and a fatherless child. Light and dark. The earthen plane and the ethereal realms. A burst of bright light. A dark, never-ending vat of emptiness that would suck every joyful moment right out of me.*

I shudder at remembering the way I felt when the vision thundered through me. I'd never felt so empty.

This staying within the Seven Kingdoms of Heaven blows.

"Let's skip town. Me and you," I offer. "I'll take you somewhere, and we can forget about all of this. We don't need them,

Sparrow." I tug on his hair at the base of his skull, tilting his face up. "We can go bird-watching on the earthen plane. Whatever you want."

"And if I die?" he asks. "Your mother's feather revealed blood and death."

"We could make it work. Somehow. The king of Hell owes me one favor."

"You would risk my life on the word of a liar?"

"I'm a liar. I've lied." I release Sparrow's hair and try to step away from him, but he holds me tight around my middle. He knows I'm not pureblood Angel. I am part darkness. I can lie like the greatest of sinners.

"That's not what I meant." He lets go of me and stands. His green eyes shimmer and soften.

It breaks me a tiny bit when he gets that sad, faraway look in his eyes. I want to pull him to me, hold him and kiss him, and . . . and . . .

"How many times do I have to die for you, Meg?" Sparrow asks.

"I don't want you to die for me. I never asked you to die for me."

In one swift movement he grips my chin between his fingers, snakes his free arm around my back, and pulls me tight against his body.

"That's what makes it worth it. You not asking. I do it because I love you. I've loved you longer than you've known I existed." Sparrow kisses me. He's so intense. Always been this way.

Sparrow pulls away and rests his forehead against mine, inhaling deeply. "I should go."

I grip his arms. "Where?" I can't stand the thought of him leaving me behind.

"I have to go away. Fix this mess."

"Don't leave me here. Take me with you." I search his eyes, begging. I'm not below begging. It's worked for me in the past. I promised to stay within the Seven Kingdoms of Heaven, but I'm not staying in Gabriel's Kingdom alone.

There is a long pause, an internal struggle for him.

"I have to return to my father's Kingdom," he finally says.

"Your father?" I never wondered about where Sparrow came from or who his father is.

"Yes."

"Who is that?" I ask.

He's so nonchalant when he says, "Remiel. Another one of the Archangels."

Oh shit.

Sparrow isn't just some Legion Commander thrust off his perch; he's a frigging prince. No wonder the Council won't allow Gabriel to tell me crap about Sparrow.

Angels are Assholes

The realm of Heaven is immense, divided up into Seven Kingdoms. It's neither flat nor round; according to Sparrow, it just *is*.

We drive for a day in a Cadillac Escalade provided by Gabriel. Sparrow's wearing his Legion garb: black cargo pants, boots, and a fitted shirt. I try to imagine him in something different, something more princelike—maybe a suit or a tuxedo or a sparkling white robe—but I can't. I've only seen him in jeans and a trench coat buttoned up to his neck, or the Legion attire. Watching him now, the way he drives with his back so straight and his left elbow resting on the door, I think he'd look nice in jeans and a fitted T-shirt, or khakis and a button-down. What do the princes of Heaven wear? If it's anything like the crap Teari packed my suitcase with, I feel sorry for him. I feel even sorrier for me.

Sparrow drives down an oak tree–lined road before stopping in front of a stone building. I think it's a castle, but this building is much smaller than my father's. I haven't thought much about how castle size relates to each Kingdom, but judging on the size of this one, I'd say Gabriel is winning at something.

After we get out of the SUV, Sparrow takes my hand and leads me around the vehicle.

A tall man greets us at the bottom of the steps that lead to the front door. He has Sparrow's green eyes and sandy-brown hair. The Archangel in front of us is just as handsome as his son and needs no introduction. This is Remiel, Sparrow's father.

"Sparrow." Remiel nods. "Welcome home, son."

"Father." Sparrow shifts on his feet, and there's an assload of uncomfortable silence that goes on and on and on.

Remiel doesn't acknowledge that I'm standing next to Sparrow. I shrug his rudeness off, put my sunglasses on, and take a look around. It seems brighter here—and hotter. The sun bakes me and it's unexpectedly unbearable. It's so friggin' hot that I want to peel these stupid princess clothes off and run around in a pair of short shorts, flip-flops, and a skintight tank top. But, sadly, there are no Walmarts for me to shop at within the Seven Kingdoms of Heaven. Damn.

"I've come for answers," Sparrow finally says.

"Later." Remiel pats him on the shoulder. "Your room is waiting. Get settled. We'll talk after dinner."

Sparrow grabs our suitcases from the Cadillac. I start to follow him as he heads for his father's castle.

"You." Remiel points at me.

I freeze.

"Do not share a room with my son." He looks to Sparrow. "Still in the courting phase."

Sparrow nods.

When I think of *courting*, I think of long nights, necking at the drive-in, and picnic dinners in a field—one without cow patties to worry about. Nothing close to that has been happening in my life lately.

"You will reside in a different room." I open my mouth to say something, but Remiel scowls so hard that I snap it shut. "Someone will show you to it." His eyes narrow on me, and for an instant I feel like nothing but a feather on the wind. "I know your kind. Keep your sins to yourself and don't involve my son in them."

I think I'm supposed to say thank you or curtsy, but all I want to do is give this man the middle finger.

A woman in a blue dress walks toward us. She greets me with "You must be Meg. I'll show you to your room."

I turn to leave, but Sparrow grabs my hand. "I'll come find you. Let me just talk to him first." He reaches behind his back and plucks a feather out of his wings, then holds it out.

I take it.

"Promise?" I ask.

"Promise." He smiles.

I remind him, "A promise is a promise."

"I know." Sparrow squeezes my hand and passes me my bag before launching himself into the air, flying toward the upper balconies of the castle with Remiel by his side.

Well, that was disappointing. Like most of my time in Heaven.

The woman in blue looks me over. "You've no wings."

"No." I tuck the feather into my pocket.

"I guess we'll walk." She sounds completely repulsed by me already.

I follow her around the back of the castle to a door on the lowest level. It's like one of those houses built into a hillside with a garage underneath. That's what this place reminds me of.

And it's smaller than my father's castle. I'm not sure what that says about Remiel, but I'm definitely judging him.

The woman in blue leads me down a stone hallway. The walls are damp and mossy—the floor, as well. The woman stops at a door and pushes it open with one finger as though it is covered in filth.

"Your quarters," she says before leaving through the way that we came. She doesn't wait for my thanks or my no thanks. Guess I'm stuck with this.

I push the open door a little more and walk inside. The room is small and cold. Definitely nothing like my room in Gabriel's Kingdom, but it beats out my old bedroom in the single-wide trailer. At least this room has a bed frame and not just a mattress on the floor. I remove my sunglasses and toss my bag on the bed.

Just as I'm inspecting the bathroom and the closet, a loud shrieking laughter echoes throughout my room and the hallway outside my door.

I turn to find out what the noise is. A dark figure dashes by my room, slamming the door shut as it passes. I reach for the handle and twist. It's locked.

No, no, no, no, no! I hate being locked up. Spent more than enough time behind bars unable to get free. It reminds me of county jail and juvie and the Safe House. I bang on the door with my fist.

"Hey! Hey! Let me out!"

The manic laughter in the hallway continues, but no one opens my door.

...

I pace for hours, ready and waiting to pounce, when the knob finally turns. The door opens, and Sparrow steps into my room.

"What the fuck!" I yell.

He looks shocked. "What?"

"I've been locked in this room for hours. Where were you? You left me here. Of all the crap—"

"I—I didn't know." Sparrow raises his hands in defense.

"Bullshit. Where have you been?"

"Talking with my father."

I stomp out the door, eager to get out of the room where I had been confined.

"Meg. Wait." Sparrow runs after me. "Why are you so angry?"

"You promised." My hands are shaking. "You promised you'd come find me, and you never did. A promise is a promise, Sparrow. You taught me that. Remember?"

"I'm sorry. I was busy." He looks truly remorseful.

We exit through the basement door, out into the light. I quickly step back into the shadows. Why is it so hot here? I ignore the heat and remind myself that I am pissed at Sparrow.

"Busy with what?" I ask, ready to flip my shit again, angered that I can't even have the freedom here to walk in daylight.

"My father." Sparrow tucks his hands into his pockets.

"What did he have to say?" I ask. "Can he help you?"

"It's not that simple." Sparrow is avoiding all eye contact; something's off. He's keeping something from me, and I don't like it. Jim kept things from me, and then he tried to kill me. Sooner or later, Sparrow is going to spill it.

He changes the subject. "Why don't you tell me what happened," he suggests. "Why were you locked in that room?"

"Well, that lady showed me to my room, and when I was looking around, there was this crazy laughter in the hall, and then the door slammed shut. It was locked. I couldn't get out."

Sparrow stiffens.

"What?" I ask.

"That laughter . . . that was Nightingale."

"Who's that?"

"My sister."

"I didn't know you had a sister." I look up at him.

"We don't talk about her." Sparrow presses his lips together. "She's . . . odd."

Well, that's the funniest shit I've heard all day. The pot calling the kettle black and all that.

"What's so odd about her?"

"You'll see." He takes my hand. "Let's go find her."

Sparrow tugs me back into the lower level of the castle, and he starts pushing open doors.

"Night!" he calls into an empty room.

I grab onto his arm, enjoying the way his muscle tenses when I do. I've never touched anyone so freely, and I've never enjoyed anyone's touch as much as I enjoy Sparrow's.

"I thought her name is Nightingale?"

"Nickname," he replies, as he shoves open another door. "Night!"

All the rooms are dark.

"Why is she being kept in the basement?" I ask. "Or . . . is this a dungeon?"

I understand why his father would want to banish me to the basement—to piss me off and cause tension between me and Sparrow—but to keep his own daughter down here is strange.

"My father doesn't know what else to do with her."

Sparrow continues down the hall, opening another door. "Night!" It's empty inside. There's one door left. Sparrow opens it, and we are rewarded with light.

"Nightingale." Sparrow smiles wide at the sight of his sister.

I just stare, trying not to let my mouth gape open.

Nightingale is lying across a bright-pink bedspread on her stomach, wearing a black crop top and tiny red gym shorts with white piping—straight out of the eighties. She turns, pulls the headphones from her ears, and leaps off the bed. She's wearing big clunky roller skates.

"Sparrow!" The girl whistles a melodic trill before skating toward Sparrow, leaping into his arms and hugging him tight.

I guess this family has something with impersonating bird calls. Sparrow did the same when we were in Hell.

For as attractive as Sparrow is, Nightingale is even more beautiful. Her hair is brunette and long, cascading down her back, and her eyes are just as bright and green as Sparrow's.

"Night, this is Meg." Sparrow introduces me.

Nightingale looks at me, then smiles wide. "My father doesn't like you," she announces like a vapid talking Barbie doll head.

"Night!" Sparrow scolds her.

"I'm not surprised." I shrug. "I could tell. I've been treated like that before. This is nothing."

"That's the problem." Sparrow touches my arm. "Apologize to her," he tells Nightingale.

Nightingale tips her head, her mannerisms similar to the inquisitive focus of a seagull. A moment passes. "Only if you take me with you when you leave," Nightingale says to me.

"I'm not going anywhere."

She smiles. "You're going somewhere. Take me with you. I don't like it here."

"I'm not going anywhere," I repeat. I'd like to leave, though. I've only been in Remiel's Kingdom for five minutes, and I don't like it here, either.

"You will," Nightingale replies in a singsong voice as she skates around us in circles. "You will go with him. It's written in the stars." Her arms arc in the air, and she whistles the same light, melodic trill that she greeted Sparrow with; then she's whipping around the room, displaying twists and turns so fast on her skates that it makes me dizzy.

"What is she talking about?" I ask Sparrow.

"Nothing." Sparrow looks agitated. "I'm hungry."

Sparrow is always hungry. So am I.

"Let's go get dinner," he suggests.

Nightingale suddenly stops her cryptic dance. "Oh, I love dinner!" she says, following us out of her room.

Sparrow leads me around the castle. There are paved walkways throughout. Nightingale weaves back and forth on her roller skates, whistling short melodies.

We enter the castle through a patio door and walk through a library and a long hallway, before we reach the massive dining room. There's a large stone table spread with food: meats, cheeses, steaming breads, plates of vegetables, goblets of wine, and sparkling water.

Remiel is already seated at the head of the table, waiting for us. Sparrow sits; I sit next to him. Nightingale skates to the opposite side of the table from us, before stumbling into a chair.

"Hi, Daddy." Nightingale whistles a different trill to greet him.

Remiel closes his eyes and shakes his head, without responding to his daughter.

What a jerk.

Sparrow grips my thigh under the table. I think he means to soothe me, but any time he touches me, dirty thoughts fill my mind. And in that moment, Remiel's high brow rears its ugly head. He scowls at me, then looks at his son. I wonder if he can see everything in his Kingdom like Gabriel can?

He must, because he says, "Her type will leave you in a heartbeat, son. I'm sure you've already been warned of this. She'll forget you faster than you'll forget her, when your time comes."

When his time comes? I have no clue what he's talking about, but I'm so sick of this shit. I stand up, pointing a finger at the man who is supposed to be an Archangel but is actually nothing more than a giant ass.

"How dare you! He is my hallelujah, heroin, and reason to breathe." I've never said hallelujah in all my life, but forcing the words out of my lips feels strangely satisfying.

I glance at Sparrow, whose face is white as snow. Nightingale is smiling like a kid in a candy shop. Seems she's waited a long time for someone to put her father in his place.

Remiel stands. "Out!" he shouts and points to the door. "Get your sinful mouth out of here."

I only said one sentence to the guy—clearly it was the wrong thing to say. The Council is going to lose their shit over this. I guess my highway to heaven is paved in tar and disappointment.

I stomp out of the room, my stomach grumbling the entire way. I wish I had taken my plate of food.

Sparrow doesn't follow. It seems he is either afraid of his

father or completely confused. I vote for both but hold neither against him. Sparrow's having a rough time; if he can't stand up for me in this instance, I'll let it slide. This time. Only this time.

I run out of the castle toward the gardens I saw when we first arrived. Following the dimly lit sidewalk, I find myself standing among roses and daffodils and strange flowers I've never seen before. I slow myself and walk toward the small fountain that's lit up, now that it's dark.

I'm fuming. Seems it doesn't matter if King Gabriel is my father. I'm still mixed-blood. I'm sinful. I'll taint their bloodline. I'm not welcome in this place.

The sounds of a melodic whistle and roller skates sliding over smooth pavement break the night.

Nightingale skates up next to me. "He's a dick," she says, her voice chipper.

"Yup."

"Don't take it personal. He's just mad. And our kind don't trust lightly."

"Heard that before." I cross my arms and control the urge to do something bad, like rip all the blossom heads off the flowers and leave them on Remiel's bedspread. "I hate this."

"We weren't always crazy assholes." Nightingale pushes off and skates around the fountain in a blur. The snow-white feathers of her wings flutter.

"Sure."

I feel myself shutting her out. I can deal with a lot of shit, but I thought this was going to be different. My father is King Gabriel—he welcomed me here with open arms—but it seems, besides Sparrow, he is the only one happy about my presence.

Nightingale skates backward around the fountain. "You should know we are a family of cursed Angels. The only way to fix us is for Sparrow to take his turn as a Hellion. The eldest from each generation is required to do so. Sparrow has been gone a really long time, and now he has to be sent away again. Our father is an angry bastard because he never did his time when he was called. Sparrow hasn't, either. Yet. He strayed to your father's kingdom, but the curse caught up with him. That's why Sparrow's brains are scrambled. That's why mine are, too. It affects all the children—each generation until someone finally goes. Mine and Sparrow's children would be crazier than each of us." Coming to a stop in front of me, Nightingale frowns. "No one will touch me up here. I'm plagued. An aberration."

I swear to God I feel my heartbeat stop. Sparrow can never be a Hellion. Not after what they did to me.

"You look sick," Nightingale says. "You should go find him."

I close my eyes, focus on Sparrow, and—*poof*—I'm out of there.

When I open my eyes again, I'm standing next to Sparrow in some weird war room decorated with maps and strange weapons. Remiel is there, as well, and he doesn't look happy to see me.

"This is no place for your kind," Remiel says. "Blasphemy that you were allowed within the Seven Kingdoms of Heaven in the first place. Council knew better."

Jim's father on the earthen plane didn't like my blood, either. They'll never get my stains out.

King Gabriel was right: these guys are assholes.

Ignoring Remiel, I turn to Sparrow. "A Hellion? A *Hellion*? How could you keep this from me?"

"He is the heir to the throne," Remiel replies before

Sparrow opens his mouth to speak. "He will do his time. *He* will heal this family, and he will not taint it with your mixed blood."

"I didn't ask you," I say.

Remiel looks like he could kill me. "And I didn't invite you to come here. You don't belong. You are darkness, sin, and wickedness."

"Stop," Sparrow tells his father. "I'll do it. I'll set things right. This is my duty."

"Sparrow, you can't," I say.

"I have to." He won't look at me.

The darkness may be calling, beckoning me from the distance between realms, but that is not a place for Sparrow. We barely survived last time we were there.

Remiel starts talking. Going on and on about the Council and pride and—bullshit really.

I take Sparrow's hand.

Poof.

We're in my room in the basement of Remiel's castle.

"I have to go, Meg." Sparrow touches me. I notice this time that his head cocks to the side, just a tiny bit. Almost a nervous tick, if I didn't know better.

"You hid this from me?"

Sparrow nods. "I can't help it now. It was easier to stop before. Control the muscles." He sighs. "I have to fix this." His fingers twitch. "I'll be fine."

"Those are Hellions."

"It will be okay."

"Those are not the boys of summer, Sparrow. These are the Hellions! You know what they did to me."

"I know. I know. And you're bad to the bone. I know what your blood is to them. Rubies and jewels to those who are damned. But you're mine, Meg. And I'm yours. I can tell you're grinding at the bit to get out of here. At least we can go together now."

"I swore on your life I wouldn't leave."

"My life won't be worth much if I don't fix this." His head "tics" to the side, and Sparrow presses his lips together, like he's trying to control it but losing fast. "Our life won't be worth anything. I'll only get worse. Worse than when you found me in Hell, and I had no memories. Teari assured me this is a one-way ticket to madness. If my father had gone, I'd be fine. But he didn't. This rests on my shoulders now. I want a future with you." He steps closer. "It will mean nothing if I'm crazy. I will not let this curse taint our children." His hand falls to my lower abdomen.

I was pregnant once—thought I could never be again—but Teari fixed me.

"I want my sister to have a family, as well."

The door bursts open, and Nightingale glides in.

"They're going to turn him bad, Meg." Her voice sounds haunted. "They're going to turn him into a bad, bad man. He needs it to rule, to know darkness and light. They're going to turn him into a *monster*!"

Nightingale never stops circling on her skates. Faster and faster she goes. It makes me dizzy.

"No," I say. "No. No. No!" I want to scream and cry at the same time.

"Night, stop it!" Sparrow shouts.

"You already have it, Meg. You teeter on the fringes. But Sparrow has only known good and honor. Our kind must learn or suffer the consequences." Nightingale stops in front of me. "Let him go, Meg. Let him fulfill his destiny."

"I can't have Sparrow turn into one of them. It's my worst nightmare."

Nightingale cocks her head to the side and studies me for a moment. "Take me with you."

"No."

"Well then, he's your monster now," Nightingale replies. She whistles a light melodic trill before skating out of the room.

"How much time do you have?" I ask Sparrow.

"I'm not sure."

"Hours, days, weeks?"

He shrugs. "A few days at least. I already agreed to it. They'll call on me when one of their Hellions dies, and I'll take its place."

I strip off my stupid princess clothing and throw on my last pair of tight jeans and a wide-necked T-shirt. I've kept this outfit folded up under my mattress in my father's Kingdom, waiting for the perfect time. This is as good a time as any to shed my fake Angel skin.

Sparrow's eyes widen in surprise at seeing me in my old clothes. I grab my bag and turn to Sparrow. He's still wearing his Legion issue garb. It will have to do for now.

"Okay." I take his hand. "We're going to get away. *Angele Dei, illumina, custodi, rege et guberna.*"

"Meg—"

Poof.

A Dollar and a Daydream

We're back on the earthen plane, standing on a sidewalk outside a thrift shop.

Gabriel is going to be pissed.

"What do we do now?" Sparrow asks after looking around.

I turn to face him, surprised that I can no longer see his wings. I almost forgot they aren't visible here. Angels and Demons, their wings and horns and scales aren't noticeable on the earthen plane.

"We need a car."

"But you can *poof* us anywhere," Sparrow points out.

If these are the last days of us together, of him knowing me and me knowing him, then I want to savor them.

"I have to conserve my energy in case I need to *poof* us in an emergency."

"Okay." He smiles, believing me.

God, I'm so selfish.

"We need wheels." I look him over. "And you need something else to wear. You look like Black Ops in that getup."

Sparrow tips his head to the side and turns just slightly, like he's listening to something.

"Wait here." He spins, runs down the street, and turns the corner.

Where the heck did he just go? I wait on the sidewalk alone. A few people pass, eyeing me skeptically. I shiver as a cool breeze blows. I wish I had a coat. I adjust my bag on my shoulder.

Finally, an eggplant-purple van rounds the corner. It's a Dodge Caravan, straight from 1999. Sparrow's driving and going about seven miles per hour. He has no idea how many guys at the trailer park drove one of these suckers. All it needs is a light bar and a volunteer firefighter sticker across the back, and I'd swear we were standing on a dirt road in upstate New York.

I smile as Sparrow gets out and walks toward me. He changed his clothes—must've gotten them from the thrift shop or the garbage bin or, heck, maybe they were in the back of the van. He's wearing jeans with a matching jean vest. And he looks really good. Like, Bon Jovi good. But people are going to stare. I wanted to keep a low profile in case we run into any Angels or Demons who have escaped their realm.

"You can't wear that," I say.

"Why?"

"I mean, you look spectacular. Like you walked out of a music video from 1985, but you can't go walking around in a Canadian tuxedo."

Sparrow's eyebrow tips up. "Canadian tuxedo?"

"Yeah."

"Sweet." He smiles and smooths his hands over the denim fabric.

I bite my lip and stare a little longer. Who cares? He looks hot.

"Wear it. But I'm driving," I warn.

I've already experienced a time when Sparrow couldn't remember how to drive. With his mind fading, I don't want to be the passenger when it all goes to shit and he forgets what the brake pedal does.

Sparrow sits in the passenger side and clicks his seat belt on. He reaches out and touches the dashboard. "We don't have these things in Heaven."

"Minivans?" I ask.

Sparrow shakes his head.

Of course not. I don't think Cadillac ever made a minivan.

I motion to the back of the van. "We could fit, like, six kids back there."

Sparrow turns, focused on something in the backseat.

"What?" I ask.

He reaches behind me and comes back with a pale-orange feather duster. From the glint in his eye I can tell he's enamored with the thing. Maybe this feather obsession is never going to go away. It's kind of cute—and fucked up.

"It's a feather duster, birdboy."

Sparrow looks at me quick before running his long fingers through the column of feathers.

"For cleaning."

"Tragic." He brushes the duster across his face. "It's really soft."

I know what he's thinking: he could put those suckers in his pocket and stroke them all day long.

I wish he'd put me in his pocket.

Sparrow touches the feather duster again.

I put my seat belt on.

"Did you steal this van?" I ask, settling my hands on the steering wheel.

"It was running. I didn't break anything," he replies innocently.

Perfect.

"I need to get my tattoo fixed." I point to the quill on my shoulder that was faded by Teari and her healing. I know just the place.

"Ready?"

Sparrow's eyes lock on the ink, and he licks his lips. "Sure." His head "tics" to the left.

My heart sinks.

I pull away from the curb, focusing on the road and not my slowly deteriorating Sparrow.

Doing whatever we want here should be easy. I have loads of money on the earthen plane. My mother left me millions before John Lewis murdered her. He tried to murder me, as well, right before I turned twenty-five and the lump sum was due to be handed over to me. Jim, my ex-fiancé, was in on it, too. The jerks.

Deciding on a place to go, I know that I don't want to go back to Gouverneur: too many bad memories, too many people I don't trust. So I get on the highway and head for the little town where I went to college in downstate New York.

Sparrow fondles the feather duster the entire way. It makes me a little jealous. Living the past week in a chastity belt has been killing me, especially with Sparrow being dangled like a steak in front of me the entire time. Heaven was the worst case of torture—look but don't touch.

At least the food was good.

After we pull into town, I park around the corner from the tattoo shop.

"Come on." I motion for Sparrow to get out and follow me.

He holds my hand as we walk down the sidewalk to the shop entrance. A bell jingles as we walk inside.

"Help you?" the guy behind the counter asks.

"Yeah. I need to get this ink fixed." I pull the neck of my shirt out and show him the faded quill.

The guy's eyes flick to the tattoo and then to Sparrow. "Slow day here. College kids are on break. Can fix it now."

"Perfect."

I follow the guy behind the counter. Sparrow stands in the waiting area, looking at framed pictures of tattoos on the wall.

The guy shows me to a seat, then preps my skin and his workspace. Thankfully, the neck of my shirt is wide enough that I don't have to take it off.

The guy begins darkening the quill across my collarbone. The pinching feeling, sharp at first, lessens gradually, as I watch Sparrow study the pictures on the wall. When he finally turns to me, his eyes zero in on the tattoo. I check the mirror and see how much darker it is; looks like Teari never messed with it in the first place.

Sparrow's hand moves to his pocket, and I'd bet money he has one of the feathers from the duster in there.

I wink at him.

He smiles.

The world stops spinning.

"All done." The tattoo guy starts cleaning up.

I inspect the quill in the mirror again. "Much better."

I pay the man with my bank card, and then we leave the shop and head toward the minivan.

After we're buckled in, I turn to Sparrow and ask, "Does it look better?"

As he nods and blinks, I am reminded of the day we slept on an outcropping of rock to avoid the walking dead of Hell. Sparrow was scouting below us; his long lashes brushed his cheeks as he blinked, and his hair curled at the nape of his neck. I thought, *A crazy man shouldn't have those features.*

"What now?" Sparrow asks.

I snap out of it. "Okay. Um. We should do something. What have you always wanted to do?"

He looks out the window thoughtfully. "I've always wanted to suck on a chili dog."

"What?" Laughter bubbles up inside me.

"You know, like 'Jack & Diane.' I love that song."

I exhale a breath of air and hold in more laughter. "I'm sure Jack and Diane got divorced thirty years ago. You know how old that song is?"

Sparrow's face drops.

"I'm joking. Holy hell. I'm joking. Okay." I turn the ignition. "Chili dogs it is. You can be Jack. I'll be Diane."

Sparrow smiles. "You can even sit on my lap," he offers.

This is way better than the Seven Kingdoms of Heaven.

...

We stop at three mini-marts before we find one selling chili dogs. The hot dog skin looks overly tanned and tough but smells delicious. We get giant fountain drinks and sit at one of the booths by the window. Sparrow eats his chili dog in three bites. As I'm working on mine, he's watching.

"You want the rest of this?" I offer. "I can get something else."

Now that I have money, I can afford all the fried food and sweets I want. And soda. It's been too long since I've had soda. I'm going to buy a case of soda before we leave here.

"I want it." Sparrow licks his lips.

"The food up there is delicious." I motion toward Heaven. "But there's no beating mini-mart fare."

I hand him the rest of my chili dog, then get up to order a cheeseburger from the counter.

When I return to my seat, Sparrow is chewing and watching the leaves blow outside the window.

"It's cold out there," he says.

"Winter's coming." I take a bite of my cheeseburger and sip on my drink.

"Winter . . ." His eyes flick to mine and then back out the window. His right thumb and index finger of his free hand twitch.

"We should probably get some coats." I shove the rest of the cheeseburger in my mouth and stand. "Come on." I take Sparrow's hand and drag him around the store with me. We collect Twinkies and Sno Balls and chips and a case of orange soda.

At the checkout the clerk gives us a look as he bags everything up. "This crap will give you a heart attack." He glances at the fresh tattoo on my collarbone.

I know what he's thinking. The same everyone else thought of me my entire life: white trash. I should let him know I'm a princess and Sparrow is a prince, and I'm a millionaire.

"Sixty-two dollars and three cents," the clerk says.

I shake it off, slide my bank card, sign the receipt, take our snacks, and leave.

"There's a Hilton extended-stay hotel nearby. Want to crash there for the night?" I ask Sparrow as we're setting our bags in the back of the minivan.

"If that's where you want to stay."

We get in the car. Sparrow is oddly silent.

I drive to the Hilton. The hotel isn't really big, but it still looks out of place in this little town. I park the van; we grab our bags and walk in. The lobby is all dark tile, white columns, and beige decor. I've never stayed in a hotel like this before.

The girl at the desk smiles. "Welcome to the Hilton. How can I help you?" Her eyes flick twice to Sparrow, and even though she's talking to me, she keeps looking at him.

"We need a room."

"A double?" she asks sweetly.

Doesn't she wish. I want no doubt left in her mind that Sparrow's mine, and if these are my last days with him, I'm going all out. I splurge on the king suite.

After paying for the room and signing the papers, the girl hands me the key cards.

"Enjoy your stay."

We follow the floral-patterned carpet to the elevators. Sparrow pushes the button to the third floor. He turns, a grin spreading across his face. Sparrow could stop a train with his smile. I wonder if he realizes that?

"What are you thinking?" I ask, shifting the bag of sweets to my other arm.

His smile widens, and his green eyes hint of trouble. "We're no longer in Heaven."

"No."

The elevator dings.

"Gabriel can no longer see," he says.

I smile. "Let's find our room."

We step off the elevator, take a left, and follow the hall to the end. Using the key card, I open the door to the suite, and we walk in. The hotel room is huge. A full kitchenette and table, a living room, and there's an open double door revealing a giant bed.

I drop my bags on the kitchen counter. Sparrow hefts the case of soda up onto the table and sets his bag of food there, as well.

We turn to each other. He looks so good dressed like that, even if it is outdated. He's tall and muscular and very attractive.

"I don't want you to be a Hellion," I tell Sparrow in a moment of weakness and truth.

"I don't want our children to be crazy."

"I'm sinful," I warn.

"Soon, I will be, too."

I run at Sparrow and leap into his arms. He catches me as if I weigh nothing and walks toward the bedroom as I cling to him. I pull my shirt off and toss it on the floor. Sparrow buries his face in my neck, whispering sweet words, snowy owl words. I missed this about him. No one ever spoke to me like this before. Just him, only him. The tip of his nose rubs against the sensitive skin of my ear.

"Say yes," he whispers. "Only if you say yes. You have to say yes. Remember?"

I grip his shoulders; he stands at the end of the bed.

"Yes." My eyes search his. "God, yes. Hell, yes."

He drops me on the bed. The denim getup disappears as he strips. I lick my lips. A naked Sparrow is a beautiful sight. His body has angles and planes that I've never seen on another man.

Sparrow reaches for the waistband on my jeans, flicks the button, and peels them down my legs.

"So beautiful," he says as he throws my pants over his shoulder.

Sparrow bends, his hands drop to the mattress on each side of my head supporting his big body, and he kisses me. His mouth is hot against mine, demanding. I've waited too long for him. My legs part. His hips press against the edge of the mattress to support his weight. Sparrow's featherlight touch moves down my arms, across my abdomen. He hooks his fingers into the waistband of my panties, and in one quick motion he rips them off.

My eyes flick open and meet his.

"I've been dreaming of doing that." He smiles and kisses me again. Then he is trailing tiny kisses down my body. "I've dreamed of you like this. The entire time we were in Heaven. Damn them for keeping us apart."

He kisses the inside of my thigh, and I jerk upright.

Sparrow glances at me, his eyes heavy and dark with desire. And then he moves, forcing me to back up on the bed until my head hits the pillows. His head dips to kiss me, his tongue spreading the seam of my lips, dipping into my mouth.

Sweet Jesus, I forgot how good he tastes: sweet from the soda, salty from the chili dog. And there's simply Sparrow, the part of him that tastes like Christmas and cake batter. I remember that filthy dream I had of him when I was in the Safe House. This is so much better.

I run my hands down his back, but Sparrow is quick to grab them and secure my wrists above my head with his large hand.

"I want to touch you," I whisper and wiggle, trying to free myself.

"Slow down." He nips at my shoulder. "I've been waiting for this for far too long." He kisses and nips his way across my body. "Patience, Meg. You always rush."

I have no patience. I want him now—fast and hard. My body feels like it's on fire.

Sparrow's mouth is on my rib cage, licking the anchor tattoo there. He kisses his way to the heart on my right hip, licking the tattoo there. His head dips lower, and he presses our hands against my abdomen, immobilizing me.

"Sparrow." I breathe his name, pained.

"I know, Meg. Trust me. I know."

And then his mouth is on me, and there's fire in my veins. Stars and lights burst behind my closed eyes, and I grit my teeth, trying not to scream.

Sparrow moves over me, finally letting go of my wrists so I am free to touch him wherever I want.

"I love you," he whispers as his body covers mine.

I can't talk, can't barely think. This is what he does to me.

His hips push against mine. I moan. Within moments we are coated in a thin sheen of sweat. Sparrow whispers things in my ear again, sweet words. My body aches for him, and then he does that thing with his hips, twisting and thrusting. Something in my center shatters. I arch my back, tighten my legs around him, and call his name.

Sparrow collapses, his face buried in my neck. We're both panting like when we're running from the dead in Hell.

After, he rolls and tucks me against his side. Being with Sparrow is better than anything. Better than life itself.

His finger brushes the birthmark on my inner thigh. The ouroboros, Lucifer called it. I have yet to learn its significance.

"Don't do it," I warn.

Sparrow smiles before he starts to hum "Bed of Roses."

He may be teetering on the edge of insanity, but this is the Sparrow I grew to love.

...

I wake startled from a dream in which all my teeth fell out. There was nothing left but the pink gums of my mouth, and I looked like one of those women back at the trailer park in Gouverneur with nine kids and a thrift-shop purseful of food stamps.

I jerk upright and run my tongue over my teeth, ensuring that they're all there.

"What's wrong?" Sparrow reaches for me, his voice groggy.

"I had a dream that they all fell out." I touch my two front teeth with my finger.

Sparrow laughs. "That's Nightingale cursing you for leaving her behind."

"She can do that?"

Sparrow shrugs. "We can all do a little something."

Sparrow can do something amazing. He saved me from the Hellions by bursting his feathers off his wings. The feathers fell like razorblades and cut the Hellions to bits.

Nightingale can influence people's dreams? Wonder if she had anything to do with that filthy dream I had about him taking off his trench coat when I was in the Safe House in Hell?

The Safe Houses are where the newly dead can go to repent, their last chance to ascend to Heaven.

I run my tongue across my teeth one more time. They're all there. I may not have had much growing up, but I had my teeth. I prefer to keep them intact.

Sparrow rolls, wrapping the blanket around him like a burrito. I get up and shower.

Sparrow's eating a Twinkie when I walk out of the bathroom wrapped in a towel. I grab the second one from the package on the table and take a bite out of it.

"What do you want to do today?" I ask as I chew.

Sparrow hands me a can of orange soda. "Not sure."

"There's a pool downstairs. Want to swim?"

Something flickers across his face.

The last time we were near a pool together, I was washing off the splatter of the dead after nearly killing him. My trigger finger twitches, and I close my eyes. I almost shot Sparrow dead that day. He was teetering on that rocky cliff after I blew out the brains of one of the walking dead. The creature was trying to eat his face, and I panicked—remembered things I tried to bury. I hope Sparrow forgives me for that.

He must've, since he's still standing here.

"I don't have a swimsuit," Sparrow replies.

"You shower. I'll run down to the hotel gift shop and get us some swimsuits."

I pull on jeans and a T-shirt over my damp skin before grabbing my bank card and room key. The shower starts in the bathroom, and the sounds of Sparrow moving around in there echo. I head for the elevator, worried that he might not be there when I get back. I don't want to leave him, not for a second.

The gift shop only has a one-piece tropical-print suit and a pair of swim trunks with palm trees all over them. I pay for both and then dash back up to the room.

Just as I'm walking through the door, Sparrow's stepping out of the bathroom with a towel wrapped around his waist.

"How was it?" I open the bag from the shop and hand him the swim trunks.

"Lonely."

I smile. "Next time."

His left shoulder "tics" hard, nearly throwing him off-balance. I start to go to him, but Sparrow holds his hand out, stopping me from coming closer.

"It's fine," he says, looking away.

Something breaks inside of me, watching this torture overtake him. I want to hide him away and protect him, or hurry up and get his time as a Hellion over with so he can go back to normal. Whatever his normal is.

A tiny emotion flashes through my heart: what if I hate Sparrow's normal?

I shake my head and reach for the bag with my bathing suit. We change, grab towels from the closet near the bathroom, then head to the pool. The uneasy feelings of sudden loneliness and loss begin to creep up on me.

The smell of chlorine lingers in the hall. Sparrow reaches around me and pulls the door to the pool area open. He waits for me to walk through. I toss my towel on a chair and head for the water, trying to figure out the right thing to say to him at this moment. This threat of him becoming a Hellion is creating a ridge between us, and I don't like it at all. I've never had anyone in my life quite like Sparrow.

As I'm dipping my toe in the pool, trying to figure what to say, Sparrow touches my arm, and I hear his sharp intake of breath. I look up and find Gabriel standing on the other side of the pool.

Oh shit.

"Brats." Gabriel's voice echoes throughout the pool room.

"Just like your mother, running away" comes next. "Goddamned kids." He's staring me down with his electric-blue gaze. Before I can say one word, he's standing next to me in a flash. "You swore on his life not to leave the Seven Kingdoms of Heaven." Gabriel points at Sparrow. "On. His. Life."

I step back.

"My father didn't tell you?" Sparrow steps forward. "The other Council members know."

"What?" Gabriel asks.

"He didn't do his time."

"Hellion?"

"Yes."

Gabriel frowns. "It's the curse then?"

Sparrow nods.

"Fucking idiot," Gabriel mumbles as he walks in a tight circle. "Fucking idiot!" Gabriel turns to face us, angrier than a hornet. "He never went when he was called?" Gabriel asks Sparrow.

"No," Sparrow replies.

"Imbecile!" Gabriel clenches his hands into fists. "You have the curse. And your sister—is she crazier than a shit house rat?"

"Yes. He keeps her locked up."

Gabriel nods, understanding. "Your banishment must have delayed the curse catching up with you or we would have known years ago." He looks Sparrow up and down before walking toward him and placing both of his hands on Sparrow's broad shoulders. "Darkness must taint your soul. This must happen. All Archangels who ever did an ounce of good paid their dues as a Hellion."

There is a dark glint in my father's eyes.

51

"Does that mean you, too?" I ask, curious as to how many of the Archangels have walked on the dark side.

Gabriel glances at me. "Yes. That is where I met Clea."

Holy crap. He met my mother when he was doing his time as a Hellion. I know what the Hellions did to me; does that mean . . .

"No." Gabriel's tone is harsh. It's as though he read my mind. "It was of her own free will. Clea was more. I brought her back with me when I finished my time. Lucifer was pissed." Gabriel suddenly laughs loud, and it echoes throughout the poolroom, making my ears ache. His eyes close for a few seconds, as though he's remembering the past. He sighs. "This is noble." Gabriel pats Sparrow so hard on the shoulder his body jerks. "And you will go together."

"I swore—" I start to say.

"It is forgiven," Gabriel declares.

"But Clea's feather showed you something." Clea gave a feather to each of us, but Gabriel still hasn't told me what he saw. "Was it a warning?"

"Now is not the time to discuss that." Gabriel presses his lips together, refusing to tell me. He turns. "Sparrow?"

"Yes, sir."

"Christ, boy. Remiel is pissed that you took off without a word. Don't forget what you're made of." Gabriel flicks him hard on the forehead. "Sparkles and fluffy clouds and shit." Gabriel turns to face me and frowns. "The owl is the bringer of death." Then in a flash, Gabriel is gone.

The owl? Is that what Clea's feather revealed?

I suddenly don't feel like swimming any longer. I turn to Sparrow, taking his hand in mine. "Let's go back to the room."

Poof.

...

"We could have taken the . . ." Sparrow's lips move, and his brow furrows, like he can't remember, but he's still trying to get the words out.

It feels like there is a stone in my gut.

"Elevator?" I ask.

Sparrow nods as he tosses his towel over the back of a nearby chair. He moves around the room, opens a can of soda, digs through the bag of snacks, pulls out some chips, and starts eating.

I do the same, both of us staring off into space as we chew. The snacks are good. I kinda miss the delicacies of Heaven fare, though. Thinking of food reminds me of the hunger that was never sated in Hell. We have to go back to that. I touch my stomach, remembering the nights of searching for a safe place to eat or sleep. Sparrow killed a deer for food. He helped keep me alive. Something inside me tells me that this time it's going to be very different.

I think of Noah. The last true friend I had before Sparrow. He got busted for possession and died in a bus accident on his way to the prison in Auburn. I met back up with him in Hell. Noah never repented, so he turned into a walking sack of flesh and tried to eat my face. Sparrow cut his hand off, and that was the first time he saved my life.

That's all I've had, Sparrow and Noah. There was Jim, but he doesn't count. Anyone who killed your unborn baby and let seven Hellions rape and try to murder you definitely doesn't fall under the category of "nice guys I dated or was engaged to."

Sparrow sits at the table across from me. He's eaten an

entire bag of chips, and now he's reaching for a package of Sno Balls.

The countertop is littered with empty soda cans. The paper bags we carried our snacks in are crumpled and nearly empty, too. I should have gotten more food.

Angst wells up inside me. I suddenly want to do something bad, something very bad. The darkness inherited from Lucifer feels like it's going to burst out of my body. I want to steal something or deface a sign or go to a bar and—

"I want another tattoo," I announce as I stand up.

Sparrow smiles. He stands, moves closer, and runs his finger around the quill on my collarbone. "Of what?"

I shrug. "I'm not sure," I say. But I do have an idea.

Sparrow frowns. Going back to the tattoo parlor and letting a stranger put his hands on me for more than a quick touch-up is a big deal. He knows I don't like to be touched.

"I don't like that man's hands on your body." Sparrow grips my hips and drags me toward him. He kisses me—hard at first, then so desperately that I can barely breathe. It's like he can't stand to lose me. I can't stand to lose him. Sparrow pulls away and holds my face. My throat feels thick. I swallow down the words I decided not to say.

"Don't forget me, Meg. Don't forget that I love you more than anything. The things they'll make me do . . ." He presses his forehead against mine—doesn't finish whatever he was saying. Instead, for the next hour Sparrow shows me exactly why I shouldn't want anyone else's hands on my body, except for his.

...

There are snowflakes in the air as we head to the tattoo parlor. I called the guy who darkened my quill earlier, and he had an opening available.

"Christmas is coming," I say as I drive the minivan.

"Yeah." Sparrow smiles, but his hands are all over the feather duster that was left in the car. He tugs a feather out of the duster and shoves it in his pocket.

I pretend I don't see that. Other people might be thrown off by what he's doing, but it's way easier to watch than when we were in Hell and he was plucking feathers straight out of the birds' wings. Alive or dead, he filled his pockets with hundreds of feathers.

Sparrow's humming "It's My Life" as I park the van, and we get out. We walk to the tattoo parlor hand in hand. He holds the door to the shop open for me, and, as I pass by, he does something strange: he whistles the eerie tremolo of the loon.

My favorite bird is the loon. Sparrow knows this. He hasn't mimicked its call since he asked me what my favorite bird was not long after we first met.

Before I can say anything about it, the guy at the counter says, "Hey again." He checks out Sparrow's outfit. He's still wearing the Canadian tuxedo, since I never got us new clothes. "Cool threads, man."

Sparrow whistles something that sounds like a blue jay call.

The guy at the counter looks confused. I should tell him not to mind my man, who has apparently decided to communicate with birdcalls.

Just then the lights flicker. In the millisecond of darkness, the tattoo man looks as though he's backlit with blue light.

I blink, and the lights come back on—full force—and there is nothing but a normal guy standing in front of me.

Maybe I'm seeing things from all the junk food I've been eating over the past twenty-four hours. Never experienced anything like that before, but my blood sugar is probably at a critical high.

The tattoo guy watches me intently. "Are you . . . ?"

"What?" I ask, but the guy seems to change his focus.

"There's a book over there. Pick out what you want."

I head for the books filled with tattoos. I have an idea of what I want already. After flipping a few pages, I find it: a dainty watercolor of a sparrow in flight. Just as beautiful as Sparrow is handsome.

"Where ya want it?" the tattoo guy asks. He glances at Sparrow, seeming uneasy.

I could go full tramp and get it on the small of my back or maybe my butt cheek. But I want to see it. I want it close. "Here." I point to the space over my heart.

The guy nods and motions for me to follow him.

I sit in the reclining chair as the tattoo guy preps his tools and then my skin. I have to take my shirt off this time and pull my bra down a little bit. Good thing I'm not self-conscious.

Sparrow stiffens and watches from the waiting area. The look on his face is one of possession and near jealousy.

The tattoo man starts working his magic. I feel the familiar sting of the needle, the annoying burning sensation.

Sparrow's eyes are riveted to mine the entire time.

I'm not sure how much time passes before the tattoo guy leans away from me, assesses the tattoo from a few different angles, dips his tool in a new ink pot, and adjusts some coloring. He presses a towel to my skin, then moves away.

"Think it's done." He hands me a mirror.

I inspect the ink. The tattoo looks better than I expected.

Pinks and blues and yellows all come together, with the wispy outline of the sparrow. Reminds me of a sunset.

"Perfect." I smile.

Now I will always have Sparrow close to my heart.

I put my shirt on and get up to pay the guy, then take Sparrow's hand, and we walk out the door to the minivan. Just before I let go of his hand to walk to the driver's side, Sparrow pulls me against him and kisses me hard on the lips.

"You like?" I ask.

"Love." He smiles and releases me. His hand moves to his pocket. I bet he's stroking off to a handful of feathers. It wouldn't be the first time.

We get in the van, and I start it.

"Christmas is coming," I remind him. "Should we get presents?"

The first time I got a real present on Christmas, I was fourteen and Noah bought me a hemp-twine bracelet with teal beads. I didn't have anything for him. That was the year we spent a summer in juvie together; the thrill of doing 120 miles per hour down the thruway was almost worth losing two months of my life.

"What if I'm not here for Christmas?" Sparrow asks.

Gripping the steering wheel, I drive past the hotel.

"We'll do Christmas tonight."

I drive to the mall and get a few hundred dollars from the ATM. I give Sparrow a handful of twenties.

"Get me something. Meet me back here in thirty minutes."

I don't care if he gets me nothing at all. I want to do something for him.

We walk in opposite directions. I head for the nearest home store and find the largest, fluffiest down comforter I can find.

After tugging the plastic case off a shelf, I pay for it, then leave the store to find a shadowed corner.

Poof.

I'm back in the hotel room. I rip open the package, then search the kitchenette for a sharp knife. After finding one in the third drawer, I cut the down comforter open and shake the feathers all over the bed. I shove the empty fabric back into the packaging and stuff it in the closet.

Housekeeping is going to be pissed.

Poof.

Back at the mall, I head to the spot where I'm supposed to meet Sparrow. On the way, I pass a few vendors selling food. It all smells too good. I stop to buy a bag of warm pretzels, a box of cookies, fresh popcorn, and caramel corn. I consider ice cream, but I know it will melt.

When I find Sparrow, he glances at the bags in my arms.

"Hungry?" he asks.

"It all smelled too good."

"I would never let you starve."

My heart cracks. He's said that to me before.

"I'd never let you starve, either." I force a smile.

We make our way to the minivan, and I drive us back to the hotel. Sparrow is quiet, and the van smells like the mall food court. I eat a pretzel as I drive and offer Sparrow a bite, but he seems distracted. Maybe he's regretting running off with me in his last days. Maybe he's regretting me altogether.

I park the van, get out, and walk around the side to collect the packages of food. Sparrow stops me as I'm opening the door. I look up; the sunset is ablaze behind his head in a fiery orange and yellow and blue. He's never looked more like an

Angel than he does at this moment. He opens his mouth but stops, glances at the bags, and seems to refocus.

"Were you going to say something?" I ask.

He kisses me, soft and sweet; his warm tongue on my lips nearly melts me. When he pulls away, his hand gripping my shoulder, he says, "I'm running out of time."

Oh, good feeling gone.

I grab the bags of food and drag Sparrow to the hotel. Thankfully, the guy behind the counter barely acknowledges us when we enter. I'm grateful for one less distraction. The elevator doors open for us as though it had been waiting for us to arrive. Sparrow pushes the button to our floor. As the elevator rises, he stares at his wavy reflection in the metal doors.

We step off the elevator, and I turn to stop Sparrow, my hand on his chest. "I just want to warn you that your present is in there."

"And yours is right here." He holds a small box between his index finger and thumb.

I take the box and open it. Inside is a silver ring with a black stone. It's just some cheap costume jewelry straight from China. Probably give me lead poisoning if I licked it. But the stone looks real enough, like a little chunk of shiny coal.

Sparrow takes the ring out of the box and pushes it onto my finger. "Don't let me forget, Meg." His eyes search. "Don't let me forget you." He kisses me quick.

I tug him to our room and open the door. After leading him to the bedroom, I step out of the way. "Merry Christmas." I reveal the bed covered in downy white feathers.

Sparrow's face lights up. His head jerks to the side, and he closes his eyes, ashamed. Then he starts stripping off his clothes.

"What are you doing?"

"I want to feel them on every inch of my body."

Sparrow runs and dives onto the bed. White feathers burst into the air, surrounding us. It's like a feather snowstorm. I pick up a handful to throw at Sparrow. He does the same. Feathers are floating everywhere. One sticks to my lip as I'm laughing. When I try to pull it away, Sparrow blasts me in the face with another handful.

We drop down onto the mattress, breathing heavy and laughing. As the feathers settle, Sparrow glances out the window. He stands and moves toward it. The snow is falling just as hard outside as the feathers were in here.

I get up and move to him.

"I can't believe there's already five inches of snow out there." Sparrow opens the curtains wider, watching as though he were an enamored toddler.

"You've never seen snow before?" I ask.

"Not like this."

I lean forward and whisper something in Sparrow's ear that has to do with measuring.

Sparrow freezes. "You say the filthiest things."

I smile and beckon him closer.

...

"I'm bored with white." Sparrow holds up one of the down feathers. "We need colorful ones."

"Let's go get some." I roll toward him. "You want to go now?"

Sparrow reaches out, his fingers slide over the ring he gave me, and no doubt he's remembering our time collecting feathers from every bird imaginable.

Fun times.

"Let's go," I say.

Concern furrows his face.

"What's wrong?" I move off the bed.

Sparrow stands and starts getting dressed. "Nothing."

Suddenly feeling pressed for time, I get up and get dressed, run my hands through my hair, and check the new tattoo on my chest. It looks like it's going to heal well. I grab my bag.

We collect the food and what's left of our case of soda and leave the room. While I'm checking out, I take a look at all the local-interest pamphlets displayed on the side of the counter. There's one for a bird sanctuary. I take it.

"Thank you for choosing Hilton," the clerk says with a smile as I sign the credit card receipt.

"Thank you." They're going to be cursing my name when they see the mess we left in there.

I meet Sparrow at the car and hand him the pamphlet on the bird sanctuary.

He smiles.

After taking a quick look around, I start the van and begin driving out of the parking lot, heading for the highway.

"Meg..."

I pull over at the sound of fear in Sparrow's voice.

"Spar—" I begin to ask.

Oh no! He's fading—his entire being is fading before my eyes, his transparency increasing until I can see the pleather of the seat he's sitting in.

"I think I love you." His voice is strange—faraway sounding. "I love you, right?"

"Yeah. You told me you do." I get an uneasy feeling in my gut. The tattoo on my chest burns.

Sparrow tips his head to the side, and his fingers slide through the soft feathers of the duster on his lap. "This world is moving too fast for me." He looks at me and blinks. "What's your name again?"

I die inside.

He drops the feather duster on the floor.

Poof.

He's gone. Disappeared before my eyes in a puff of dust. The only thing left in his place is a single feather.

"Sparrow!" I scream.

The Hellions have called.

Hellfire and Brimstone

The honeymoon is over. I can feel it in my bones. I had a few weeks of comfort and puppy love with Sparrow. Nauseatingly sweet. Almost changed who I was. In the moments since Sparrow's disappearance, I think back and wonder, *Who was that person?* Having him taken from me like this, I feel the old Meg slam full force to the forefront of my being. Someone is going to pay. I grab my blade and my wallet, and look longingly at the snacks piled up in the back seat.

I get out and strap the blade to my thigh and then focus. Sparrow can only be in one place.

I *poof* myself to Hell.

Hell is the dark and dingy reflection of Earth. Everything here is the same: countries, cities, towns, and stores. And the walking dead are everywhere, moaning and shuffling, knocking into each other like cows in a crowded pasture.

I'm standing just outside the burning caves, ready to run inside the dwelling and rip everyone on two legs to shreds. Before I get a chance to follow my instincts, my mother's figure appears at the entrance to the caves. She floats toward me, her lips a bright cherry red, her hair and eyes dark as night, her skin a ghostly porcelain white. She touches my face with cold fingers. "Child?"

"Where is Sparrow?" I ask in near hysterics.

"Oh, child." Clea reaches for me.

"No!" I move away from her, but the walking dead surrounding us keep me from getting too far.

I touch the weapon strapped to my thigh. It hums to life, ready to protect me.

"Meg." My mother's voice is soft and demanding. "Easy. Things are *happening* in there."

"They took him. They took Sparrow!"

The dead prevent me from running away like I want to. Instantly I am reminded of the months I spent in the county lockup of Hell, alone, with the dead grabbing at me through the bars of my cell. I ate fresh rats to stay alive. I shiver.

"Calm yourself." Clea reaches both of her arms out. "Child, what's done is done. It is required. He's still yours. Together you will be invincible, I promise you this. But he is undergoing the change and needs time."

"No." I want to scream so loud that every soul in Hell will hear me. "I want him back! Now!"

"You need distance. Come with me."

I start to shove her and move away, but my mother, although truly dead, is the daughter of Lucifer; she has more power down here than I ever will. I give up and allow her to walk me away from the entrance of the burning caves.

"Where are we going?" I ask.

"He needs space. The change will take over. He needs distance from you. This time is dangerous."

Of course it's dangerous. The Hellions are the warriors of Hell—worse than Demons. Stronger, viler, and more vicious.

In a wisp of smoke and hot air Clea transforms into a giant bird. My mother can shift into an Argentavis, a strange mix between a vulture and a crow and as massive as a dinosaur—Sparrow thinks it's awesome.

Clea motions for me to climb on her back.

"Hold on," she warns, once I'm settled.

In a forceful thrust we are airborne, flying over sepia forests and writhing shadows. I grip the feathers on her back, holding on tight while her giant wings flap, sending us higher and faster.

She's done this before, taken me for a ride as distraction. It's soothing, like a mother rocking her child. Something I never got to experience since Clea died the day I was born. Strangely, I am calmed by the heated wind blowing past my face and the hearty thrum of her beating wings.

"I birthed you on a forbidden plane, so you are unaware of these things," she says as she soars. "Sparrow is special. His soul is pure. He needs this. He needs to be tainted by darkness so that he can be a great leader one day."

Everyone keeps saying the same thing. It's annoying.

"I like his soul the way it is," I say.

"We know." She flaps her wings, thrusting us higher and faster.

We know? Who else knows this? Who is *we*?

"Calm your mind," she soothes.

I grit my teeth.

"Have you ever watched a sparrow and a hawk in flight?"

"No." I couldn't give a crap about a sparrow and a hawk right now. I want *my* Sparrow.

"The sparrow will fight a creature ten times its size to

defend its nest." She pauses for a moment, gliding through the thick, heated atmosphere. "Have you ever watched a sparrow and a crow? You know what the difference is?"

"I have no clue." I never paid much attention to birds in the past. Never really cared about bird fight club.

"The hawk is out for blood. The crow is simply antagonizing."

"And?"

"Don't turn this into a bloodbath. Sparrow will protect you at all costs. It's in his nature. Give him time to recover from the change."

I say nothing.

"You will be invincible together," she adds.

Flapping her powerful wings, she takes me farther and farther away from where I want to be.

...

By the time Clea returns me to the burning caves, it is dark, and the dead lie in sleeping piles on the ground. Clea lands. I slide down her side, feeling centered when my feet connect with solid ground. In a gust of wind she returns to the form of my mother—nearly my dark twin, the princess of the underworld.

I am tired from traveling between realms and from gripping so tightly to Clea's feathers. My fingers ache.

"I'll take you to your room." Clea holds out her hand.

She is strangely solid yet ghostlike. Her skin feels cool as I put my hand in hers, which reminds me that she's actually dead down here—nothing but a soul in its final resting place.

When we step inside the burning caves, I am reminded of the pleasant smell of this place: woodsmoke and pine. I inhale deeply. It's warm here—not as warm as Heaven, but the heat from the forever-burning fires deep under the caves keep the temperature ambient.

This place shadows Centralia, Pennsylvania, in the earthen realm. When humans in the earthen realm set a landfill on fire in Centralia, little did they know they were igniting fires that mimicked the burning caves of Hell, and these fires would never extinguish.

My footsteps make muted sounds on the carpet-covered rock. Clea leads me down the main hallway. I shiver as I pass the wooden door that leads to the Hellions' lair. I was there a few weeks ago. Jim had me strung up like a turkey, ready to drain my blood for him and his Hellions so they could escape Hell at will. That's what my blood does. Sparrow says it's worth rubies and jewels to the souls down here. A little bit can get them out; a lot can keep them out for good.

"They won't bother you," Clea promises as we descend a wide stone staircase.

The deeper we go into the cave, the more castlelike it becomes.

"Lucifer has forbidden any of them from touching you." She gives me a look. "Including Jim."

In a cloud of smoke, a giant figure appears on the steps before us.

"You called?" Lucifer towers before me. His giant wings stretch wide. They're darker than the shadows at night, just like his eyes. He smiles at me, and I notice he's wearing the same leather pants and vest as the last time I saw him. It's a badass getup, but he scares the shit out of me.

"Daddy." Clea touches Lucifer's arm.

Something comes over the giant man when his daughter

touches him. He is no longer so imposing and intimidating. He softens, reaches out, and touches her cheek.

"Can she have the suite?" Clea asks.

"Yes." He nods before turning and walking away from us. The man is massive and dark, his body taking up most of the hallway. God forbid anyone try to walk by him—there isn't any room.

"Let's go." Clea pulls me along.

We step off the stairs and turn down another stone hallway. Near the end, Clea stops in front of a large wooden door and pushes it open.

"This is your room."

I step inside. The space is just as massive as my room in Gabriel's castle; the only difference is that everything is stone and decorated with dark draperies in reds and blacks and purples. There is a large mattress on a frame set low to the floor. There are doors leading to the bathroom and a walk-in closet. A fire burns in the hearth without wood to fuel it.

"One of the nicest rooms in the castle." Clea walks around the bed, inspecting. "Almost as nice as mine."

There's a velvet couch along the far wall and a table and chairs near the windows. The place is like a small apartment. I'd probably never need to leave.

Feeling dusty and grimy, I yawn, rub my hands over my face, then take in the condition of the jeans and T-shirt I've been wearing for the past few days.

"You need clothing here." Clea looks me over, and it's as though her gaze sees straight into my soul. I think nothing of it, since it's a gift all mothers possess. "I think I know your style."

As long as it's none of the princess crap Teari filled my closet with, I'll be happy with almost anything.

Clea crosses the room and opens the closet door. She snaps her fingers. "I think this will do."

I walk into the closet to take inventory. There's plenty of jeans, dark T-shirts and tanks, a few leather jackets, leather pants, vests like I've seen Lucifer wear, and boots. This is way better than my closet in Gabriel's Kingdom.

I pull a low-cut tank off a hanger, take off my T-shirt, and try it on. Perfect fit.

"Is this new?" Clea points to the sparrow tattoo on my chest.

"Yes." I reach for a thin leather jacket and pull it off the hanger.

Clea waves her hand over my new ink, which is still a bit sore and red around the edges. When her hands move away, the skin is completely healed—reminds me of the time Gabriel healed Sparrow after he was attacked by the Hellions.

"Thanks." I put the jacket on and move away from the closet. "How can you do that?"

"Some of us have magic."

My attention turns to the large window and glass door near the bed. I make my way toward them and pull the curtain back. The view stretches for miles and miles.

"Where are we?" I ask. "I thought we were in the caves, but it looks more like a castle now."

"We are at the back of the caves. It's built into a mountainside."

I push the door open and walk out onto the balcony. There is nothing but darkness, the world below illuminated by the full moon. Bats fly in the valleys between the trees, frogs chirp, an owl hoots, a cool breeze blows. I shiver and zip up my jacket.

"Beautiful. Isn't it?" Clea asks.

"Yes." It doesn't glitter like Heaven, but there is something about this place that satisfies a dark part of my soul.

For a few moments there is nothing but the sounds of night in Hell before I ask, "Gabriel was a Hellion?"

She nods. "A handsome one at that."

"You left here?"

"I did. But, I'm sure you've found out already, things are not perfect within the Seven Kingdoms of Heaven."

They're definitely not.

"I am pure darkness. Full-blood. The Council did not want me there. It did not matter that I was carrying the half-blood child of an Archangel."

"They didn't want me there, either," I say.

Clea smiles, nodding. "In time. All will be right." She floats away from me. "Sparrow's change is done now. Make yourself at home." She pauses at the door. "But be careful, Meg. This is Hell, and wickedness is rampant."

Doesn't sound much different than Gouverneur or Heaven.

Clea leaves my room.

I stand on the balcony for a few minutes longer, my hands gripping the stone railing. The darkness that called me while I was in Heaven has finally quelled. It was nearly unbearable there, not so bad on the earthen plane, and now that I'm here, I can barely sense it.

I decide to find Sparrow.

I cross the room and tug on the door handle. Nothing happens. That smothering feeling of being trapped and having no control overwhelms me. I wiggle the door back and forth, slamming it against the frame, but it does no good. I kick at it, and when it still doesn't budge, I cross the room again and walk out onto the balcony. Leaning over the railing, I search for other means of escape. I could climb over and try to rappel down the rock—but before I decide much, I hear a clicking sound behind me, and I turn to find my door slowly opening.

"Watch yourself, child," my mother's voice echoes in my mind. A warning. It's nice to know that she's not going to lock me up in this place, but the threat still makes my blood boil.

I leave my room, close the door, and walk down the hallway that Clea brought me through. I climb the stone stairwell, turn at the landing, and look down. The stairs descend into a dark abyss. Strange sounds rise up: the chomping of a thousand jaws, the tearing of leather, writhing thuds, and . . . screams. That's definitely screaming.

I turn away and run toward the Hellions' lair. There are dull echoes and movement from the shadows and doorways as I pass. Both soothing and frightening. I pause in front of the lair for a moment before reaching for the handle and pushing the door open.

The lair is just like I remember: leather furniture, wet bar, giant TV, billiards. It's nothing but a giant bachelor pad. Chains dangle from the ceiling where Jim strung me up before he stabbed me in the chest. I fucking hate Jim. As I scan the room, I notice seven menacing figures standing on the far side of the room—dark warriors awaiting commands. I recognize a few of them as the Hellions that invaded my house and tried to kill me that quiet afternoon nearly a year ago.

Sparrow's there, as well, and—holy hell—he has gone to the dark side. His downy-white wings have been replaced with dark, leathery skin stretched over bone. He's wearing tight leather pants, a black vest, and boots. He looks like a big biker dude. But with his skin so pale and his bright green eyes, he doesn't look as dark as the other Hellions.

If all Sparrow has to do is his time down here, I think I might like it a little too much if this is what he's going to look like. It's way better than the Legion gear and that old trench coat he used to wear. Makes something deeper than my trailer park roots tremble at the sight of him.

I touch the ring he gave me, rotating it with my thumb.

Don't let me forget, Meg. Don't let me forget you.

I move toward the one Hellion I know, the one who didn't try to murder me.

"Sparrow?" I grab his hand and turn to lead him away.

He doesn't follow, only stands as still as a stone, jerking me to a stop. Shivers of unease travel up my spine. I look up to face him, not liking what I see. Sparrow's face is hard, his eyes dark; he tips his head to the side, a quirky and familiar movement.

"Sparrow?" I ask.

He flicks my hand off his and grabs my wrist, hard enough to leave bruises. "Who are you?" he asks, his voice deep, unfamiliar.

In the second that it takes him to say those three words, I die inside. Every tiny shred of hope that I had for this new life with him, it shrivels and turns to dust.

"Aw, that sucks, Meg." Jim chuckles from behind me. "Guess your momma forgot to tell you that part. Birdman don't remember you."

I swallow hard and consider reaching for my blade.

"Don't worry your trashy little head. He'll slowly come back to himself—a little darker, though. The change is rough on the cherubs. Twists their gizzards or some crap."

I die a little more inside.

"Clea warned me," I reply as I turn to face Asshole Jim.

Jim's gray eyes and blond hair are the same. He would still

be handsome if it weren't for the fact that half of his face is burned off. Sparrow and Gabriel did that to him when they came to my rescue. Serves the jerk right.

Jim's smile is lopsided as he says, "Welcome back."

I want to punch him in his stupid, deformed face.

Instead I reply with, "Screw you." I'm glad Sparrow nearly killed him. I wish he had succeeded.

Jim touches his cheek. "Like this look?" he asks.

"You're almost as pretty as you were before you became a complete jackass."

Jim smirks and steps closer. I back up, remembering how terrible he actually is. Only one kind of man beats his pregnant fiancée. Only one kind of man kills his own unborn child, his own flesh and blood. And that kind of man is standing in front of me.

Jim raises his hand before it comes down hard but stops just before touching me. "Your grandpappy may have forbidden me from touching you," he whispers, slapping my cheek lightly. "But we still crave your trashy blood."

I settle my hand on my weapon and straighten my shoulders in an effort not to look scared shitless. Lucifer has threatened to kill Jim if he touches me. And I may hate everything about Jim and the Hellions, but I have to put up with them until Sparrow is done here. This entire situation is more fucked up than the day I found out who I really was. What I really was.

Craving control, I change the direction of the conversation and ask, "Will he remember what he does as a Hellion?"

Jim shrugs. "Don't know. There's a chance he could start to remember. But, to tell you the truth, it's been so long since we've had a winged prince down here I can't remember all the details."

My heart aches for Sparrow. Whatever he does in the name of my grandfather, there is a chance he'll remember.

As a member of the Legion, he protected man in the name of God—even killed. Down here I'm sure the things he's going to do are dark and wicked. The memory of the Hellions invading my home and assaulting me flicks through my memory. I can't imagine Sparrow doing something like that, participating in something so evil.

Jim snickers. "Don't worry. Your grandfather frowns upon the things the Hellions did to you. I doubt birdboy will be involved in anything like that."

It takes me a moment to realize that Sparrow still has a grasp on my arm. I wrest it away from him and turn to Jim. "Go fuck yourself."

I stomp out of the Hellion's lair and head outside. Since it's night, the walking dead sleep. The smell of rotting corpses wafts around me, churning my stomach. They'll rise with the sun and begin their foot-dragging and moaning all over again. Poor bastards should have just found a Safe House and repented. Now they've missed their chance to ascend.

Walking further from the entrance to the cave, I notice the tree Jim knocked me out of when I came back here with Clea's bones. The tree is upright again, its craggy branches devoid of any leaves. Strange.

Out here there's nothing but the moon, the sleeping dead, and the echoes of night. I glance down at the watercolor tattoo on my pale skin, the colorful sparrow battling the haze of Hell. It looks amazing in the moonlight.

I take a deep breath and swallow down a scream of frustration. I let myself get sucked into the sweet promises of Heaven. All the glitter and purity, it's bullshit. I just wanted someone to call my own. I forgot who I was, what I came from. All in an effort to hold on tightly to someone I barely know and figure out where I belong. And now it's all fucked up.

Somehow, I have to make Sparrow remember.

But first I need to get some sleep.

...

Sparrow

A fire burned deep in Sparrow, one bred of dark needs and insatiable power. This was nothing like the bright, pure light he was familiar with. Both were warring within his soul; it made his head hurt, his heart ache. Something was *missing*.

"Birdman's awake." He heard the soft chuckling of a man.

Sparrow sat up, moved to his feet, and stood in robotlike movement. Sparrow was towering over the man with the viciously scarred face. *Jim.* That was his name. And like a collar tugging around his neck, Sparrow knew that Jim had complete control of his soul. Sparrow didn't like it. He turned his head and twisted his neck to try to lessen the feeling. Instead, it tightened further.

"Soon you won't even feel it. Can't give you free run of the place." Jim had a lopsided grin.

Although he couldn't remember details, Sparrow had a feeling he was the reason for the scars.

Jim poked Sparrow in the stomach and made a sound of disappointment. "The change went easy on you, cherub. Others came out darker skinned and vicious. Drooling at the chops." Jim thumbed toward the grouping of six Hellions. They watched Sparrow, eyes half-lidded with menace. These were now his brethren. "But they weren't princes," Jim added as an afterthought.

Sparrow caught a glimpse of himself in the mirror over the bar countertop. Of what he remembered, he knew that he looked different now. There were darker shadows to the angles of his face; the wings on his back felt tight and heavy. He had a feeling that learning to fly with these was going to be drastically different from the last time.

There was tension in the room as Jim inspected Sparrow, walking around him as a panther would its prey. Finally, Jim turned his back and collected something from a cupboard along the wall. He turned and threw clothing at Sparrow.

"New uniform." Jim motioned to a door. "Go get dressed." His tone was clipped and annoyed.

Sparrow walked away, clothing clutched to his chest. Through the door was a large room where there were cots and nothing else. Sparrow had the feeling that the Hellions had no personal belongings. They were warriors, used and discarded; those wasted would be refilled by other souls waiting in the annexes of Hell.

Sparrow chose a bed at the end of the room, dropped the clothing on the cot, and began removing what he had on. His fingers felt strange when he tried to unhook the buttons of the thick vest he wore. Angry blood pulsed underneath his nail beds. Frustrated, he gripped the material at his neck and ripped it apart. Next went the pants. He threw the torn material in a nearby trash can.

Sparrow dressed in the leather pants and vest. Both had a thickness that rivaled the skin of his new wings. There were ties on the back to accommodate the bony appendages coming out of his spine; he cinched it tight and found security in the clothing, which conformed to his body so well. Last were the boots, large and steel toed. Sparrow tied them tight around his ankles before he left the room.

The other Hellions were standing near a pool table. Not playing but just standing, murmuring in dark-tongued conversation.

Sparrow sensed something, movement outside the lair that he was now to call home. The door burst open, and a young woman walked through. Dressed in jeans and a leather jacket, her hair was short and dark, her eyes a fiery blue as they searched the room and landed on him. *Mine,* her eyes conveyed as they roved over his body, pleased.

Sparrow felt something as she advanced. They were linked, somehow, but right now he couldn't place how she fit into his life. He couldn't remember her—wanted to, but instinct told him this was not the time or the place.

The other Hellions were watching, and although Jim never moved, Sparrow felt the invisible coil around his throat tighten.

"Sparrow?" she asked as she grabbed his arm.

Every muscle in Sparrow's body stiffened with her touch. Jim made a grim face. Sparrow's throat tightened. In a movement that felt familiar and right, he tipped his head to the side to study her with interest.

"Sparrow?" she asked again.

Her voice was a pinpoint of sunshine calling him across vast darkness. But something was wrong, and Sparrow did the only thing he could at the moment: flicked her hand off his arm and grabbed her wrist. "Who are you?"

Jim chuckled, and Sparrow felt the coil around his neck tighten, nearly choking him. He didn't move. An image of Jim with his hands on *her* crossed Sparrow's memory, and he was filled with a rage darker than anything he'd ever felt in his life.

She argued with Jim, and the interaction made Sparrow want to react, pull her behind him, and thrash at the Hellion leader. But he couldn't. He was a Hellion now, and whatever his burden now was, it prevented him from lashing out at his commander.

Sparrow didn't listen to the words they said to each other; he was too interested in the softness of her wrist underneath his fingers. Her skin was smooth and strong, familiar. Sparrow had the compelling urge to tug her away and hide her deep in the dark recesses of the burning caves. Save her for himself. But he didn't—couldn't. He wasn't in control; Jim was.

With a strong jerk she tore herself away from Sparrow and stormed out of the room. Jim followed, a few leg lengths behind her. Sparrow wanted to stop him—wanted to run out of the room, pick her up, and fly off into the night. But he was held in place by an invisible force. Jim slammed the door closed behind her as she left the lair.

Turning, Jim's cool gray gaze landed on Sparrow. His crooked smirk made another appearance.

"Remember her?" Jim asked as he thumbed toward the closed door.

Sparrow said nothing.

"You'd do good to forget her, Birdman. Nothing but trouble, that one."

Sparrow didn't know what to think, but something deep within him implied that Jim was wrong.

The clanging of metal caught his attention. Sparrow turned and focused on the chains hanging from the ceiling in the center of the room.

"Remember those?" Jim's voice was dark.

Sparrow stood still, never conveying a thing. Something tugged at the edges of his memory; it had to do with the chains and blood and that woman who was just here.

Jim laughed as he walked across the room, turned the radio on, and poured himself a tumbler of amber liquid from the bar.

The steady beat of techno music thudded heavily in Sparrow's chest as Jim watched him from across the room. The other Hellions stayed where they were. Sparrow was apart from everyone, and he had a feeling that it would always be so. He might be a Hellion now, but he'd never be truly accepted as one of them. That was fine with Sparrow. He didn't trust these creatures as far as he could throw them, and judging from the bulging muscles of his biceps and the hollow echo of strength in his center waiting to be fed, that was pretty damn far.

...

Meg

I wake with a startle and sit up straight. I had another dream that my teeth fell out. I run my finger along the inside of my mouth and make sure they're still there. After wiggling my finger over my canines, incisors, and a few molars, I'm relieved that none of them are loose.

Damn Nightingale.

I throw myself back onto the bed and stretch. The sheets are black satin and feel smooth against my skin. I could stay in this bed all day. My stomach growls—scratch that.

I get up and head for the bathroom. The tiles are dark slate with bone-colored pieces mixed in. It's not as big as the one in Gabriel's Kingdom, but it will do. Still beats the tiny bathroom

I had to share with John Lewis when I was a kid. I strip and get in the shower.

The water comes out like heavy syrup. I stick my hand in the spray and rub my fingers together, waiting for it to warm. The water is soft. Reminds me of the sulfur water at my old friend Sara Shepard's house.

I try not to think about Sara and what a terrible friend I was to her.

I get clean, then get out and dry myself. At the mirror, I style my short hair with my fingers before heading to the closet. Running my hand over the clothing, I settle on a pair of dark blue jeans, an off-the-shoulder top in red, and the leather jacket I wore yesterday.

In one of the drawers I find Clea has provided me with some skimpy underthings. Sweet Jesus, I've never worn thin, lacy stuff like this before. I mean, I've gone a few days with nothing plenty of times, but this—I hold up a pair of skimpy panties—this stuff will get a girl in loads of trouble. Clea definitely didn't get this at any of the stores I've ever shopped at. I choose some underthings that don't feel too trampy and get dressed.

As I'm pulling on a pair of leather boots, my stomach growls louder than before. Damn, I'm hungry. I really should have eaten something before going to bed last night. The last time I had a real meal was before we left Gabriel's Kingdom. I regret living off junk food on the earthen plane for the past few days. I'm starving.

I cross the room, pick up my blade and holster, and strap it on before leaving my room in search of food.

After walking up and down the hallway, I don't find a kitchen—only locked doors and empty rooms. I take the stairs and check the next floor down. Nothing. I go down another floor. Still nothing. My stomach grumbles louder. I try the next floor down. Nothing again. The deeper I go into the castle, the darker and dingier it gets. The noises get worse—the snapping-jaw sound louder, the ripping sound faster—all adding to my angst.

The rumbling in my stomach echoes along the rocky hallways. This is like a bad dream. I stop and rub my eyes, just to make sure I'm not still sleeping. When I open them again, the dark hall still stretches before me—the world's simplest maze with no chunk of cheese at the finish. I'd kill for cheese right now. I keep walking, my search turning frantic the hungrier I get. My hands start to shake; after a lifetime of eating high-fructose junk, my blood sugar has never been this low.

I turn shadowed corners, check locked doors, run down the main stairwell to more of the lower levels, searching no matter how badly the sounds from the abyss below scare me. A few hours have passed, at least. I can't do this much longer. After checking every level for a kitchen of some kind, I think to ask the creatures I pass in the halls, but they shy away from me, pressing themselves against the walls as though I am a leper. If only they could see themselves. The creatures of Hell are a strange-looking bunch: horns and scales and odd tufts of black hair.

Part of me wants to call out to Clea or Lucifer, but I can take care of myself. I didn't make it this far in life by crying when I couldn't find something I wanted. I didn't cry when John Lewis sold all my stuff that time I went to juvie, didn't cry when my sneakers were two sizes too small in middle school, didn't cry when ...

I continue searching, feeling like I'm stuck in a labyrinth, until I find myself standing outside of the Hellions' lair. I know there's alcohol in there. I could get a beer or something stronger to stop my guts from aching.

I don't even have to knock; my stomach rumbles to announce me. The door swings open, and Jim's standing there.

"Hey, Meg." He looks me up and down approvingly. "Looking for something . . . or someone?"

I remember this tone of his voice. Back when we were engaged and living together, he'd use it on the days he decided to be nice. Never on the days that I burned dinner or forgot to water the flowers. Hearing this tone was always a rare event.

"Where the hell is all the food in this place?" I ask. I reach out and grip the doorframe, but my arms feel rubbery and weak.

Jim laughs loudly. "They didn't tell you?"

Heavy metal rock music is playing from the stereo system.

"Tell me what?"

He steps away from the door and opens it wide so I can enter. He's wearing jeans and a dark button-down shirt. As soon as I step past the threshold, I know that this is a bad idea, but I can't seem to help myself. I spent plenty of my life hungry, but nothing like this. I can't take it one second longer.

Jim motions for me to follow him to the bar area. He opens a small stainless steel fridge under the counter. There are rows of pint-size bags. Jim selects one, then reaches into the cupboard along the wall and takes down two glasses. He opens a drawer, pulls out a pair of scissors, and cuts the corner off the bag, then he pours the contents of the bag into the glasses.

It's red, thick.

I blink.

That's blood.

Jim turns, holding out a glass for me to take.

"There's only one meal in the bowels of Hell. It's the only thing you'll ever need down here. Better than that shit you used to cook."

I want to slap him but instead take the glass. Maybe I should ask for bourbon. I hate bourbon, but at least it would fill my stomach. The liquid in the glass smells coppery and strangely tempting. My mouth waters. I swallow down the little bit of saliva that's coating my throat, working up the courage to do something. My stomach twists.

Jim lifts his glass, drains it in one swallow, and licks his lips. "I've never known you to shy away from a good dare. Do it. I promise you'll like it."

I move the glass closer to my lips. This is fucking crazy. I sip. Shit, it tastes good. Really good. I take a large swallow and wipe my mouth. There's something so wrong about this, but it feels so good and right. The grumbling in my stomach stops immediately. Warmth floods my veins, and my stomach feels full. I'd rather have a buffet in Heaven, but this—I've never felt like this after gorging myself on Heaven fare.

Jim steps closer. "It feels good to be gangster. Doesn't it?" There is amusement in his voice.

"Gangster?" I stare into the glass, wanting to drain it while being completely disgusted with myself at the same time

"You know." The corner of his mouth that still works tips up in a smile. "Criminal, dark, sinner, a villain. That's you through and through."

I look away. Suddenly I feel dirty. Drinking blood is for vampires and shit. What the hell am I doing? The urge to down the remainder in the glass then rip open another bag with my teeth is strong.

"Say it." He steps closer, much too close. "Say it feels good."

I don't want to admit it, but I've never felt sated in Hell, until now. "Yes." I respond through gritted teeth.

"Yes, what?"

"It feels good." I drink the rest of the blood in my glass before slamming it down on the nearby bar. "*So good* to be gangster."

"Knew it." Jim spins away from me. "Now comes the fun part." Mischief glints in his gray eyes. Jim crosses the room and opens a door in the back of the lair. "Boys. It's dinnertime."

The Hellions enter. I stare at Sparrow, shocked; he looks like he's lost about ten pounds. Jim crosses the room again, this time opening the front door to the lair.

There's a line of women standing out there.

"Fresh meat." Jim makes eye contact with me. "Newly dead. Their blood is still warm. Haven't turned yet." He ushers the women in. "Feast." He orders the Hellions.

"What about the blood in the fridge?" I ask.

"The fresher the blood, the stronger they are." Jim points at the Hellions.

A few of the Hellions step forward, grab a woman, and latch onto her neck or arm. They are sucking her blood. My eyes are glued to Sparrow. He's just watching the other Hellions, until he takes a step forward. It feels like my stomach is filled to the brim with heavy stones.

Jim laughs.

Something in my soul shrivels and turns to ash.

Oh, hell no.

Fuck this.

Fuck Jim.

Fuck Sparrow.

I'm out.

Poof.

I leave the burning caves and find myself at the small castle on the lake near the Canada of Hell, where I once spent a night with Sparrow. That seems like forever ago.

I can't look at Sparrow. Can't go near him. I don't know what to do with myself. I want to kill something or break something or go to a bar and take home the first guy I find who doesn't look like he has a venereal disease.

I hate this. I hate this. I hate it!

A loon calls from across the lake.

My heart cracks.

I am stronger than this. John Lewis didn't remind me each morning that I killed my mother the day I was born so I'd grow up weak. *You killed her, and don't you forget it.* His words echo in my memories. He said I burst from her womb so fast that I took the placenta with me, and she bled out before help could come. Later on I learned the truth. I didn't live through all that bullcrap so I could give up so easily now.

I kick at a rock and send it flying into the nearby bushes. It hits something with a thud. Branches tremble; a moan echoes. One of the walking fleshbags ambles out, reaching for me, moaning like a tipped cow. I grab the blade from where it's secured on my thigh. I didn't make it through months locked in a jail cell while the dead threatened to eat me just to let Sparrow sucking the blood of some newly dead woman break my spirit.

The blade vibrates in my hand, then slices like butter as I chop the head off the walking corpse. I wait for another one to walk out of the brush.

By the time I'm done releasing my frustrations on the dead, night has fallen. They'll be sleeping in piles, no longer a bother until sunrise. I walk out on the nearby dock and collapse to my knees. The sleeves of my leather jacket are coated with the fluids of the departed, sticky and thick. I strip off the jacket and dip the sleeves in the water. As I scrub away the gunk, I want to scream.

The loon calls again, an eerie tremolo that echoes over the water. Dark and haunting. Reminding. Something fluttering on the edge of the dock catches my attention. It's a dark-brown feather. I tug it out from the splinters of weathered wood and tuck it into my pocket.

Shaking the water off my jacket, I stand and look out over the dark lake. I don't understand how this went so wrong.

I walk toward the small castle. The water around the moat is still, as the dead underneath sleep. I shouldn't have come here. I know better than to return to the scene of the crime. Not that we committed any crimes here. I just know that this place is going to remind me of *him*.

I push open the heavy wooden door and secure it closed behind me. Nothing will try to get in at night, but in the morning they might try. I'd rather be safe than sorry.

I make my way upstairs and find the room that we stayed in together. There are soot-covered sticks in the fireplace and an unburned pile of wood in the corner of the room.

I throw my jacket on the bed to dry. After pushing a dresser in front of the door, I stand in the middle of the room and take a few moments to calm myself.

When shit went south before, I packed my crap and went to college. I tried to run from my demons, but they just caught up with me when Jim showed at that party and took me to bed.

The way I see it, I've got three choices: go back to Gabriel's Kingdom with my tail between my legs and learn how to be a glittery princess, go back to the earthen plane and vacation in Bora-Bora and meet some new people, or go back to the burning caves and keep my eye on Sparrow.

Going back to Earth sounds good. I've got plenty of money for the first time in my life. I could start over.

I look around the bare room. But there'd be no Sparrow. He is the first man who has ever shown me love and caring and truth. Am I ready to drop that and run? I spent twenty-five years of my life being nothing but trailer trash; going back to that isn't high on my bucket list. I'd be wealthy, but I'd still be the same old me—can't rub out trailer. Lord knows I've tried.

I open the window and push the only chair in the room closer so I can gaze over Hell at night. The chair has a high wingback; Sparrow tried to sleep in it last time we were here. Back then, I had to promise him I wouldn't try to unbutton his coat to get him to sleep in the bed with me.

I drop down, exhausted. A cool breeze blows in the window, and the sounds of night soothe me, until I fall asleep curled up in the chair.

...

Sparrow

They left Sparrow alone in the lair all day. Locked him in the room with the cots and took off. Hunger was tearing him apart. Sparrow's insides were on fire, sparks lit his veins, and a deep grumble that wouldn't stop echoed in his throat. Sparrow could barely control his body or his mind at the moment. The thoughts in his brain tumbled among the woman who had showed up and tried to drag him away, the sneers from the other Hellions, and the fact that they had detained him when they left.

It was hours before they finally returned. Jim instructed the other Hellions to rest. They each fell onto a bed, sleeping soundly.

Sparrow couldn't tell where the others had been—didn't really care. All he knew was that he couldn't sleep. He was wired, ready to move. The pressure around his neck was tight and left him digging at his skin in an attempt to relieve it, but nothing helped.

The Hellions didn't rest for long, before Jim finally ordered them out of the room.

One of the Hellions, a large beast with scars on his face, growled as he walked by Sparrow, "Dinner's here."

Sparrow's stomach clenched at the thought of food.

They exited the room. He could sense that *she* was there before Jim crossed the lair and opened the front door.

Sparrow could sense her unease, and it was all he could do not to move toward her and do *something*. He knew better and didn't look in her direction when her eyes fell on him.

A line of women entered the room. Sparrow could tell by their smell that they were freshly departed. Their blood was tainted with death. He was so ravenous his mouth watered.

Then, in the blink of an eye, *she* just suddenly disappeared from the room.

"Bitch," Jim murmured, staring at the empty space where she once stood.

Jim crossed the room, took a Bloodwhore by the neck, and bit down. His mouth was coated in blood when he let the body drop to the floor.

The other Hellions drained the Bloodwhores dry, drinking until nothing but husks remained.

Sparrow stepped forward, ready to feast with his fellow warriors. He touched a short, pretty-faced girl, who was standing in front of him, waiting. An offering. Sparrow's stomach heaved as his skin touched hers. He shoved her away, and the girl's wide eyes filled with relief.

Jim's hollow laughter filled the room. "You deny her?" Jim asked. "You'll starve, Birdman. Can't go back to your legions of pigeons if you're deader than a doornail. Eat."

Sparrow stood still. He was hungry, famished. His eyes glanced to the refrigerators across the room. He could see that they held bags of blood.

"Oh no," Jim tsk-tsked at him. "You eat fresh. I need you strong like the others." He motioned to the other six beasts who were wiping their faces. Blood smeared their skin and teeth, their venomous smiles.

The only thing Sparrow felt now was disgust.

...

Meg

My eyes flutter open to the sound of moaning below the window. I lean forward and see the dead have collected outside the castle. Strange. I didn't make any noise to attract them. I lean back in the chair as memories of my dreams flash through my mind. There were a lot of images of Sparrow sucking on some chick's neck. I touch my face and find my cheeks are wet. Shit, maybe I was making noise in my sleep.

Next time I see Nightingale, I'm going to choke the life out of her.

"Child?" Clea appears, scaring the shit out of me.

"Oh God." I grip my chest. "You can't do that to me."

I wouldn't mind Clea being here right now if it weren't for the look on her face. She knows I found out about the blood sucking. I hate it when people look at me with pity and sorrow. Reminds me of those doctors when I woke up from my coma in the hospital, after they read my medical chart in front of me, their faces drawn in sympathy.

"Don't look at me like that," I snap.

"Are you going to stay here now?" she asks. Looking around the barren room, disgust veils her face.

"I'm not sure." I didn't think this place was that bad. There's a bed, a fireplace, and no Sparrow touching his lips to another woman's neck. I think this place is pretty perfect, actually.

"I'd like you back at the caves." Clea moves her dark hair over her shoulder. "It's safer for you there."

"Safe?"

"If fresh souls out here learn what your blood can do . . ." She shakes her head. Anyone with a little bit of my blood can cross the planes, just like I can. They can get out of Hell. They can return to the Earthen plane.

Go back to Lucifer's castle . . . "I don't know if I can do that," I say.

"It's not so bad." Clea stands and walks closer. "The blood."

What do you say when your mother tells you drinking blood isn't so bad? It's like I'm twelve, and she might as well hand me a beer or a joint. I lick my lips, remembering the smell of the blood, the way it felt sliding down my throat. The fullness. My face twists in revulsion.

"Don't feel that way about it. This is what we are." Her voice is soft, understanding.

I look up at Clea, as disgusted with myself as she is of the room.

"This is why I birthed you on Earth, so you'd have choices. Down here blood will keep you sated. But since you are half light, you can survive by other means. The darkness will always be there, though, wanting its fill."

Well that explains why I could barely contain the darkness while I was in Gabriel's Kingdom. Explains why I could never eat my fill when Sparrow and I were trapped down here the first time.

The dead moan from below the window.

"And Sparrow?" I ask.

She sighs. "He is a Hellion now. He needs it until his time is done. It will keep him strong. They are dangerous creatures with dangerous undertakings. You don't want him weak."

"And the Bloodwhores?"

She tips her head. "Is that what this is really about?"

I play with the ring on my finger. "I can't do it." I shake my head.

Clea kneels at my feet and looks at me with large dark eyes. "There is something highly sensual about it."

I snap to attention.

"I very much enjoyed feeding from Gabriel." Her voice is soft with cherished memories.

I choke. Oh God. I didn't need to know that. No kid wants to hear their parent's stories about sucking each other's blood.

Clea smiles. "Sorry." She stands and floats back to the bed to sit again.

"I can't watch him feed from other women." The thought of it makes bile rise in the back of my throat.

"Oh, child." Clea makes a movement, an expression of relief. "Sparrow refuses to drink from any of them."

I touch the tattoo on my chest, my heart thundering under my fingertips. Sparrow is supposed to be mine, and I am his. The change just screwed up the parts of his brain that used to remember this.

Clea stands and holds her hand out. "He's weak from the change. And he has refused every Bloodwhore." She wiggles her fingers. "Come. You must return. He needs you."

I hesitate, remembering the way he gripped my arm two days ago and asked who I was.

"He doesn't know me."

"Give him time. Come."

I stand, move to grab my jacket off the bed, then take her hand.

"Take us back."

I whisper the words and return us to my room in the burning caves. *Poof.*

After moving away from Clea, I hang my jacket on the back of a chair.

"This entire situation reminds me of some dirty vampire movie." I touch my teeth. "I don't have fangs," I warn her.

"They'll come out just before you feed, then retract like they were never there."

Oh, the things I've learned in Hell. I run my tongue over my teeth, trying to feel anything different.

"I'll send him to you." Clea leaves.

I open the window to let the air in and sit on the edge of my bed, unsure of what the heck I'm supposed to do with myself.

Sparrow is going to suck my blood. I contain a shiver. What if it hurts? What if he doesn't like the taste of me? We've barely spoken two words since he took his role as a Hellion. What am I supposed to say to him?

Don't let me forget you. Using my thumb, I roll the ring on my finger.

There is a knock on the door.

"Come in," I say.

The door opens, and the Hellion that is Sparrow steps in. He seems larger and darker. He closes the door softly behind him and waits.

I'm not sure what to do.

There is a heck of a lot of awkward silence before I ask, "Do you remember me?"

Sparrow's eyes roam over my body. If he remembers anything, he says nothing.

I notice he looks pale, gaunt. Like he's starving.

Let's get this over with.

I reach for my blade; I cut the soft skin of my inner forearm. It's so sharp I barely feel a thing.

Sparrow's nose flares. He moves so fast that I barely see him until he has my arm in his hand. His mouth lowers to the deep cut, and it's like I am no longer in the room; there is just Sparrow and his meal.

He latches on, his teeth on my skin, the sharp pinch of pain, the movement of his tongue. Sparrow sucks. The feeling intensifies. My knees weaken. The sensations confuse me. It's strange. Even though I'm slightly repulsed, heat floods my body. I want to rip all of Sparrow's clothes off and jump his bones.

Feeling lightheaded, I drop to my knees, my arm still held

above my head by Sparrow. His grip loosens, and I feel his tongue brush over the cut.

I feel so weak that I can't help but close my eyes.

...

Sparrow

"Come with me." The daughter of Lucifer held her hand out to Sparrow.

Sparrow glanced at Jim, awaiting orders.

Jim waved his hand in annoyance. "Go. Her authority trumps that of the commander of the Hellions." The distaste in his voice was strong.

Sparrow followed Clea out of the lair. They moved down the hall.

"You should not have waited this long," Clea said as they turned at the stairwell. She touched his arm, her icy fingers threatening to send a chill throughout his body. "Refusing the others, it was the right thing to do." Clea smiled. "You have instincts, follow them." She floated down the stairs; Sparrow followed. After walking down the hall, her hand hovered over the knob of the wooden door in front of them. "She is my child." Clea's black fathomless eyes were anything but kind at the moment. "Do not forget this."

Sparrow knew it was a threat, a reminder.

Clea knocked on the door and waited for the voice on the other side. She pushed the door open and shoved at Sparrow's back. "Close the door behind you," she said softly. "This thing between you both is private. Keep it that way."

Clea was gone. Sparrow walked into the room like a trouble child. *She* was there. And she was anxious. He could smell her fear; it was sweet, soft, and cakelike. Sparrow could remember the taste on his tongue, sweets that he had eaten not too long before the change. Was it with her?

"Do you remember me?" Her voice was soft, demanding.

While her skin was milky white, she was tainted with dark; he could sense the part of her soul that was like him now. And then, something else he didn't quite understand. He wanted to remember, but he couldn't. Something in his brain was begging for him to remember. It was as though the morning rays of sunlight were reaching for him, but he couldn't quite grasp them.

She sighed, reached for the blade strapped to her thigh, and used it to cut her wrist.

Sparrow could smell her blood as soon as the blade first grazed her skin. He was starving—should've eaten days ago—but couldn't bring himself to touch those other women. But this one standing in front of him, she was right. Her blood called to him, rich and sweet, commanding. Sparrow moved as though she was some celestial being, her gravity drawing him.

He fed, filling the void in his center, and when he was done, she lay limply on the floor. Sparrow was horrified—sated but completely horrified, given Clea's warning. And then, as though Jim knew the moment that Sparrow had taken his fill, he called Sparrow away.

Sparrow fled the room in a blur, moving faster than ever. Her blood, fresh and alive, made him faster and stronger than he had remembered ever being.

...

Meg

"Oh my. Oh no." My shoulder is pushed, and I am rolled onto my back. Clea slaps my cheeks with her cold hands. "Wake up." She slaps harder.

I groan. My mouth feels dry.

"Wake up, wake up." Clea shakes my shoulders.

I open my eyes and feel the hard floor on my back. "What happened?" I try to sit up, but my head spins.

Clea reaches out to support me. "He took too much."

I move my arm. With blurry vision I see that there is only a faint mark from where I cut it. Small dots from Sparrow's teeth surround the area.

Clea looks panicked. She touches my forehead. "He left you like this?" she asks.

I try to shake my head, but the world spins and my stomach heaves.

"He shouldn't have left you like this." She stands. "Can you walk?"

I try, but I don't have the energy to lift my ass off the floor. I want to do nothing more than curl up on the stone underneath me and drift off into an hours-long nap.

"I'll get help."

Clea leaves and returns with two men. At least, I think they're men. Like the other creatures of Hell, they have horns and scales, but they look very humanlike. They cross the room with swift strides and reach for me.

In an instant I am reminded of the day the Hellions came for me. They chased me up the stairs, burst through the locked door to my bedroom, and did terrible, terrible things to me. Things no man should ever do to a pregnant woman. I panic, try to scramble away, and slap at their hands.

"No! No. No. No. Don't touch me." I reach for my blade

and hold it out to protect myself, the tip grazing one of their chests. "Go away! Go away!"

"Child?" Clea frowns.

Next, the memories of a childhood with John Lewis flood my vision. He hated me—let me know it each day after I turned twelve. Never laid a finger on me before that, but there was something about the number twelve that gave him the permission to let loose. An old scar on my leg throbs where he threw a butter knife and it stabbed into my skin.

I panic and start swiping at the men. "Get them out!"

"Out." Clea makes them leave. Before she closes the door, she shouts into the hallway, "Daddy!"

In a puff of smoke Lucifer appears in my room. He bends down and touches the middle of my forehead with his index finger, and I'm out.

The Devil Watches Over His Own

Clea is sitting on my bed. She looks worried. I vaguely remember trying to attack the men she brought in to help lift me off the floor.

I stretch my arms and legs, then realize I am in bed wearing nothing but my underwear.

"Who did this?" I ask, gripping the blankets to my chest.

"Your grandfather." Clea reaches out and brushes my hair away from my face. "You look just like him, you know. The eyes, the hair." She smiles sadly.

"Who?"

"Gabriel."

I pull the covers up to my chin. I resemble him *and* her, different features at different moments.

Lucifer bursts into the room. He looks at Clea. "I feel your sorrow." His voice is deep and thunderous, as though he is making some heartfelt confession that he can no longer hold in.

Clea looks away from her father.

Lucifer focuses on me, taking an intimidating step forward. "I saw why."

"How?" I ask.

Lucifer touches my forehead with his index finger. "I saw. Everything."

He must mean he saw the many reasons why I don't want anyone to touch me. Perfect. Then he probably saw how I despise being pitied. He must have; he doesn't give me that look like the doctors did.

"Hellions are forbidden from touching you, but Sparrow is different. There are very few whose touch you trust."

I nod.

Lucifer glances at Clea. "I will do this only because I lost one child due to my stubbornness." He snaps his fingers.

Noah Cooper appears in my room, looking much different from the last time I saw him. No longer one of the walking dead, he's all dark hair and brown eyes, as handsome as he was when we were dating in high school. Noah stands before me smiling his lady-killer smile with perfect white teeth. He resembles a ghost now, just like Clea.

"How is he whole again?" I ask. "Last time I saw him, his soul had turned."

Lucifer smiles. "I have power over the souls here." Lucifer walks in a slow circle around Noah. "This is one of the few you trust. He will be responsible for finding you nourishment and attending to you after your Hellion feeds."

My Hellion? Shit, now that just sounds dirty.

"So, he's like my manservant?" I ask, motioning to Noah.

Lucifer nods.

"Why?"

"You have the ouroboros. This is important."

Not so long ago, Lucifer was the one who finally told me what the mark was on my thigh. But he has yet to explain its true significance. I only know that the mark is part of the reason why I can travel between realms so easily.

I nod in thanks.

Lucifer disappears.

Clea looks nervous.

"Meg." Noah whispers, his face stretched in disbelief.

And then I am staring into Noah's deliciously chocolate-brown eyes. With all the food I've had since I woke from my coma and shit got real fucked up, I have yet to have chocolate. Noah disappears, then reappears, with a Hershey bar in his outstretched hand.

Well, fuck me. I am surrounded by temptation down here. But that is Hell, I must remind myself. Temptation until your soul is owned by the devil.

"I think I should go," Clea mutters as she stands and floats out of the room.

Noah watches her before turning. "I'm sorry I tried to eat your face. This whole dying and going to Hell thing doesn't come with a manual."

"You could have found a Safe House and repented. The Deacons would have taken you in," I point out. "You could be in Heaven right now."

Noah tosses the Hershey's bar onto the bed; he moves across the room and sits down at the table near the window.

"Where's the fun in that?" he asks. "Besides, the astral plane is so lovely."

"What's the astral plane?" I ask as I stare at the chocolate bar. My stomach growls.

"Eat it." Noah waves at me. "This is my duty as your manservant."

I rip open the wrapper and eat the chocolate bar in less than a minute. It tastes amazing, chocolaty and gooey; I wish I had a glass of milk. I'm still hungry.

"The astral plane is a place of souls and dreams." Noah stands and claps his hands together. "What do you want? Soda, chips, turkey sandwich?"

"Sure." That sounds way better than milk or the Twinkies and Sno Balls I ate for the few days before we showed up here.

Noah disappears. He's gone for longer this time. I lie down and wait, inspecting the marks on my arm. Sparrow was definitely not himself. The change must've screwed him up pretty good. Nothing new for Sparrow, though; seems messing up his brains is the thing to do, lately. Poor guy. I am kinda pissed that he sucked me dry and didn't have the courtesy to pick me up off the floor. When he finally comes around, I'm going to make him pay for that.

Noah returns and hands me a brown paper bag. I open it to find everything I asked for inside.

"How did you get this?" I ask.

"Scoured Hell."

"Seriously?"

He nods. "Soda's past the expiration date, but who knows what they put in that crap. Sure the turkey's on its last day, but it smelled fresh enough. And I think chips will last forever, as long as the bag is sealed."

I wrinkle my nose.

"What?" Noah asks innocently. He inspects his fingers. "Last time I saw my fingers, Rick was chewing them off. Your grandfather knows some pretty nifty magic."

Rick was a friend of Noah's, one of the newly dead. They were surviving together, until they turned.

I open the bag of chips. "That wasn't just my grandfather. He's Lucifer."

"Oh." Noah looks at me with disbelief for a moment. I remember him making the same face when we were kids, when he didn't believe something I told him, like the things John Lewis did to me. "That explains a few things."

I bite into the sandwich and open the soda.

"So that makes you . . ." Noah taps his finger on his bottom lip, waiting.

"The granddaughter of Lucifer." I take a bite of the sandwich. The turkey's pretty good. Not even slimy.

"Okay. That's cool." Noah moves to the chair next to my nightstand. "You should eat. Sleep." He tips his head to the side, and his eyes narrow on me. "And you should probably wear more clothing around me. I may be dead, but I'm not *that* dead."

I pull the blanket tighter around me. "You're dead enough to know that nothing under this blanket is for you."

Noah chuckles. "Still so tough, Meg." He smiles at me. "Thanks for doing whatever it was that brought me back."

"Nothing, besides being scared shitless of letting the goons down here touch me."

Noah moves from inspecting his fingers to his forearms and biceps. "You always were strange with that." He flexes his left arm and tests the muscle with his index finger of his right hand. "Just not with me."

"I know what to expect with you." I take another bite of the sandwich and shake chips into my hand. "Would you stop feeling yourself up? It's making me uncomfortable."

"Been a while since I had this body." Noah folds his hand

behind his head and kicks his feet out, crossing them at the ankles.

As I eat, Noah reminisces about all the things we got in trouble over as kids: hotwiring cars, stealing model helicopters, skipping school, parties, having premarital underage sex in absurd places.

Jeez, we did a lot of bad shit.

When I'm finished eating, I'm disappointed to feel that my hunger is not fully satisfied. I could eat more—tons more, loads more. A glass of blood would cure it, but I'm not ready to go back there.

"You should sleep," Noah suggests. "I'll watch over you."

"Thanks, manservant." I smile at him before lying down again and burrowing under the soft satin sheets.

...

I dream that I have a beak—no teeth, no lips, just a perfectly smooth bird beak with a pointy tip. Nightingale is whipping around me as fast as lightning on her roller skates, whistling a daunting trill. I open my beak to speak to her, but the only thing that comes out is a dull, throaty squawking sound.

I wake with a startle, my hand flying to my mouth.

Goddamn Nightingale.

After reassuring myself that I still have lips and teeth, I get up and head for the bathroom. I strip and shower, and after washing every inch of my skin, I wrap myself in a large towel and step in front of the mirror. I brush my teeth—scrub them until they're smooth—and comb my hair, then head for the closet.

Noah's sitting next to the window. His eyebrows rise as I

step out of the bathroom. I walk the few steps to the closet, open the door, and walk inside.

Noah is behind me in a heartbeat.

"Didn't have threads like this back in Gouverneur." He touches the clothing on the hangers.

"Nope." I take a pair of dark jeans from the shelf.

Noah opens one of the drawers. "Shit."

I turn to him. He's holding up something that looks like red string.

"Is this even considered underwear?" He winks. "These would look nice under those jeans." He holds out the string.

"I don't think so."

Noah digs through the drawer inspecting all the scraps of fabric Clea supplied me with. "Never wore dirty underthings like this for me, Meg."

"I couldn't afford that shit when we were kids." I pull a gray top from its hanger. I didn't have a bank full of money until I turned twenty-five.

"What's there to afford? It's just string." Noah closes the drawer. "I could go get some fishing line and make you something."

"Get out of here. I need to get dressed."

Noah looks me up and down. "I *am* your manservant. I'm sure my duties include helping."

"Out."

He's gone in a flash. I close the door and get dressed.

When I leave the closet again, Noah is sitting across the room on the small couch along the wall.

"Shit, Meg." He stands. "You look good. How come you never dressed like that when we were together?"

107

"I couldn't afford these clothes on my budget of food stamps and stolen cigarettes."

"I would have bought you something like that. If you hadn't run away to college and left me behind."

I rest my hand on my hip and thrust my other thumb toward the closet door. "Sure. I'm betting you could have afforded all that with your small-town drug dealer budget. Selling weed didn't exactly pay your bills. I remember that much. You lived in your grandmother's basement."

Noah frowns. "Way to ruin the mood."

"There was no mood."

His eyes narrow on the new tattoo on my chest; the wings of the sparrow peek over the low collar of my top.

"New ink?" Noah asks.

"Yeah." I'm not sure I could handle explaining Sparrow and the tangled mess we're in right now.

My stomach rumbles.

Noah straightens his back. "What do you want? Pancakes, hot cocoa, bacon?"

That sounds amazing. "Sure."

He's gone.

I walk to the small table near the window. There's a lot of moaning from the walking sacks of flesh below us. And there are shouts in the distance, probably new souls trying to figure out where the heck they are. I did the same when I woke up in county lockup and realized I was alone. The jail was empty except for the dead. I spent weeks trapping rats and eating them. I shudder. It was days of staring at the spoon outside of my cell before I finally worked up the courage to reach for it. It wasn't a rock hammer, but it would do. I dug through the crumbling cement wall in the back of my cell, made my way to the basement of County, and escaped through the sewer cap. The whole time all I could think of was that move *The Shawshank Redemption* and how Andy never gave up after all those years. When I finally reached street level, I ran to my house for supplies. I know how those fresh souls feel; I lived it for a short time.

I sit at the table until Noah appears again. He's holding a steaming plate of food and a mug.

"You know how hard it was to find this?" He sets breakfast down, then sits at the chair opposite me.

"How hard?" I ask as I dig in.

Noah looks away. "Luckily some old lady knew how to make pancake mix from scratch. Had her whip up a short stack before she turned into a gooney. Some weird dude in the woods killed a pig and cut the bacon fresh. Found the hot cocoa—"

"Stop. I've decided I don't want to know where this came from." I try not to think about a dead old lady cooking my breakfast.

When I'm done eating, I push the plate away. I stand, find the thigh holster for my blade, and strap it on my leg. I secure my weapon, then find the thin leather jacket I've been wearing thrown across one of the chairs near the door. I put it on, then turn to Noah.

"Shit, Meg." Noah stands. "That's hot."

"Shut up." I reach for the door handle and smirk, tipping my head toward the blade. "It's better than a Beretta."

"Don't know about that. Those guns saved your life once."

"Yeah. I did shoot seven Hellions and Jim."

"Where you going?" Noah asks.

"You my manservant or my nanny?"

He shrugs. "Pretty much the same thing."

"I'm not going to stay locked up waiting to be someone's Hungry-Man TV dinner. Let's go find some trouble."

Noah smiles wide. "That's my girl."

We head for the entrance to the burning caves, but the droves of stinking, meandering meat sacks drive us back. They keep a few yards' distance from the opening, never entering.

"We should wait until night," Noah suggests.

"But I'm bored now."

"Hang on." Noah dashes out of the cave and sprints around the dead to a pile of gravel. He grabs a handful before running back to me. His cheeks are flushed. "Okay. Come on."

I follow him back to my room and out on the balcony. Noah bends and pours the handful of pebbles on the floor.

"What are you up to?"

He smirks up at me before taking three of the pebbles and moving toward the railing. Noah leans over and throws a rock. Moaning erupts below.

I move to look over the railing. There's a group of the dead far below my window. It must be fifteen stories or more down.

Noah tosses another pebble. They shift and moan, searching for the source of the noise, hoping for a fresh neck to bite into.

"That's cruel."

Noah shrugs. "You're bored."

A bird flutters by; it's more of a shadow, but it gives me an idea. I bend and take a handful of pebbles.

"What are you doing?" Noah asks.

I lean my hip on the railing and hold my hand out.

"Try it," I suggest.

He grabs a handful of stones and mimics my stance.

We stand like this for minutes.

Noah turns, raises his eyebrow in question, then yawns exaggeratedly.

A bird flutters down and lands in his open hand.

Noah's eyes widen.

"Ye of no faith," I mock.

It's a robin, which pecks at the stones a few times before ruffling its feathers and flying away in frustration.

"Cool." Noah smiles.

I'm still on the fence about staying down here with Sparrow, but I'm not going to continue to be bored out of my mind all day long waiting for him to come feed off me. I just need some distraction, some time to think things over for a little bit.

"Manservant. Can you get us some birdseed?" I ask.

Noah disappears, returning a few minutes later with a plastic bucket filled with seed. "You don't even want to know where I found this." He hefts the bucket to the corner of the balcony and sets it down.

"You're right. I don't."

I take a handful of seed and move back to the edge of the balcony.

Noah does the same.

"Is this what we're going to do all day? Let birds eat out of our hands?"

Three chickadees land on the railing. They hop closer and closer until two flutter up to my hand to eat. The other takes flight and hovers around Noah's hand before landing and pecking at the seed.

"Why not?"

"The Meg I knew would never do this."

"Maybe I've changed."

Noah chuckles. "People don't change, Meg. They just suppress it all."

"That was deep."

"And I wasn't even under the influence."

We watch the birds, laying out seed and letting them eat from our hands until night comes.

After all the birds have gone, Noah presses the lid on the container of seed. He moves to stand near me. Our elbows are resting on the stone railing as we both stare off into the moonlit vastness of Hell, until there is a knock on my door.

"Come in," I shout.

Sparrow enters my room, and my nerves kick up a notch. I notice he's gaunt again. Starving. He stands motionless near the door, a deep rumble echoing from his chest as he looks warily at Noah.

"You should probably leave," I warn Noah as we both step into the room.

My manservant is gone in a flash, and it is just me and Sparrow. My heartbeat quickens as I reach for my blade and cut my arm.

Sparrow moves just as quickly as before. He latches on. I feel his teeth on my skin, the sharp pinch of pain, and the movement of his tongue. He sucks. The feeling intensifies. My knees weaken. My core burns and quivers. Sweet Jesus. I drop to the ground...

I come to as Noah's lifting me off the floor. "Knew that guy was fucked in the head," he's muttering as he sets me on the bed and covers me with blankets.

"You don't understand. He can't help it," I say. "He's not normally like this."

"How is he then?"

I try to shake my head, but it only lolls to one side in exhaustion. "Different," is all I say before I fall asleep.

...

Thankfully, Nightingale doesn't permeate my dreams this time. When I wake, Noah is nowhere to be seen. I check my arm and find there is a small pink scar and a smear of blood across my skin. I get up and shower.

After getting dressed in a pair of form-fitting sweatpants and an off-the-shoulder sweatshirt, I move to the balcony.

The sun is rising in an explosion of pinks and grays.

"Breakfast." Noah's voice startles me.

I turn to find him setting out food on the small table in my room.

"You didn't ask me what I wanted," I point out as I walk toward him.

Noah makes a noise. "Know you well enough. Coffee, chocolate chip pancakes, and sausage."

I sit. "Coffee?"

Noah sits across from me. "Some crazy teenage chick south of here found a truck filled with unopened cans of Folgers. She was smart enough to set up a little French press by herself. Could smell it ten miles away. Had her make you a cup before she turned." Noah's expression turns thoughtful. "Strange, isn't it. Last thing these people spend their energy doing is preparing gourmet coffees and making chocolate chip pancakes and sausage out of wild boars."

I drop my fork and stare at him.

"What?" Noah asks innocently.

"I was really enjoying this, until you told me all that."

"I just don't understand."

"Some of us really like our food. It's comforting."

Noah shrugs, moves his hands behind his head, and leans back. "I can't eat, so it doesn't matter to me anymore."

I look down at the breakfast he brought me. Wasting it would be a tragedy. And I'm hungry. I pick up my fork and start eating again.

"Never found much comfort in food anyways."

"What then?" I ask, taking a very unladylike mouthful of pancake.

"Thick blunt packed with Kushberry that's been hang dried in a fifty-degree room for about four weeks." He sucks in a breath and closes his eyes before exhaling slowly. "That's comforting."

I take a sip of my coffee, which is really quite good, and let Noah daydream about his pastimes of smoking weed and doing nothing productive.

When he finally snaps out of it, I find him leering at me as I'm rubbing the last of my sausage in the puddle of syrup on my plate.

"What?" I ask without looking up.

"Dressing down today? Is this you letting go?"

I sigh and eat the piece of maple-soaked sausage. "I just didn't feel like getting dressed." I set my fork down and finish off the last of the coffee.

Birds are settling on the balcony railing, cocking their heads expectantly at us and blinking their beady eyes. A few of them chirp, beckoning us to set out seed.

"I guess it's time to feed them." Noah stands.

I follow him to the balcony.

...

I lie awake in bed, my brain buzzing too fast to sleep. All I can think is that it's been three days since I last saw Sparrow. Maybe he regrets almost draining me and leaving me on the floor like a sack of bones, twice.

Noah's gone for the night. We've spent our days training the songbirds and playing cards. I keep asking him to find me a Jeep so we can go driving one night, but he keeps making excuses. Mostly he says Clea will kill him all over again. I don't care; I don't like being cooped up here like a zoo animal.

I want a beer and a party, something to drown my sorrows in and forget.

Knowing the one place where I can find alcohol here, I get up and leave my room. By the time I reach the stairwell, I wish I had something more appropriate on. I'm wearing nothing but a long T-shirt and underwear. Oh well, I've worn less into Walmart. A string bikini and flip-flops somehow got past their "no shirts, no shoes, no service" policy.

The castle is empty; nothing lurks in the hallways at this ungodly hour. I climb the stairs and make my way to the Hellions' lair, then push open the door to find the place is empty. I focus on the bar and see the bottles of liquor lined up neat. There's a glass-front fridge, half of it filled with beer bottles, the other half with blood. I lick my lips.

Just as I'm reaching for the door, I hear footsteps behind me and smell a familiar scent.

When I met Jim at that party in college, I thought it was hot, him smelling like embers and rock dust. Little did I know he smelled like Hell. Back then I didn't know he was the child of Lucifer's head Demon, raised on the earthen plane after his father smuggled him out of Hell. He hunted me down, knocked me up, and dragged me back to the tiny town I grew up in. I hate him for it. I hate him more for trying to kill me twice.

"Don't turn around," Jim says.

No problem with that. I can't stand the look of his face, even before it was half-melted off. I know he's leering at me. I feel him pinch my shirt and lift it so he can see my ass.

I freeze.

"Don't touch me," I warn. "I'll kill you." I grip my thigh looking for my blade. There's nothing there but bare skin. Shit. This is not the kind of trouble I was looking for.

"Not touching. Just looking," Jim assures me. "Have to see what's so wonderful about you. Birdboy won't touch none of the Bloodwhores. Thinks he's better than the rest of us."

"I don't give a shit."

Jim leans in close, and I feel his breath on my neck. "I'd fuck you nice and hard like I used to if I knew your grandpappy weren't watching."

I want to kick him in the nuts and chop his head off. But I can't do that right now. Besides telling me not to go around unarmed like an idiot, Clea warned me that Jim's dad will kill me. Really kill me. Vine doesn't care if my grandfather will kill him back. But if I had my weapon, I could hurt him a little—toy with him like he did to me all those years.

I wish Sparrow were here—my Sparrow, not what they turned him into. He'd kill Jim all over again for even suggesting he was going to touch me.

Jim lifts my shirt higher, getting an eyeful, I guess. I wasn't expecting company. I just wanted a stiff drink, forgetting for a moment that the beings around here don't sleep at night.

I have to turn this around and get in control of the situation again. I wonder if a guy could die of blue balls?

I bend, throw out a hip real sluttylike, and listen to Jim suck in a sharp breath. The underwear is black and lace and barely there. It was meant for Sparrow to see, not Jim. It's nothing Jim hasn't seen before, though, I remind myself.

I had better plans for tonight: I was going to try to seduce Sparrow when he came to feed. Get him to do me like he did me on the floor of that church back when we were nothing but two lost souls, who had no one but each other. Talk about backfire. My old Sparrow'd be pissed right now. He'd get all hot and bothered. I bet his downy white wings would even ruffle.

I pretend to take forever to choose a beer. I couldn't care less what it tastes like; I just want something numbing. Settling on Michelob Light, I take two.

"What's wrong, Jimboy? Gotta roll a quarters in yer fly?" I let the trailer drawl work real hard.

"Fuck, Meg." Jim tugs at my shirt again, lifting it higher. I hear him step closer, feel his heat on my ass.

I stand, ramrod straight, beers in hand. "Don't fucking touch me." I look over my shoulder.

Jim drops the shirt and steps away, hands up. "If you weren't such a slut, walking around here half-naked, tempting us all . . ."

I turn, facing him for the first time since he enticed me with a glass of blood days ago. "Us?"

Jim tips his head to the shadows where seven forms stand. Shit, Hellions. I didn't see any of them when I walked in here. But then, I wasn't really thinking about the trouble I could get in. I was only thinking of the pain caused by Sparrow not remembering me—using me up and tossing me away every time he wants dinner—and I wanted to numb it.

I take my beer and run out of the lair. I run all the way back to my bedroom, slam the door, and down the beers in a few long swallows. I wait for the buzz to hit me.

When my lips feel numb, and my fingertips, too, it still doesn't help. I miss Sparrow even more. And the emptiness of barely understanding what the heck is going on down here threatens to consume me.

The glowy, glowy glitteriness of Heaven gave me a headache like no other, but this place is breaking my stupid heart.

Burn and Rust

"Watch this." Noah whistles; a yellow finch lands on his hand.

"Show off." I sit in a chair that I dragged to the balcony earlier.

Songbirds peck at the seeds spread across the railing.

A large gray bird lands, and Noah moves away.

"What?" I ask.

"That's a mourning dove."

"So."

"My grandmother said mourning doves bring bad luck." Another mourning dove lands. "And they always come in twos."

"Your grandmother had a contact buzz from the years you spent growing weed in her basement."

Noah throws seed at the doves, and they fly away. "I'm not taking any chances."

"What chances do you have?" I ask. "You're already dead. And in Hell."

"You never know. I get on Lucifer's good side, maybe he'll give me a promotion."

I shake my head. "No. You'll be my manservant the entire time I'm here."

Noah turns. "How long will you be here for?"

"Not sure. Until Sparrow is done serving his time as a Hellion."

"And then?"

I look over the Kingdom of Hell. "I'm not sure."

Noah sits next to me in another chair. "So we found each other in the afterlife."

"I'm not dead. I can just pass through realms." I point at him. "You're dead."

Noah gets super quiet.

Crap. I think I hurt his feelings.

"Do you think I'll ever see Jack again?" Noah asks.

Jack is Noah's older brother. He's a state trooper on the earthen plane, who saved my ass when John Lewis tried to smother me with a pillow after I woke up from my coma. He also smacked John a little too hard upside the head with his billy club, giving Jack a one-way ticket straight to Hell. I'm not sure Noah knows any of this. Why depress him further?

"Maybe you'll see him again," I reply.

Noah watches the birds.

Minutes later he asks. "How long has it been since Sparrow visited you?"

I think back. "Four days."

Noah whistles low. "I thought three days was bad."

"I know." A feather falls off a yellow finch. I pick it up and twist it between my fingertips. "On that note, I should probably go find him."

Noah salutes me. "Good luck, Captain."

I kick his chair as I pass.

Before leaving my room, I stop at the closet and open one of the small drawers; inside there's a handful of feathers I've collected over the past few days from birds that have fed on my balcony—gray and black from the chickadee, steel gray from the mourning dove, brown from a finch, red from a cardinal, blue from a jay. I set the yellow feather inside, close the drawer, and head for the Hellions' lair.

I'm not sure what Jim is keeping Sparrow busy with, but I'm already tired of him coming to me starved, then nearly draining me dry. So far, three days has been his max. If he waits any longer, no amount of pancakes or pizza will bring me back when he's finished sucking every last drop of blood from of my body.

I push open the door to the Hellions' lair.

Sparrow is standing at the bar; he's humming some dark languid tune. I stop to listen. It's "House of the Rising Sun."

He's humming my number one hated song.

It's Jim's favorite.

Figures.

Being down here is changing my lovely Sparrow into some dark albatross. I want to take him away, then shake him until he remembers everything. He'd be pissed if I did it; this is the only way to relieve his family of the curse.

Let's get this over with.

I slice my arm.

Sparrow turns; his dark wings flex. He's haggard—too thin for his big frame. His green eyes, once glittery and bright, are now dull. He's holding a bottle of bourbon in his hand.

Is that how he's doing this, filling his gut with liquor?

"Dinnertime," I murmur.

Sparrow's nose flares. The bottle drops to the ground and shatters. Sparrow latches on. I feel his teeth on my skin, the sharp pinch, his hot tongue. He sucks. Oh shit. My knees weaken. My core burns and spasms. Sweet Jesus. I drop to the ground.

"Sparrow?" I whisper.

Jim laughs from somewhere in the room. I didn't see him when I first came in here. There's a heck of a lot of growling, and I have no clue where or who it's coming from.

"Sparrow . . ." Words get caught in my throat.

Sparrow's eyes open, and he looks down at me. His gaze settles on the tattoo on my chest. He swallows. Sucks again. Closes his eyes. I notice a bulge in the crotch of his leather pants. Good to know I'm not the only sick freak turned on by this.

The edges of my vision start to blur. My breathing turns shallow. I reach for him but I can barely move my free arm. If I could talk, I'd have some choice words for Sparrow right now.

"Stop." Noah's booming voice fills the room.

Oh goody, my manservant is here.

Sparrow drops my arm, and I fall to the floor.

At least now I know four days will almost kill me. I put a pin in that shit and remember it for later. If Sparrow won't come to me willingly, then I will come looking for him.

Noah lifts me off the ground and walks back to my room, muttering a string of curse words the entire way.

"Why in the hell would you walk into the lion's den and offer yourself up like a goddamned piece of bloody steak?" Noah's pissed.

"I didn't want him showing up here and sucking me dry in the heat of passion . . . or hunger."

"Every Hellion was in that room. You're lucky they all didn't take a drag."

The sound of Noah kicking my door open echoes in the hall. He spins to kick it closed again—much harder than necessary—before crossing the room and dropping me on my bed.

Noah starts walking away.

"Where are you going?"

"To tattle to your mother."

Shit, he's going to tell Clea what I did. "Don't—"

"Go the fuck to sleep, Meg. You're in deep shit."

I sink into the bed and listen to the door slam again before closing my eyes.

...

Sparrow

"How much have you remembered?" Jim stood before Sparrow, waiting.

Sparrow shook his head. Admitting this truth shamed him. Sparrow could remember nothing—just an urge of feelings that had not yet come to fruition.

"Better off." Jim downed a shot of bourbon, hissing through his teeth after swallowing. He passed a shot glass to Sparrow, who swallowed the liquor down in silence.

"Not as good as that trashy whore's blood. Is it, cherub?"

Sparrow grunted. He felt too weak to talk—hadn't been back to her since the second time he had left her a heap of bones on the floor. The guilt tore at him; it ripped a hole in his soul and threatened to drown him. He'd seen Clea since then; her sinister stare was all the punishment Sparrow needed. Clea knew what he had done.

Sparrow was famished. For the past few days they had been all over Hell collecting stone blocks. Jim had sent Sparrow to gather them, saying Sparrow was the only one who could step foot on the hallowed ground.

Even in the dim sunlight of Hell the labor was intensive. The only positive Sparrow found from the hours spent pounding on thick rock was that the walking dead kept their distance. He didn't have to send their tortured souls away with the sharp end of his blade.

Jim moved away, and Sparrow poured himself another drink. The burn of the bourbon was nearly useless when it came to sating his hunger; though, it did dull the haze threatening to overtake him.

Sparrow began to hum a song he'd heard repeated over and over again in the lair. As he stood there, drowning in his own darkness and shame, doing his best to forget and remember, the door to the lair burst open.

Sparrow knew who it was before he turned around.

She was there. Electricity enlivened the air between them.

Sparrow turned.

She cut her arm and murmured something. Stood there, bleeding for him. Sparrow knew that the other Hellions in the room would be on her in a second. The dark hunger overtook him. Sparrow dropped the bottle in his hand and crossed the room in a flicker of haste. He couldn't remember her name or who she was to him, but Sparrow wouldn't let the other Hellions touch her. She was his; he could taste it on his tongue as he fed from her.

"Sparrow . . ." He heard her call his name, her voice weakening. When he finally opened his eyes, he saw the colorful ink on her chest, and a fire lit within him, something stronger than the power of turning into a Hellion. Sparrow sucked, filled his bloodstream with her blood, lapped at the soft skin of her arm, and badly wanted to drag her away from the lair and into a dark room to have his way with her.

"Stop!" A voice boomed, and a force shoved Sparrow away.

Noah. Sparrow knew the ghost standing before him. Their darknesses were linked, just like his and the other Hellions. But Noah had some strange power: he was tainted with astral magic that would protect Meg at any cost if her life were in danger.

The ghost bent and scooped her off the floor. Sparrow watched, blood dripping from the corner of his mouth, wanting nothing more than to tear Noah's hands off her. But the collar around Sparrow's throat tightened, and Noah's magic kept him at a distance.

Jim laughed.

The door slammed closed behind Noah as he walked out of the lair.

Sparrow stood frozen in place. He licked his lips, tasting sweetness. He knew he was in trouble. This was a depraved bloodthirst that he could barely control.

Jim moved in front of Sparrow. "Bet you're strong now, Birdman." Jim poked his finger into Sparrow's chest. "That was lovely." He glanced down. "Perhaps you should go take care of *that*." His eyebrow rose, the one that wasn't burned and scarred. "Or I could bring in one of the Bloodwhores to relieve you of your angst. They'll do anything you want. The empty promises we've made them ensure it."

Sparrow said nothing, wanting to simply remove Jim's head from his neck and force the man to shut up. He could do it.

Sparrow had the strength now, but that invisible collar tightened around his neck as though Jim could read his thoughts; it was holding him back.

"Now that you're strong, get back to work." Jim reached out and swatted at the bat wings on Sparrow's back. "Let's see how heavy a load you can carry now that those stupid fairy wings are gone."

...

Meg

You know you're in trouble when Lucifer and your mother are standing in the room waiting for you to wake up.

"No feeding in the Hellion's lair!" Lucifer roars.

I think my heart stops beating. No one moves or breathes for long seconds.

Clea looks down at me with a frown.

"House rules," Lucifer continues. "They are already tempted enough by the smell of you lingering throughout the caves."

The king of Hell disappears in a puff of black smoke.

"I will bring him every day, twice at the most. This cannot happen again." Clea touches my hand before standing and floating out of the room.

I feel my face flame red. There's nothing like being reprimanded as an adult. That was worse than any punishment John Lewis handed down to me as a kid, and they didn't even hit me.

Noah disappears in a flash and returns with two steaming microwaveable pizzas and a six-pack of soda. He sets them down on the bed.

"Eat," he demands, before crossing the room and pulling a chair closer to my bedside.

I hesitate. I've never been this hungry before.

"You want more?" Noah's brows rise in question "Want me to get you a nice refreshing tallboy of blood?"

"Shut up," I sneer, before biting into a slice of pizza.

...

There's a knock on my door. Noah sets his cards down on the bed. We've been playing rummy to kill time. He wouldn't let me get up except to shower and use the bathroom—said I needed to conserve my energy.

"Come in," I shout, setting down my cards and giving Noah a wary look. The memories from yesterday are still fresh.

Clea enters; Sparrow follows. He looks like a puppy that's been kicked.

Poor bastard.

I move off the bed and stand. Sparrow refuses to look at me.

"It's time," Clea says. She beckons Noah. "Come. Leave them."

They leave us standing in the room together. He looks agitated.

Don't let me forget, Meg. Don't let me forget you. My thumb rolls over the ring band on my finger.

"Sparrow?" I ask.

He looks away and licks his lips.

"Remember me yet?" I ask.

The strange wings on his back twitch. I miss his feathers. These look wrong on him.

"Stop staring at my wings," Sparrow finally says, his voice

deep and rhythmic. "It's rude. I feel like you're undressing me with your eyes."

"Maybe I am."

His eyes lock with mine. He's still across the room.

I sigh and reach for my blade. After cutting my skin, I stand there with my arm stretched out, waiting.

The blood pools and starts to slide.

Sparrow's eyes never leave mine.

A bead of blood forms into a large drop and stretches toward the floor, the gravity of Hell beckoning it to fall away from my body. Just as it separates from my arm and hits air, Sparrow moves. He slides on his knees, catching the drop of blood in his mouth, then grabs my arm and pulls it to his mouth, latching on and sucking.

Heat floods me. Christ, seeing him on his knees like that does something to me. Sparrow's hot tongue slides over my skin; his teeth pinch. I draw in a breath. He sucks like a baby to breast, his eyes closed and jaw moving.

This time he doesn't drain me dry. He moves his mouth away, his tongue sweeping over the wound, sealing it instantly.

Sparrow stands, towering over me. He turns to leave.

Don't let me forget you, Meg.

"Wait!" I run to the closet and open the drawer where I've been stashing the feathers I've collected. I select a small black one and run back to Sparrow.

"Here." I hold the feather out to him.

Sparrow's fingers grip the end of the feather. He looks confused, then pissed. He drops the feather on the floor and walks away.

Son of a bitch.

Noah's standing outside my room as Sparrow walks

through the door. He glares at Sparrow before entering, carrying a box of donuts and a carton of milk.

"Manservant at your beck and call." Noah kicks the door closed behind him. His eyes roam over me. "See you're still standing. Birdman didn't suck you dry. Good thing your mother intervened."

I bend to pick up the feather and walk back to the closet, replacing it in the drawer.

"Found these donuts in the back of a convenience store. Thought they'd be the first to go. Powdered sugar's probably clumpy." He raises the jug of milk. "Have no idea how this isn't expired." He opens the cap and sniffs, then jiggles the jug. "Probably safe to drink." He crosses the room and sets everything down on the table.

I sit in a chair, take one of the donuts out of the box, and shove the entire thing in my mouth. My eyes burn. I choke a little on the powdered sugar.

"I don't do the Heimlich," Noah warns. "You choke on that shit, you're going to have to save yourself."

I flick the cap off the milk, letting it bounce to the floor before drinking straight out of the jug. It's hard to feel thankful for much right now, but I'm thankful when I don't get a mouthful of sour chunks of curd.

...

Sparrow

Turns out Sparrow could carry a heavy load of rock immediately after feeding like he did. But as the day went on, the weight of the rock became nearly unliftable. With each stone he transported, the thrusting of his wings moved him less and less through the thick atmosphere of Hell.

As time passed, launching from the ground turned difficult, followed by the distance of flight, and when he landed, he stumbled and fell to one knee. Lurching and nearly breaking one of the stones, Jim swore and finally sent the other Hellions to help.

By the time they made it back to the burning caves, Clea was waiting there, and she was pissed. "Sparrow." Her tone was clipped and dark. "Come with me now."

Jim waved him away with an annoyed gesture.

As Sparrow walked, the invisible collar around his throat grew tighter and tighter. It was nothing compared to the ache in his gut.

Sparrow walked away from his fellow warriors and followed Clea.

When they were a good distance away, headed toward the entrance to the burning caves, Clea said, "I thought better of you than to do that to her." Her gaze was a splinter wedged deep in his skin; he'd never get over that glare. "You are not evil incarnate like the others. You should be remembering." Clea stopped him and touched his shoulders, which towered above her. She looked deep into his eyes. "What did that little prick do to you?"

Sparrow stood silent. He didn't know—only had a feeling that something was warring within his soul, threatening to tear him apart.

Clea stood a moment longer. "Perhaps it's the stronghold of the curse. We'll have to give it time." She started walking again. "Come."

Sparrow followed her to the bedroom door he knew to be *hers*. Clea knocked, then pushed the door open.

She was there, standing in the middle of the room wearing the same thing as the day before. She looked pale, nervous, scared of him even, and he felt like shit because of it.

Clea was gone; the door shut. *She* continued to watch him before slicing her wrist and tempting him. Sparrow didn't waste a drop of her blood, and he found that it was much easier to stop himself after having fed the previous day.

After Sparrow pulled away from her and stood, she handed him a small dark feather. A memory assaulted him: he was standing somewhere very bright, gripping a large black feather in his hand and visions were flashing behind his eyes . . . *War. Battles without end. Confusion. Darkness and death. Light and dark. A white-hot explosion between ethereal realms. Pain and loss. Abandoned children. Isolation. A vast plane of emptiness filled with sand and the burning heat of the sun where he was left alone with nothing but his frequent state of madness.*

Sparrow dropped the feather and stormed out of the room.

...

Meg

"What time's dinner?" Noah throws a handful of seed over the balcony.

"Hey. You're going to have to go out and get more of that," I threaten. "Especially since you still haven't gotten me that Jeep so we can go driving." I shift in my chair and prop my feet up on the balcony railing.

"Answer the question?"

Manservant is getting bossy.

"I don't know." I tap my toes on the railing and pull my

shorts up, revealing more thigh, soaking up the sun, and hoping for a tan.

"You're going to burn his dinner," Noah warns.

I swat at him.

"I can hear your skin crisping up already." Noah laughs and throws another handful of seed.

"I'm bored." I stretch my legs.

Noah leans back in his chair and clasps his hands behind his head. "Don't know about that. You're pretty set here. Better than we ever had it as kids. Even if that crazy dude is sucking your blood on a nightly basis."

I point at Noah. "You trusted him at one point. I remember that much. When I found you, before you turned into a walking sack of flesh, you told me you trusted him more than those other chuckleheads you were holed up with. Said he saved your ass on more than one occasion."

Noah rubs his chin in thought. "Maybe."

"You said it. He saved my life, too."

"And then?"

And then everything continued to get further and further fucked up. I roll the ring band with my thumb.

"He has to do this. We have no choice."

"You'll forgive him after?" Noah squints at me.

"Yeah." Or at least I hope so. Because other people who treated me so shittily, I didn't hesitate one second before cutting them out of my life.

"Sound pretty sure about that."

"Before the change, he told me to remember him and remember that he loved me more than anything." I think hard—pull up the memory of Sparrow in that Canadian tuxedo standing in the hallway of the Hilton outside our hotel-room door.

"That's some deep shit."

"I don't know." I shake my head. "This could be one giant mistake. I forgot who I was for a while." I look away from Noah and stare at the dark forest.

"Who are you?" Noah is watching me closely.

"I'm having a hard time remembering. The empty promises of Heaven really did a number on me."

Long moments pass before Noah speaks again. "You think things between us could have been different?" he asks.

I shake my head. "No. We got in too much trouble."

He reaches out and touches my arm. "I'm sorry I never stood up to that bastard when we were kids."

"It's the past. Can't change it." I stand and stretch, and consider lying out on the balcony in my underwear to get a tan. "Besides, we're here now."

"Yeah." He throws another handful of seed; the dead moan and groan from below.

"Those walking meat sacks are going to eat the songbirds, and then all my entertainment will be gone."

Noah wipes his hands on his pants before folding them over his stomach.

"It never gets this bright here. I think I'm going to sunbathe." I strip off my shirt and lay it down on the stone floor in the sun. I settle on my stomach and rest the side of my face on my shirt.

Noah clears his throat.

"What?"

"Don't fry up like an egg and get all wrinkly. Sparrow Man won't be able to bite through your leathery skin."

I reach out to swat Noah, but he disappears.

Laying my head down again, I close my eyes and drift off to sleep with the heat of the sun on my back.

I dream of Nightingale, and she's pissed. "Why didn't you take me with you?" She's standing in front of me, screaming. Her face twists, angry and red. "Your monster's coming!"

My eyes flash open.

It's dark now. I shiver in the shade that coats the balcony. I get up on my knees, grab my shirt, and stand.

A large shadow moves in my room.

"Hello?" I ask.

The bedroom door slams.

I push the curtain aside and walk into my room.

Maybe it was Noah snooping around. I check things over: look in the bathroom, then the closet. I open the drawer with the feathers. There's more now, hundreds. I've been collecting handfuls of them every day. I shouldn't be doing it—worse, I shouldn't be doing it in secret after Noah leaves for the night.

Realizing that Sparrow should be here soon, I take a red cardinal feather out of the drawer and tuck it in my pocket. As I leave the closet, walking in a circle, the hair on the back of my neck stands up. Something seems off.

I reach for my blade on a nearby table.

There's a knock on my door.

"Come in," I shout.

Clea enters; Sparrow trails in behind her. She notices the weapon in my hand, and her brow wrinkles. "What's wrong?"

I set the blade down. "I think someone was in here while I was sleeping."

Sparrow suddenly seems interested in the place. He walks through the room, inspecting and sniffing like a guard dog.

"They have been forbidden from touching you." Clea's cold hand settles on my arm.

"I know. Just . . . I saw a shadow."

"Was it Jim?" Clea asks.

Sparrow's head whips in our direction.

"I don't think so. The shadow was too big."

Clea bites her lip. "All will be well. I must go." She leaves.

Sparrow turns to face me as the door closes.

I walk toward him, holding out the cardinal feather.

Sparrow takes it, holds it in his hand—his face impassive.

"What are you doing?" I ask.

"Searching for a fuck to give." His eyes narrow on me.

The Sparrow I know doesn't say shit like that. I do. Maybe this is the darkness taking hold, tainting his soul like everyone tells me it's supposed to.

I never said anything asshole-ish like that to him when we tramped all over Hell searching for his beloved feathers. My hands curl into fists.

"You're a jerk," I reply.

Sparrow takes an intimidating step toward me. I stand taller and consider running for my blade on the table. I've faced worse than a Hellion Sparrow. I've faced off against seven of them and lived to tell the tale. He doesn't scare me. Well, maybe he does. A little bit.

Sparrow takes my arm, pulling it away from my body toward his mouth. The movement is much gentler than his words just were. He licks the pale, vein-laced skin of my wrist before closing his eyes and sinking his teeth in.

Fire burns in my core even though I'm still a little heartbroken after what he just said. The mixture of emotions is confusing. Tears well up behind my eyes. I swallow them down. Girls like me don't cry; we get a beer and drown our sorrows.

I look down and away.

Sparrow stops, and I turn to face him again.

"Dinner was good." He looks me up and down, licking his lips.

"Get the hell out of my room." I growl, pointing at the door.

Sparrow turns on his heel and marches out of the room

Noah's waiting in the hall. "Take it that went well." He glares down the hall at Sparrow.

"Don't ask."

I start looking for the cardinal feather, but I can't find it on the floor. I stand up straight when I realize that Sparrow must've taken it with him.

"You don't know how far I had to go to find this." Noah holds up a steaming calzone on a plate and two bottles of beer. "Was in the back of a freezer in some dude's camper. Had to light his stove with a match to cook the sucker. And these." He holds up the beer. "Had to cut a bitch for 'em."

I take one of the beers, pop the top, and drink the entire thing without stopping.

"That bad, huh?"

I motion for him to pass me the next one.

...

Sparrow

The thought of Jim in her room angered Sparrow beyond belief. He was quick to inspect each and every corner of her bedroom. Someone was definitely just here; he could smell it, sweet and pure like the scent that lingered on her. It wasn't Jim, but it was someone. He couldn't control the anger, knowing it was the darkness within him taking hold, twisting him away from the man he used to be.

Clea left, closing the door behind her, trapping the two of them alone.

She walked toward him with something red in her hand. She held it out. A red feather. Sparrow gripped it between his fingers, unsure of what she wanted him to do with a feather. He remembered the visions from the last one. This one didn't assault him as the other one had. Instead, on the peripheries of his mind, he could see *her*, smiling on the shores of a lake, at him, gripping fistfuls of feathers in his hands and shoving them in a backpack. It didn't make sense, so he pushed it away and focused on the young woman in front of him.

She was afraid.

Sparrow took a step toward her, towering over her as his eyes appreciated both what she wore and the ink that marked her skin. He wanted to touch the tattoos: the colorful one on her chest and the black quill across her slender collarbone.

Sparrow thought that there were more; there had to be more hidden on her body in places he couldn't see because of her clothing. He had half a mind to strip her bare and look his fill. But Sparrow didn't have the time; he was too hungry from his day of labor with the Hellions.

Sparrow knew the words he said to her were not nice, but he liked the way fire lit her eyes when she was angry.

She didn't offer her arm to him this time; instead he closed the space between them and took her narrow wrist in his large hand. Her heartbeat beckoned him, and he knew the pain he'd caused her moments ago by saying those words would taint her blood. He could taste her emotions as he drank; there was pain, but there was more—something that made his leather pants feel impossibly constricting.

Slowly, he was getting better at this. When she ordered him out of her room, he smiled inwardly, anticipating the next time he'd see her.

Sparrow was finally full. Pain tainted her blood—sated his hunger faster than her fear had on previous occasions.

...

Meg

"Did you figure out who was in your room?" Noah is lying on the floor doing sit-ups.

"No." I roll to the edge of the bed. "Why are you exercising?"

"Gotta keep fit for the ladies." Noah grunts as he does another sit-up.

"Did you find a pretty one with scales and horns?"

Noah starts doing leg lifts. "No." His face is turning tomato red.

"Don't give yourself a hernia. I don't know what health care is like in Hell, but I get the impression the deductible is sky-high."

Noah's feet hit the floor with a thud. "I'm so out of shape."

"You spent your teenage years and early twenties smoking doobies all day."

"So?" He moves to his feet.

"And now you want to get fit?"

"Yeah." Noah starts doing jumping jacks.

I don't think any amount of exercise will change anything. Noah already looks good. I don't know what this is about.

"You bore me." I roll out of bed and hit the shower.

Today I decide on finally wearing the leather pants Clea loaded my closet with. I pair them with a vestlike top. When I walk out of the closet, Noah whistles a catcall.

"Shut up."

"Got a date?"

"With the songbirds." I head for the balcony. After setting out a line of fresh bird food, I sit in one of the chairs and wait for our friends to arrive.

A blue jay lands first, then a group of chickadees, four sparrows, the mourning dove couple, and a yellow finch. I tell Noah what each one is as they arrive.

"How do you know what kinds of birds these are?" Noah sits in the chair next to me.

"Sparrow taught me about them."

"Oh. How about that one?" Noah points to a small gray bird with a pointy beak, black-and-white-striped head, and orange-colored chest.

"I'm not sure what that is."

"Hm." He sounds disappointed.

I stand. "Wait here."

"Where you going?"

"Just wait here." I run to the bathroom and lock the door.

Poof.

I'm in Sparrow's house in Heaven. I wonder if he has *Birds of Hell*. I don't have time to look. I run to his bookcase and take *Birds of the Northeast*.

Poof.

I'm back in Lucifer's Kingdom.

I unlock the bathroom door and head to the balcony. Sitting in my seat, I open *Birds of the Northeast* and begin searching.

"Bathroom reading material?" Noah asks. "You should really wash your hands."

I reach for the seed bucket and throw a handful at him.

Laughing, Noah stands and brushes the seed off his clothing.

I find the bird. "Red-breasted nuthatch."

"Sounds like a shitty band name."

"No." I show him the picture in the book and point at the bird on the railing that he asked about. "It's right here."

"Oh." Noah smiles. "Cool."

I sit back in my chair and flip through the book.

"When did we become bird-watchers like two old ladies in a nursing home?" Noah asks.

"Right around the time you refused to find me a Jeep, so we can hit the streets and find some trouble."

Noah throws birdseed, while I look at the book.

"What time's dinner?" Noah asks.

"Whenever he shows up."

"Hm."

"What?"

"I'm just surprised by how well you've behaved. The Meg I knew wouldn't sit around her room all day and wait for her big, bad boyfriend to show up and suck her blood."

I shrug and pull the book to my chest, wrapping my arms around it. "It's not so bad. And I'm not getting my ass beat every day."

"True."

"I have my mother here. They accept me way more than any

of those jerks in Gouverneur and Heaven ever did. Eventually Sparrow will come around. I hope."

I stare out over the treetops.

"What do you think the Hellions do all day?" I ask.

Noah rolls seed between his fingers. "Probably kill things and kick ass." He sets the seed on the railing. "That's what I'd do."

"I worry about what he's doing with them."

"You probably shouldn't think about it."

Noah tips forward and crawls to the ground. He starts doing sit-ups.

"Again with this?" I ask.

"You bore me." He winks. "Got my eye on a sweet young lady with snakes for hair."

"You're kidding me."

Noah flashes his lady-killer smile. "I'm not getting any younger."

I'll let someone else notify him of the fact that he's not aging, either.

"What if she has snakes for pubic hair?" I ask.

Noah stops with the sit-ups and makes a face. "Way to ruin it for me."

I shrug. "Just want to put it out there. We're no longer in hickville. Weird shit goes on here. This is Hell, after all."

There's a loud knock on my door.

"That's my cue. Happy dining." Noah's gone.

I walk into my room and hide *Birds of the Northeast* in my nightstand.

"Come in," I yell.

The door opens; Sparrow steps in. He looks on edge, more so than usual. He's also hours earlier than normal.

"Hello." I force a smile

Sparrow crosses the room lightning fast and grabs my arm.

"Sparrow?" I ask.

"I dare you to move." Sparrow's fingers tighten on my arm. "Run from me."

What the . . . ? "I dare you to go fuck yourself." I want to punch him in the throat. Maybe that would make him remember me and stop the bullshit. "I'm not going to run from you. That's messed up. You know what the Hellions did to me last time I ran from them."

Sparrow's stare is blank, like he has no clue what I'm talking about. His eyes narrow on my chest before he moves, his arm wraps around my waist, and he pulls me tight against his body.

"Sparrow?"

"Sorry."

"For what?"

His eyes search mine. "This."

His teeth sink into the flesh of my upper arm.

I grip onto his shoulders. "Oh" escapes my lips.

He sucks.

I bite my lip and try to center myself before I lose it.

Sparrow stops and seals the wound with the flick of his tongue. He doesn't let go of me, though. He lifts me, carries me to the bed, and sets me down before turning to leave.

Perhaps chivalry is not dead. But Sparrow might be if he doesn't cut the shit, fast.

...

Sparrow

"You should tell your Bloodwhore to run next time you see her." Mischief glinted in Jim's eyes.

Sparrow wanted to clock the guy, but his arms were too tired from flying stone hither and thither all day. The only thing Sparrow wanted to do was eat and sleep. The muscles that powered his wings ached, his arms throbbed, and his head and chest felt like they were ready to explode. Sparrow knew his heart was trying to tell him to remember something, but the confusion was too deep, and the weariness drove him to lose interest in figuring it all out.

Tell her to run. It was a command—one he couldn't ignore. The collar around his neck tightened, until he could barely breathe. Sparrow knew he had to repeat the words; he didn't have a choice.

Her large blue eyes were wary of him.

But this was something else. Sparrow could feel fear sparking off her, the way her eyes found his, the thundering of her heart. He didn't miss the way she toyed with the ring on her finger. There was something familiar about the silver band and the small black rock that the pad of her thumb rubbed against. But he couldn't remember.

He craved her pain, her fear. He wanted the damn collar to loosen, and only saying those words would make it so.

Sparrow said the words, regretting them instantly when he saw the pain and anger on her face. She yelled at him—said things that made his blood boil with need.

"You know what the Hellions did to me last time I ran from them," she yelled at him.

A spark of remembrance flared within him but never came to fruition. They had hurt her; that was all he could gain from it. Sparrow couldn't help himself. He was hungry, tired, famished, and sore.

The apology that left his lips would do nothing to soothe her; he knew this as his eyes scanned her soft arm. He wanted to feed closer, wanted to taste the larger veins that were nearer to her heart, warm and savory. His eyes flicked to the bird on her chest. It was a sparrow. He is Sparrow. His teeth sunk into the flesh of her bicep.

...

Meg

I let myself sink back down on the mattress and press my hands over my face. This is getting to be too much for me to handle.

A large, dark shadow moving on the balcony catches my eye. I hope it's Noah with something to eat. When I get up and pull the curtain back, there's nothing there.

My door opens, and Noah walks in. He's carrying a large bowl filled with steaming liquid.

"Some newly dead idiots started a commune to the east." He sets the bowl on my table. "They got chickens and cows. Someone planted a garden. Poor suckers spending their last of their days farming for their lives, making this soup only to never enjoy it." He pauses. "Hey, Meg. You okay?"

I let the curtain fall back into place.

"Peachy."

Noah frowns. "You can tell me."

I sit at the table and swirl the steaming soup with a spoon. "You're not my therapist."

Memories flood me . . . giant men kicking my front door

open and chasing me through my house. They chased me all the way upstairs—kicked down that door, too, after I tried locking myself in the bedroom. Did terrible, terrible things to me, then hauled me up by my arms and tossed me down the stairs like a rag doll. I don't regret pulling the gun out of its hiding spot on the steps and shooting them all dead.

Run from me. I have half a mind to hunt Sparrow down and stab him with my blade. Or maybe I should hunt Jim down. That bastard probably had something to do with that entire interaction. My Sparrow knows better. He hated when I brought it up—felt guilty for not being there to protect me.

"Tell me, Meg," Noah urges. "Whatever happened, it's eating you up."

I drop the spoon and push away from the table.

"Did you know Sparrow was assigned to watch over me and my mother on Earth?"

Noah shakes his head.

"He was. But he fell in love with me. He fell in love and abandoned his post in shame. My mother died and he was banished to death down here. When I met you here the first time, and Sparrow was with you, he was dead. A fallen Angel stripped of his wings and his memories. After you changed into a walking sack of flesh, we stuck together. Sparrow helped me and I helped him. We survived together until we both found out the truth."

Noah watches me, his face placid.

"Sparrow was cracked in the head but sweet and honest. He was so strange back then, but the only man who's ever been good to me since we broke up." I feel tears threatening to break. "And now he's a giant asshole." My chin quivers. I clear my throat and swallow it down. "I think I'm starting to hate him."

"Ah, Meg." Noah reaches for me, drags my chair close to his, and wraps his arms around me. "This entire situation is fucked up. I mean, I never thought you'd grow up to be a sparkly vampire."

I swat at him.

Noah pets my head. I try to twist away, unsuccessfully, since he just tugs me tighter to his chest in a strong bear hug.

"In all seriousness, my grandmother used to say 'broken hearts are like broken bones; they'll heal if you let them.'"

"When did she tell you that?" I ask.

"When you left and went to college downstate. You packed your shit and never looked back."

Silence fills the room. I don't know what to say. I won't apologize for leaving and going to college. I wanted to make something of myself. In the end it all backfired, but at least I tried. I rest my head on Noah's shoulder. He wraps his arms around me again, and I fall asleep.

...

My teeth are gone; my gums, smooth and pink. Someone hands me a pair of dentures that look like they were made from Chiclets, Play-Doh, and superglue. *"You should have taken me with you!"* Nightingale screams.

I jerk awake and find the sheets are damp with sweat.

I look out the window to find night invading the late-afternoon haze. I throw the covers back, get out of bed, and run to the balcony. I missed the songbirds. I rub my face and thread my fingers through my hair. What the heck? I slept most of the day.

I shower and get dressed in a pair of jeans and an oversize T-shirt. Just as I'm leaving my closet, there's a knock on my door.

"Come in," I shout.

The door opens and slams closed. Sparrow's here. My stomach feels tight. I don't really want to see him after last night. He really upset me.

Sparrow moves toward me. He smells fresh, like he just showered. There's dirt on his boots. Makes me wonder what Jim has him doing if he has to shower before he comes to see me.

I never move. Sparrow advances until he's standing in my personal space. He pulls me tight against him, like he's some Neanderthal devoid of words, and buries his face in the crook of my neck. I freeze, afraid he's going to feed from my jugular.

Sparrow's hand slides down my side to cup my ass, then around the front. His fingers slide over my jeans to the space between my legs. I suck in a breath, waiting.

"Your sex is on fire, baby." The words sound strange coming from him. Sparrow doesn't say things like this.

"When you say it like that, it sounds like I have chlamydia." I giggle, but when Sparrow moves his head to look in my eyes, my breath catches. He doesn't laugh. "Do you remember me?" I ask.

Sparrow doesn't answer; instead he kisses me hard. His tongue spears between my lips, tasting, demanding. If he weren't holding on to me so tightly, I'm sure I'd drop to the ground from swooning.

I feel a sharp pinch as Sparrow sucks on my tongue. My hands grip his shoulders as he presses his body against mine. Oh Lord, this is sinful. Heat spreads; sweat beads on the back of my neck and down my spine.

Sparrow's fingers press firmer into the vee between my

legs. He rubs, applying just the right amount of pressure. Sweet Jesus, this is hot. He moves his hand. I'm close, so close—

Sparrow releases my mouth and pushes me away. There's a smear of blood on his lips. He licks it away before turning and stomping out of the room.

I'm not sure what the heck that was. An apology for last night? A little afternoon delight? I have no clue. What a dick.

Noah appears. He wrinkles his nose. "You're breaking my heart, Meg."

"Why?" I wipe the taste of Sparrow off my mouth.

"It smells like sex and blood in here."

He drops a box onto the table.

"There was no sex," I assure him.

Noah turns. "Well, something's got you all hot and bothered. I brought tuna melts. Canned tuna, processed cheese, and bread with enough preservatives to stay fresh for a thousand years."

"I wish you'd stop telling me this shit."

He shrugs. "Thought you should know."

I sit and eat.

"Cards?" Noah holds up the box when I'm done.

"No."

"Birds?" He points out the window.

"Change of plans tonight." I stand and grab a clean top from the closet. I glance out the window as I pull it on. It's twilight.

"The dead will be sleeping soon. Let's go have some fun."

Noah snickers. "I think you just had enough fun for the both of us."

"Definitely not." I slip on a pair of boots.

"What are you looking to do?" Noah stands. "As your manservant, I aim to please." He winks. "Just not like that."

I haven't boned him since I was seventeen, and we no longer have that kind of relationship. He definitely knows this after our conversation last night.

"Not happening." I stand up straight. "Let's party. I need to burn off some frustration."

"Oh." Noah walks toward the door. "What kind of party are you looking for?"

"Booze and weed. Your specialty."

"Oh, Meg, you're killing me." Noah takes my hand, and we walk down the hall, heading for the stairwell.

Just as we're heading up, Clea floats down the steps.

"Child?" She asks, focused on my hand holding Noah's.

"What?" I drop his hand. "We're just going out."

"You think that's a good idea?" she asks.

"I don't see why not." I take another step up.

"I'll keep an eye on her," Noah promises.

Clea's eyes narrow on Noah. "It's dangerous for you," she reminds me.

This is stupid. I'm an adult. An immature one, but still.

"I'm going. We'll be fine. I'll be back in a few hours."

Clea drifts to the side and allows us to pass. "Steer clear from the newly dead," she warns. "Word is out about you. The Deacons are gossiping."

My back straightens. The Deacons run the Safe Houses. They have their ears to the ground, looking to pay their penance and buy their way back into Heaven. When I was here before, they threatened to turn me in for a bounty of 150 souls.

"Noah's coming. I'll be fine," I assure Clea. "We won't be out long."

Clea crosses her arms and watches as we walk up the stairwell and turn down the hallway leading outside.

We pass the Hellion's lair on the way out. The loud rock music pauses for a second as we walk by the door.

I grip Noah's hand and tug him along faster before one of them can come out and stop us.

We cross the threshold and step out onto the rocky ground at the mouth of the burning caves of Hell.

"Where do you want to go?" Noah asks as we walk farther away.

"How do you feel about New York City?"

Noah laughs; then his face drops. "You're serious."

"Come on, we've done worse. Remember that time you taught me how to hotwire a car, and we set off for Six Flags with no money in our pockets?"

"That was different."

"How?" I take his hand. "Watch what I can do."

Poof.

We're standing in Times Square—the Times Square of Hell, of course. It's just darker and dirtier than the one on the earthen plane.

There's chain-link fencing and barbed wire lining the streets and alleys. Behind that, the dead shuffle and moan. People walk by us: some look normal—the newly dead—and others have the scales and horns of Demons.

"Let's find a party." I take Noah's hand and start walking.

"You sure this is a good idea?"

"I never asked you that when you were getting me into all that trouble when we were kids." I try to ignore the smell of trash and sour milk, but it's overwhelming here. From behind the nearby fencing, the walking dead moan but keep their distance.

We follow the crowd and find ourselves in front of a tall industrial building. Lights and music pulse from inside. There are bouncers with giant twisted ram horns protruding from their foreheads. They stop no one from entering.

We enter the building with the crowd and walk through a short vestibule loaded with coats and other pieces of clothing. There's a single high heel; a pair of Chucks; and something thick and gleaming, dripping down the wall. Noah pulls me to the side as soon as we make it to the large warehouse section of the building.

Wow. The creatures of Hell sure know how to throw a rave.

There are strobe lights flashing in every color, as a fast techno beat pulses from the speakers throughout the room. The place is one giant dance floor. Bodies gyrate, sway, and shimmy against each other. The scene is something out of a dirty movie. Cages suspended from the ceiling hold scantily clad women with tails and black eyes. Their bodies pulse with the music. There's a bar along the far wall, and behind the counter are row upon row of Devil's Springs vodka. Go figure.

"Let's get drinks first," I suggest.

Noah leads me to the bar and waves the bartender down.

The guy takes one look at us and pours four shots of vodka. "On the house," he says with a smile. I catch him looking at the quill tattoo across my collarbone.

Noah turns to face me. "Sorry, there's no weed." He hands me a shot glass. "This might burn."

We take two shots each.

The music pumps louder. I feel the beat in my chest, beckoning me to do something other than stand at this bar poisoning my liver.

"Let's dance." I drag Noah out onto the dance floor.

The place is packed tight. We have to squeeze between bodies rubbing against one another before we find a spot where we can stand together.

In no time at all we're dancing like we're dating again. I've forgotten about Sparrow getting me all hot and bothered and being a giant dickweed.

Noah puts his hands on my hips and grinds against me; he smiles and whispers something in my ear. The music is too loud, and I can't hear him. Needing some space, I move away. It's so hot I can barely breathe.

The music stops—abrupt silence in its place. Someone screams, loud and shrill.

Noah stands on his tiptoes to see what's going on. "Shit." He takes my hand and pulls me away.

We're running between gyrating bodies who haven't seemed to noticed that the music is off. People rub against us. Someone touches my hair.

Noah tugs me along faster. "Gotta get out of here."

In an instant the party turns violent. The dance floor turns into a fight club. Punches are thrown. A big guy in a tank top punches Noah as we're running. He trips and falls.

I feel a slice of pain across my back. Turning, I find a woman with wild purple hair holding a knife out, jabbing it at me.

What the . . . ?

I try to pull Noah up, but the lady with the knife comes after us. The big guy in the tank top gets distracted by another guy and goes after him.

These people are frigging crazy.

Noah kicks the lady in the knee. She howls and throws the knife, end over end, and it lodges in my arm. I drop to the ground with a scream.

Shit!

Noah pulls the knife out of my arm and throws it into the crowd. Blood starts pouring out of the wound.

"I don't think you were supposed to pull that out."

"Take us back, Meg," Noah whispers harshly. "Take us back now!"

"I can't. Not after being stabbed and sliced up. Can't you do something?"

"Not like this. Shit. Shit. Shit. Clea is going to tan my ass."

The music blares again. Someone kicks Noah in the ribs. He groans and grips his side—tries to stand.

A foot kicks me square in the gut. I double over and press my forehead to the ground, trying to fight the urge to vomit.

Screams erupt throughout the warehouse. Something roars; there's growling. Wet thwacking sounds and hard thuds pierce the air.

"What is happening out there?" I try to hide the panic in my voice.

"We have to get out of here." Noah crawls to his feet, then reaches down and pulls me up with both hands. We lean on each other. There's blood dripping from the corner of his mouth. I didn't know ghosts could bleed. There's not much time to dwell on the thought. Blood is dripping down my own arm, and my body aches.

Three men near us go motionless before turning and focusing on me. They have scales on their shoulders and bony pieces hanging off their knuckles. The screaming around us is louder than the techno music. The men close in.

"Run. Now," Noah says.

I lean on him, reaching for the blade on my thigh. I grip my weapon as we run. The shadows of the warehouse are dark; strange noises echo. Noah leads me along the edges. The three men track us.

Noah stops.

I push at him. "Get moving."

"There's nowhere else. We're backed into a corner." He bends and picks a metal pipe up off the floor. "We fight. Unless you're ready to get us out of here."

Blood is dripping down my arm. I try to *poof* us the heck out of here, but it doesn't work.

"This is not what I was expecting when I told you I wanted a night of booze and weed."

"Me, either." Noah holds the pipe out, threatening the men who seem to care about nothing but the blood pumping down my arm. "I was hoping for some necking on the bluffs, but *you* chose New York City."

"I am never coming here again." I hold my blade out. "These New York City people are a bunch of a-holes."

One of the men lurches forward. Using the pipe, Noah hits him in the stomach with everything he's got. I move and slice the guy's head off.

Another one advances. We try the same move, but this guy shifts to the side and spins, knocking Noah on his ass and leaving me to fend for myself. He throws a punch; I duck and chop him in the leg. The guy howls, and the stump of his left leg squirts blood all over the floor.

"That's disgusting." Noah crawls to his feet and grabs his pipe.

"Better than a smashed brain." I silently thank Lucifer for the blade.

A brick comes flying toward us and hits me in the shoulder. Another smashes Noah in the knee.

"Where the hell did that come from?" Noah shouts.

I look past the one guy who's left. There are more lining up. Now blood is flowing out of the wound on my shoulder. "I think those bricks were made of glass."

"Goddamn it," Noah mutters. "I never got you in this much trouble."

He's right. I never bled this much after a night of shenanigans with Noah.

There's more screaming and shouting. Bodies start flying through the air.

"What is going on out there?" I ask.

Something booms. Sounds like thunder indoors.

"Whatever it is, it's big," Noah shouts over the music.

The last guy advances on us. I move to the side, but he catches me and slams me into the wall. I smack my head so hard I see stars. Noah's beating on the guy's back with the pipe. I swing my blade and catch the guy in the arm. He howls, then stops; his eyes widen.

I hear Noah mutter, "We're dead."

The guy is flung off me. Through blurry vision I see the seven forms of the Hellions standing before us.

Goddamn it.

Jim steps forward. "Nice job, Meg." He spins and just his thumb in our direction.

Sparrow steps forward, pushing the other Hellions away

from me. He reaches for the front of my torn shirt, taking in the blood covering my body and snarls.

Jim claps. "Well that was fun. Let's get these dumb shits out of here. You two really know how to pick a party."

Sparrow pulls me to my feet and throws me over his shoulder in a movement that's so swift it knocks the wind right out of me.

...

Sparrow

Blood rippled through Sparrow's body. The taste of her after he'd touched her, put his hands where he dreamed of for days—it still filled him. The tension had been thick; the noises she made echoed in his thoughts. The taste of her lips on his—

"Hey, Birdman!" Jim shouted. "Focus!"

Sparrow was lugging the last of the rock load. The other Hellions were tying the rock with rope for him to carry. Sparrow thought it was odd that they were careful not to let the stone touch their skin, but he knew better than to ask.

They had dug for a day at some strange dwelling a few hours' flight from the burning caves. Then Jim informed the Hellions that they needed more rock. Once again, Sparrow took the brunt of the labor. It wasn't so bad; he found solace working on hallowed ground, and the daily feedings had made him stronger than before.

When they returned to the burning caves that evening, Clea was waiting patiently for them. There was a fleet of four-door Jeep Wranglers nearby.

"Clea?" Jim asked with a snide tone.

Clea motioned for Jim to follow her away from the Hellions

and Sparrow. Clea was whispering to him and glanced hesitantly back at Sparrow.

When Jim returned, he looked pissed.

"Split up." He gestured to the Hellions. "We're going to a party."

Sparrow rode with three other Hellions. Trees and buildings were nothing but a blur outside his window. The Hellion at the wheel drove so fast that they reached New York City in just under two hours.

The crowd of the newly dead was thick, the-city-on-New-Year's-Eve thick. When the Hellions' driving couldn't get them any closer to their destination, they pulled over and parked their vehicles in a straight line along the curb.

Sparrow didn't know much about where they were going. All he knew was what he heard the other Hellions in his vehicle discussing as they drove; they were headed to a party to collect *someone*.

After the Hellions got out of their vehicles, they started moving, jogging toward the party where Jim had told them to go. Sparrow had half a mind to take flight and get there first; he could—he'd be faster.

They slowed outside the open doors of a nightclub. Screams and deadly howls erupted from inside the building. The Demons at the door stood their ground, never assisting the ones inside and never stopping Jim and the Hellions from entering.

As they crossed the threshold to the building, a desperate need to tear something apart engulfed Sparrow. *She* was there, and she was hurt. He could feel it—sense it somehow.

Sparrow moved through the crowd, shoving and tossing, his giant boots nearly slipping in the bloody sludge that coated the floor.

Other things were in there with them, monsters feeding on the freshly dead. They'd be just as strong as the Hellions, if not stronger, depending on how much they ate. Creatures struck out, scratching at them. A few of the Hellions, including Sparrow, had to fight off droves of people, dead and demonized.

"Nice job, Meg," Jim said as they cleared the back corner of the building.

Meg. Jim had said her name, and it was all Sparrow could think of. She looked terrified, huddled in the corner, her weapon bloody from battle. Pride struck Sparrow; she was strong, fighting strong. He'd always known this, something in his gut told him. But now she was bleeding, and her face was twisted in pain.

Sparrow reached for Meg. He clasped his large hands around her narrow arms, lifted her off her feet, and tossed her over his shoulder. Meg's body went limp against his back. Sparrow'd knocked her out with the swift movement. This was for the best: she didn't need to see what he had to walk through. Sparrow knew she wasn't all innocent, but even he didn't want to see the carnage of the Hell party they were wading through.

The crowd parted, mostly. The remaining Hellions fought the horde that pushed against their retreat, leaving a trail of blood and ichor. Jim waltzed behind the row of Hellions, never lifting a finger to fight. Beastly things had eaten here—funneled the newly dead in and fed from them before they knew where they were. Noah slipped in the gore spread across the floor.

Sparrow reached out and pulled Noah up by the collar of his shirt.

They left the rave. The Demon bouncers at the door simply watched the team of Hellions as they walked away with Meg and Noah in tow.

They strode through the streets of the city for what seemed like an hour, at least, before arriving at the caravan of black Jeep Wranglers. The streets were nearly empty now. Creatures called to them from the shadows and below the sewer grates.

"I can take her back from here." Noah held his arms out.

"You will not touch her." Sparrow's hand gripped the back of Meg's thigh possessively, as she hung limp over his shoulder.

"Clea will—"

"She's safe now." Sparrow pushed at the ghost man, his hand meeting solid flesh.

Noah stumbled and glared.

"You've hurt her enough already. You're nothing like the man I first met down here." Noah glared at Sparrow. "Give her to me." Noah held his hands out again, demanding.

"No." Sparrow could feel the pulse of her femoral artery through her jeans. His hunger reared its ugly head. Fighting his way into the Hell party had taken a toll; his body was bruised and scratched. Sparrow's own blood leaked down his arms, but he wouldn't let her go. "Ride with us if you don't trust me."

Noah had astral magic; Lucifer himself had infused him with it when he bound Noah and Meg together. The ghost could tear Meg out of Sparrow's arms in an instant, but he didn't. It was as though Noah knew that Sparrow had to keep her close while the other Hellions, and Jim, were on the loose.

With his free hand, Sparrow opened the door of the Jeep and waited for Noah to get in.

Noah moved, crawled across the rear bench, and sat behind the Hellion driver. Sparrow got in next to Noah and settled Meg across his lap. She was still unconscious, her breathing shallow. Blood dripped down her arm.

The Hellion in the driver's seat turned, his eyes narrowing on the wound.

"Drive," Sparrow ordered.

The Jeep kicked into gear and pulled out onto the street behind the others.

Sparrow nestled Meg's head against his chest.

Meg. It was a name he'd recognized the second Jim said it. Sparrow couldn't remember it before—hadn't heard anyone call her by it until now.

"Put pressure on that," Noah said.

Sparrow turned to look at him.

"Her arm." Noah pointed to the puncture mark that was draining in a thick trickle of blood.

"Make it stop," the Hellion driving said.

Sparrow pressed his fingers over the wound. Meg made a soft noise against his chest. Sparrow was tempted.

"Don't," Noah warned. "She can't feed you now."

That wasn't his intention, but Sparrow could barely control himself around her normally; with her blood leaking out it was nearly impossible. He bent his head and licked the wound, sealing it.

The Hellion driver sighed as if in appreciation.

The drive back to the burning caves was long, the fleet no longer driving at an emergent pace. Noah watched Sparrow, ready to intervene.

Sparrow wasn't going to hurt her. His hand gripped her hip and pulled her closer. *Meg.* She smelled like Noah and the Devil's liquor. The thought of Noah touching her ignited a rage deep inside Sparrow.

She was his; Sparrow knew this with every speck of his being, even if he couldn't remember the details—even if Jim was slowly working at tearing them apart. After this realization, for a few minutes, Sparrow could barely breathe, and he knew it was Jim validating his hold on Sparrow.

...

Meg

I don't wake to find my faithful manservant, Noah, waiting patiently for me. Instead there is a fuming Hellion named Sparrow. He stands over me. His clothes are ripped. There are scratches on his arms, with blood and black gunk dried to his skin. His hair is matted.

"Should I thank you?" I ask.

He growls. Plainly growls like an animal.

"Thank you." The words come flying out in a rushed whisper, and I look away from him. My cheeks turn crimson. Not much embarrasses me, but last night, that was some serious shit. I can't believe we got into that mess. I'm covered in dried blood and dirt, but my wounds have healed.

Sparrow stares me down.

"What?" I ask sheepishly.

"You will rest." He points a finger at me. "Quickly. I am absolutely starving." Sparrow gives me a dark look before leaving my room.

That was a threat if I've ever heard one. I'm afraid Sparrow might bleed me dry for what I put him through last night.

Noah enters the room immediately after Sparrow walks out the door.

"Oh good, I thought he was going to suck you dry."

"He's coming back later." I swallow hard.

Noah pales. "Uh-oh."

"Right."

"I wouldn't want to be you."

"I don't want to be me, either."

Noah looks surprisingly put together for what we went through last night. "You should probably clean yourself up," he suggests.

I push myself to sit. My muscles are sore, and my stomach hurts from where I got kicked.

Noah hands me a soda.

"So, Clea tells me that you chose the rowdiest Hell party in all the land to attend." He pulls a sandwich out of a brown paper bag. "Congratulations. We're now under house arrest."

"Goddamn it." I open the soda and take a long drink.

Noah hands me the sandwich; I devour it, then wash it down with the rest of the soda.

"I'm going to shower." I stand and limp to the bathroom door, locking myself inside.

After washing the blood off, I find the only indication of the bloodbath at the rave is a few pink scars. Clea probably healed them, or maybe Sparrow licked them. Remembering his hot tongue on my flesh makes my skin flush.

I wrap myself in a towel, brush my teeth, and head for the closet. Noah's gone. Exhaustion hits me, a tsunami of fatigue. Too tired to decide on much, I grab an oversize T-shirt and a pair of underwear off the shelf. I drop the towel, dress, and then crawl back into bed.

Angel of Small Death

He's your monster now. Nightingale's words echo in my dreams. She's roller-skating around the flower garden fountain in Remiel's Kingdom. *"They're going to turn him into a bad, bad man. He needs it to rule, to know darkness and light. They're going to turn him into a monster."* Nightingale circles on her skates faster and faster before she halts in front of me. She whistles a short trill before shouting, *"You should have taken me with you!"*

I jerk awake.

There is a shadow outside my window. I stand to investigate. The breeze chills my bare legs. I reach for the curtain, pull it back, and let my eyes adjust to the moonlight.

An owl is perched on the railing of the balcony. It's brown and white and tiny—could fit in the palm of my hand. I recognize it from Sparrow's bird book: an elf owl. I don't think it belongs in this habitat. The owl turns; its amber gaze is striking. It hoots once before fluttering off into the night.

I go back to bed and lie there for a few moments, realizing that Sparrow never came back to feed, like he threatened.

I fall back asleep only to be annoyed by more of Nightingale's dreams.

...

In the wee hours of the morning I wake to footsteps in my room. My eyes flash open. Sparrow is standing near the window. He looks exhausted, his cheeks are hollow, and there are circles under his eyes. I don't know what Jim is using him for, but the guy looks like he just ran ten marathons.

"Now," he whispers from the shadows.

I am still tired and annoyed. I don't move.

"Now," Sparrow demands, louder this time.

Payback's a bitch. "I'm not getting up." I stretch my arm across the bed.

"Get up."

"No. I'm tired." I throw a pillow over my face.

The bed gives. I pull the pillow up and find Sparrow crawling gingerly toward me. I press the pillow back over my face and feel the mattress give as Sparrow lies across the bed on his stomach. He licks my arm.

I shiver. "Just do it," I mutter from under the pillow.

I feel his hot mouth on me, his firm lips sealing on my skin, his teeth pinching. There is a tugging sensation as he sucks. Heat floods my body. I press the pillow down to conceal the moan that escapes my lips. I am incredibly turned on.

Sparrow pauses, swallowing before sucking again.

And I thought Teari forbidding us from having premarital sex in Heaven was torture. This is worse. I want to rip his clothes off, and mine, too. But at the same time, I want to choke him a little for being an asshole.

Sparrow feeds until my head feels fuzzy. He stops, licks my arm, but never moves away. I lift the pillow again. He's staring at my hand. His finger touches the ring he gave me.

I press the pillow down on my face again, unable to deal with the man I knew and what he's turned into.

The door to my bedroom opens. "Meg?" It's Noah's voice.

"Leave," Sparrow growls at my manservant.

The door slams closed.

I hold my breath.

Sparrow lays his head down next to my arm. He doesn't move for a long time. When I finally work up the courage, I lift the pillow and find him passed out next to me. His face is peaceful in sleep, his muscles lax. Even the leather wings on his back lie flat.

I reach out and touch his hair. It's soft, like I remember. I want to sink my fingers into it and rub his scalp.

He doesn't move.

I roll away from him, slide off the bed, and head toward the closet. I open the drawer where I've stashed all my feathers. After selecting a light-blue one, I return to the bed and crawl next to him. I tuck the feather in his pocket, then scoot closer and close my eyes.

"I wish you'd remember me," I whisper, as I drift off to sleep.

...

Sparrow

"Faster." Jim commanded.

Sparrow was in the pit, digging alone. He slammed the shovel into the fresh dirt, tossing it to the ground above him.

The other Hellions were above, moving dirt out of the cabin to a place in the woods.

Memories of the past night came forth. The sight of Meg lying on the floor, bleeding and pale—he couldn't scratch it from his brain. Anger overwhelmed him. The fact that she'd put herself in danger and that Noah let her go—

A rock hit Sparrow in the shoulder.

"I said faster, Birdman!" Jim was standing over him. "Got a deadline to get this shit done before—"

The Hellion with the scars walked up next to Jim, interrupting. Both of them turned away, Jim never finishing his insults.

Sparrow chopped at the dirt with his shovel and lifted heavy loads of soil above him as fast as he could. His muscles ached; sweat dripped from his body in steady streams. He'd been there since dawn, and the sun was nearly setting now. Sparrow wondered if he'd have the strength to fly back to the burning caves when he was done. The others didn't have to—they were staying out here—but Sparrow's refusal to drink from the Bloodwhores meant he had to go back for Meg. It annoyed Jim, and he held nothing back when it came to punishing Sparrow. That's why he was in the pit, and he had the uneasy feeling that he'd be doing plenty more, and worse, to pay for it.

Sparrow shoveled until dark. One of the other Hellions lit a single candle to allow some light in the space. Sparrow threw a load of dirt to the floor above him. He heard it hit someone, and before he knew it, a Hellion was in the ditch with him, yelling and shoving.

"You'll pay. Stupid fairy." The Hellion punched Sparrow.

Sparrow stumbled backward. Loose soil fell around his shoulders in a cascade.

"Hey!" Jim shouted from above. "Let birdboy out."

The Hellion glared before jumping out of the pit. Sparrow followed, partially dragging himself. His arms were caked in soil. His clothing, too.

"Go." Jim waved toward the door. "Return at dawn."

As Sparrow left the cabin, Jim turned to the remaining Hellions and began a whispered conversation.

Sparrow took to the air, pleased for the rain that rinsed the dirt off him. By the time he neared the burning caves, his clothing was dried from the speed at which he flew through the warm air of Hell. He could still smell himself, sweat and body odor. Digging in the pit had exhausted him. He went to the lair first to clean up, then went to the back room with the beds and took to the showers. He scrubbed the last bits of dirt off himself, changed his clothes, and went to find Meg.

When Sparrow last left her, he voiced a warning, one that she'd have done good to remember. Memories were edging in, on the precipice; he could sense that he needed her more than she needed him. He couldn't have her going out and getting injured again. Sparrow was thankful for the warning from Clea, but he worried what else Meg would do if given the chance.

Sparrow didn't bother knocking. He twisted the handle of the door and slipped inside silently. He closed it again; glad that he could barely hear the soft click of the latch engaging.

Sparrow was hungry—could barely wait—but he forced himself to stand there a few moments and listen to the soft sounds of her breathing as she slept.

There was a shadow outside her window. Sparrow moved toward it and saw the tiny owl fluttering back and forth, catching moths in the moonlight. He had the sudden urge to capture the small creature, tug two feathers from its wings, and tuck them away in his pocket.

Movement from the bed drew his attention.

Meg was propped up on her elbow, watching him in the darkness and pale moonlight that seeped through her windows, which lit her in a sepia glow. Hunger overtook him, and Sparrow didn't trust himself to move.

"Now," he called.

Meg was insolent, making no attempt to get up and come to him. He called her again, but she refused, burying her head under a pillow like a child.

Sparrow wanted to make her pay for the scene in New York City. His muscles tensed as he moved toward her. He crawled across the big bed, focusing on her pale arm in the dim light. The pulse in her wrist throbbed, and Sparrow could think of nothing else. He fed, his gaze drifting to the ring on her finger. Often she toyed with it, and Sparrow knew it had meaning, something he couldn't quite recall. He touched the ring, hoping it would bring something to the forefront of his mind. Nothing happened. Too tired to move, he settled next to Meg and fell asleep.

Sparrow woke before dawn. Shifting up on his elbows, he looked down at Meg and found her sleeping peacefully. He moved off the bed, eager to put distance between them. As he stood, he felt something in his pocket, reached in, and pulled out a bright-blue feather.

Sparrow had a vision of Meg standing in the sunlight with a blue jay perched on her open palm. She was smiling, her eyes flicking between the bird in her hand and Sparrow. There was laughter and trust, and he was a different man. Disappointment struck. Sparrow couldn't remember seeing her smile like that since they'd been down here, and that was his fault.

Jim called—that invisible collar tugged tight around Sparrow's neck. He crossed the room, leaped off the balcony, and took off into the early-morning sunrise. Sparrow tried to focus on the steady beating of his wings instead of a peacefully sleeping Meg.

...

Meg

I dream that my hair is super long and cascading down my back in dark waves. I hate my hair long. I'm walking outside in a strange park packed tight with a horde of the walking dead. They're pulling on my hair. They wrap the tendrils around their arms and tug, making me lose my balance and fall. I smack my face on the concrete, and all my front teeth fall out. When they hit the ground, it sounds like a beaded necklace breaking and falling to the floor. *Ping, ping, ping.*

I sit up in bed. My hands fly to my mouth to make sure my teeth are still there. I exhale, relieved. I'm going to throat punch Nightingale. I can't take any more of these ridiculous dreams.

Sparrow's gone.

I get up and dress myself.

Noah walks in my room. "Morning." He's carrying breakfast: a bagel and a glass of orange juice.

I walk toward him, take the food, and eat it as quickly as I can.

"Feeling okay?" he asks.

I swallow my last bite. "I need you to cover for me."

"Why?" He leans around me and gets a good look at the bed.

"Just cover for me."

"Meg—"

Poof.

Nightingale is stretched across her bed, her head bopping along to whatever music she's listening to on headphones.

Deciding not to cause Nightingale physical harm at this moment, I clear my throat to get her attention.

Nightingale turns. A smile spreads across her face when she sees me. She rips the headphones off and jumps to her feet, skating toward me, then around me in circles. She giggles and whistles three short tweets.

"Oh, I knew you'd finally come! How are things in Hell?" she asks.

"Hellish." I run my tongue over my teeth. "The dreams are the worst."

Nightingale beams proudly. "I knew you'd get them." She throws her arms around me in a tight hug. "It's something I've been working on. Strange how I can reach you so easily. But I can!"

I stiffen. "Please don't touch me."

"Oh." Nightingale backs away. "I forgot about that." She skates across the room. "Let me get my things. I already packed a suitcase."

"Why did you pack?"

Nightingale bends near her closet, and every curve of her butt is visible in the tiny shorts she's wearing. She picks up a giant piece of luggage. "I knew you'd come for me."

I settle my hands on my hips. "Just where do you think I'm taking you?"

"To Hell." Nightingale shivers. "Oh, let me get my toothbrush!" She skates away, down the hall, returning a few moments later with a toothbrush and a tube of toothpaste in her hands. Nightingale unzips her suitcase and shoves them inside. "Okay. All ready." She stands in front of me, waiting proudly.

"Why would I bring you back there?"

"I hate it here. My father keeps me in the basement." Nightingale smiles and holds her hand out, wiggling her fingers at me impatiently.

I look her up and down. She's wearing a crop top and those ridiculously tiny shorts—and they said *I* was sinful.

"You should probably put on more clothes. That is going to attract attention," I warn.

Nightingale giggles, skates over to her closet, and removes a pair of stretch pants. She pulls them on over her shorts, then adds a fitted zip-up track jacket.

"Let's go!" Nightingale skates toward me. "Before someone alerts the Legion."

"Christ," I mutter, taking her hand.

"Oh. You shouldn't beckon him." Nightingale shakes her head, worry masking her face.

"Sorry."

Poof.

We're back in my bedroom in Hell.

"Meg?" Noah walks in. He stops in his tracks as soon as he notices Nightingale. "Fuck me. Please tell me you didn't just do what I think you did." He gapes at Nightingale, moving to get an eyeful of the downy white feathers on her back. "You are in deep shit." Noah thrusts an accusing finger in my direction. "Deep, deep shit. Mounds of it."

"Oh hell*oooooo*, handsome." Nightingale skates toward Noah, whistling the entire way. She circles him, inspecting. Her satisfied grin tells me everything she's thinking. Noah is a good-looking guy. I know this; I used to date him.

"Hide her," I order.

"I can't hide her." Noah points at Nightingale. "She's a freaking Angel. The Hellions are going to smell her a mile away."

"We could hide her in the closet."

Noah scoffs. "She's not E.T."

"The bathroom?"

Nightingale wrinkles her nose.

"You want her that close while Sparrow's in here feeding off you? From what I saw last night, you two need some privacy."

"Oh, what were they doing?" Nightingale asks as she skates around my room.

"He drinks her blood." Noah watches Nightingale, his face masked in disbelief that there is, in fact, a female Angel in my room skating around like she just stepped out of a magazine from 1987.

Nightingale turns to face me, her cheeks rosy. "Dirty girl."

"Shut up."

"Maybe you should just fuck him. I'm sure that will make him remember."

"He's your brother!" I want to reprimand her over the foul language; she is pureblood, after all.

Nightingale shrugs. "So?"

The Hellion Sparrow is definitely dark and hot, but a part of him scares me. Even if watching him suck my blood sets my loins on fire.

"He's not like I knew him."

"He never is. Won't be until the curse is lifted. And then all we can hope is that me and him don't suffer any long-term brain damage." Nightingale skates around me. "You still like him?"

"Very much."

"Take a roll between the sheets." Nightingale whistles. "It's already written in the stars. You will be together. Take advantage of his dark side. Some girls like that. I read about it in human books." She winks.

Noah raises his hand. "I'm still here. And I don't need to hear any of this."

Nobody has ever had to tell me twice to take an attractive man to bed, but this thing with Sparrow is deep and torturous.

My bedroom door bursts open.

"Brother!" Nightingale zooms across the room. She whistles the same melodic trill as the last time she saw Sparrow and leaps into his arms.

Sparrow stiffens. Confusion masks his features; his arms stiffen at his sides while Nightingale swings on him. A few moments pass before Sparrow pushes her away.

Nightingale skates backward, stopping next to me. "You should definitely bone him."

I shove her away.

"I think you both need to leave," I suggest.

"What am I supposed to do with her?" Noah points at Nightingale.

She skates toward him, grabs his hand, and twirls herself. "Take me somewhere dark." Nightingale's voice is breathy and innocent. She kisses Noah's cheek.

"Take her to Clea," I tell Noah. "And be careful. That girl is crazy."

Noah leaves the room, with Nightingale holding his hand and skating slowly behind him. She's whistling a slow, sexy tune. Someone should really let her know that Noah doesn't communicate with birdcalls.

The door closes.

Sparrow's gaze falls on me.

"Are you hungry?" I ask.

He pulls the blue feather out of his pocket and brushes it across his cheek.

"If you ever do what you did with him again, I will salt the earth and end his lineage."

My back straightens. Crap. I'm still in trouble.

"I could smell his sweat all over you last night."

"We were—"

"Never again." Sparrow tucks the feather in his pocket.

"Okay." I shiver.

I'm not sure if he just came here to yell at me or if he's hungry. I hold my arm out and offer him lunch.

Sparrow grabs my arm and yanks me toward him, hard. I knock against his chest, and it forces the air out of my lungs. His free arm snakes around my back, holding me against him. Sparrow's other hand tips my head to the side and moves my hair out of the way. He lowers his mouth.

I close my eyes.

Sparrow kisses me, short little pecks all the way down my neck. He pulls the collar of my shirt down, exposing my shoulder. He licks the skin there, then settles his firm lips. There's the pinch, the heat. My knees weaken. I press my face to his shoulder, breathe him in. He smells so good.

I open my eyes and notice the pulse in his throat. I lick my lips. Sparrow sucks harder. I whimper. His pulse beats against the taut skin of his neck. I angle my face closer. Sparrow's arm tightens around my back. I lick my lips again, open my mouth, and lean in.

Sparrow stops. His tongue brushes my skin, and he stands up straight.

"You want that?" Sparrow peers down at me.

Shit. I almost latched on and took a taste. I feel the rest of my blood drain from my face.

Sparrow catches me as my knees give out. He picks me up, and I grip the leather of his vest between my fingers, holding on for dear life. He carries me to the bed, lowers me gently, then steps back.

"Do you?" Sparrow asks again. "Is that what you want?"

"I . . . I'm not sure." I sink into the mattress, wishing it would swallow me up whole. I've done plenty of bad shit in my life, and I've never been embarrassed about anything, but sucking Sparrow's blood like some lovesick vampire mortifies me.

Sparrow smiles for the first time since he took his place as a Hellion.

"Later, baby," he promises, before turning and leaving the room.

I die inside. Both humiliated and furious, I want to run after Sparrow and punch him on the chin. But being Sparrow's very own personal buffet is exhausting. I stretch out on the bed and pull the blanket over me.

I've never taken so many naps in my life.

...

"She's awake."

I recognize Clea's voice.

I sit up to find Clea, Noah, Nightingale, and one livid Lucifer standing in my bedroom.

Lucifer steps toward me. "Do you know the shitstorm you've created by bringing her here?" He points at Nightingale. "She is pureblood, the daughter of an Archangel."

I open my mouth to say something, but Lucifer takes another step toward me, and I snap it shut.

"You broke very explicit rules. She has to go back."

Nightingale's face blanches.

Oh no, I'm not taking her back and putting up with those dreams again. And she doesn't deserve to go back. The way Remiel treats his daughter, locking her up because he can't stand to look at what he's done to her. It's no better than the way John Lewis treated me.

"He keeps her in a basement," I reveal.

Lucifer's face remains placid, like he couldn't give a crap.

"Remiel keeps her locked up in a basement like a troll. He put this curse on his own children, and he"—I point at Lucifer—"punishes them all."

"She has to go back. My hands are tied. Do it. Now." Lucifer spreads his giant wings, taking up the width of my room.

Oh, that's terrifying. Last time he did that was when I first met him, and it had me whimpering on my knees. Not this time, though.

"No." I scoot off the edge of the bed and stand. "You owe me one favor," I remind him. "I brought your daughter back to you, and in return you promised me one favor."

Lucifer quickly pulls his wings in with a snap and steps back. I move toward him. He could turn me to dust in a heartbeat, but I don't care. No one ever stood up for me against John Lewis, even though the entire town knew what was going on. I'm not going to let the same thing happen to Nightingale.

"She stays," I demand.

Lucifer touches his index finger to my forehead. After he sees what I've witnessed, he mutters something. I can't make out the words, but I don't think it's good.

"You promised," I remind Lucifer.

"Fine," he snaps.

Lucifer walks toward Nightingale. She skates backward until she hits the wall and has nowhere else to go. She looks up at him with large green eyes. Her face pales. Lucifer waves his hands over her.

Nightingale's wings turn black.

"This will mask you from your father and the other Angels searching for you. Behave," Lucifer warns her, before leaving the room in a puff of smoke.

Clea lets out a breath of relief. "I've never seen him that angry before." She floats toward me and settles a hand on my arm. "Not since I ran off to Heaven with your father." Clea turns toward Noah. "You have two to keep an eye on now. Congratulations."

Noah's face drops.

...

By dusk, Nightingale is settled. Clea put her in a room on the level below mine, closer to Clea's quarters, where she can keep an eye on the girl. She said she was worried about Nightingale disrupting *things*.

I shower and change into a T-shirt to sleep in. Exhausted

from the day, I move toward my bed, but a noise from the balcony stops me. It's a subtle hooting that I can barely hear.

I move to the window and push the curtain aside.

The tiny elf owl is perched on the railing. It's looking out over the landscape of Hell. After a few moments it turns to face me, hooting again before lifting into the air and flying away.

I let the curtain fall back into place and close the window. Hell is cold tonight.

After walking across my room, I crawl into bed.

...

There is movement on my balcony. It's late, nearly pitch-black outside on this moonless night. The curtains flutter and the glass knocks. I switch on the lamp next to my bed.

Sparrow is standing outside my window.

I get up and let him in.

"Why—" I start, but words escape me as I notice he's covered in dust and he's pale, like he hasn't been feeding off me regularly.

"Now," Sparrow whispers, his voice empty with exhaustion.

I run to the nearby table where my blade rests, cut my arm, and run back to where Sparrow stands, offering it to him. He latches on, sucking hard like a man who just ran a marathon and thirsts for water.

I reach out to touch him, but he backs away, releasing my arm. He looks unsure of what to do next.

"You should get cleaned up," I suggest.

Sparrow turns and looks over the balcony. His expression reveals that he isn't thrilled with the idea of flying away and using his usual entrance.

"You can shower here." I step back and motion for him to come in.

Sparrow takes a hesitant step, then another. What the heck is wrong with him? I lead him to the bathroom, start the shower, and leave fresh towels on the counter. I close the door behind me, listening for the sounds of Sparrow getting in the shower.

There's a loud thud, the whisper of clothing being torn, the interrupted spray of the water. A scrubbing sound. Satisfied, I move away from the door and sit on the bed.

Sparrow is in there so long that I become bored. I crawl under the covers again and get comfortable.

Just as my eyes are about to close, the bathroom door whips open. Sparrow stands there with just a towel around his waist.

Sweet baby Jesus in Heaven. I almost forgot how magnificent he looks half-naked.

He stares at me expectantly.

I don't read minds, but I get the feeling he's looking for clean clothes.

I throw back the covers and move to the door. Opening it, I call, "Noah."

My manservant arrives in a flash. His cheeks are flushed; his hair is tousled.

"Meg?" Noah asks.

I tip my head. "What have you been doing?"

"Nothing," he answers quickly. "Did you need something?"

I'm pretty sure he's lying.

"I need some Sparrow-size clothing." I glance back at Sparrow waiting at the threshold to the bathroom. He looks hungry. "And some food and drink."

Noah disappears in a flash, then returns with a plastic bag and a pile of clothes.

"Anything else?" Noah asks.

I shake my head. "Carry on with whatever wicked deeds you were occupied with."

Noah grins before disappearing again.

I turn to face Sparrow and kick the door shut. I set the bag of food down on a nearby chair and walk across the room to hand him his clothes.

He takes the clothing, looks at them, then looks at me.

I smooth my hands over my nightshirt.

Sparrow tosses the clean clothing on the floor, then whips his towel off and lets it drop, as well. There is no time for me to react before he advances, lifting me off my feet and carrying me to the bed. He drops me and reaches for the hem of my shirt.

I hold my breath and press my hands against Sparrow's shoulders. He looks into my eyes.

"Do you remember me?" I ask.

"You are Meg," he replies.

I bite my lip and nod. "Anything else?"

He grabs my hand, and his finger rolls over the ring. "I gave you this."

"You did."

Sparrow drops my hand and rips my shirt down the middle.

I gasp.

"I like you," he says.

I sure as hell hope he likes me; he's been drinking my blood down here for weeks. For Christ's sake, I've spent the past few months avoiding any of my blood spilling, and I've allowed him to take it willingly.

My heart thunders against my ribs.

"I like you, too," I say. "But you've been a Grade A jerk for a while now."

Sparrow advances. I scramble backward on the bed, unsure of what he has planned.

"That strange girl is my sister?" Sparrow asks.

"Yes."

He licks my abdomen. "She said you should just fuck me."

My mouth snaps shut. His soul is definitely tainted. Sparrow always scolded me for using that word, and I have never heard him utter it in all the time I've known him.

Sparrow pushes the scraps of my shirt away. His tongue rolls over my bare breast.

"Sparrow?"

He stops. "Is this what you want?" he asks. His head tips to the side in an odd movement that is totally birdlike and completely Sparrow. "Say yes. You have to tell me yes."

There he is. "Yes."

The lacy underwear is gone in less than a heartbeat.

Sparrow presses tiny kisses all over my body. I feel his lips, his teeth, his tongue. He's biting me all over, and while I know I should be turned off by it, with each nibble my blood simmers hotter and hotter.

Soon he has me writhing beneath him. I touch his body, which seems oddly unfamiliar to me now. The change has turned his muscles to stone; there is not one bit of softness left on him. The angles and planes are deep and taut. Sparrow stills over me. I look up. His eyes are liquid green, but now a ring of black taints the edges. He blinks slowly. He's fighting it, just as I had done during my time in Heaven.

"You are so small. I'm afraid of hurting you."

I try to control my facial features. I am actually completely average and a bit tall for most human women at five feet six.

"You won't hurt me." I run my hands down his back and open my legs wider.

Sparrow touches his forehead to mine. "Your name is Meg," he whispers.

"Yes."

"I want you more than air to breathe." Sparrow trails his nose down the side of my neck. "You tempt me."

I stretch my fingers into his hair.

Sparrow's teeth skim my shoulder. His hot tongue licks the skin; he bites down at the same time his hips thrust, filling me.

Everything tingles and burns as he simultaneously sucks and thrusts.

Sweet Jesus. I've never experienced this with him before. All rational thought leaves my mind, and the only thing I can do is *feel* and let the darkness take over. I think my body is on fire. I touch his warm skin. The pulse in his neck throbs. I lick my lips, pressing them to his shoulder.

Sparrow moves faster, harder.

I open my mouth and press my teeth against his skin.

Sparrow makes a deep noise of satisfaction.

I bite. Warm blood fills my mouth. Stars disrupt my vision. Oh, this is better than that glass of cold blood Jim handed me weeks ago. I drink. The world stops. There is nothing but the metallic taste on my tongue, the sweetness that I know is Sparrow. This is too intense. My head feels dizzy and full, like it's going to explode. I release his skin and cry out.

Before everything goes dark, I think I hear him humming.

Holding out for a Hero

I wake feeling exhausted and exhilarated. Lifting the covers, I inspect my body. There are little bite marks all over. Pink and healing. Shit. Emotions churn inside me. I cover my face, remembering what I did last night.

Rolling over, I check the nightstand for money. There's nothing there but *Birds of the Northeast*. I check the floor. The clothes Sparrow threw there last night are gone.

There's a knock on my door.

"Go away!" I shout.

Unable to face anyone right now, I throw the covers back and run to the bathroom, locking the door. I turn and inspect my naked body in the mirror. There are tiny marks all over. Logic tells me I should be embarrassed, but remembering how it felt having Sparrow's mouth on my skin squashes everything. There's dried blood on the corner of my mouth. I lick it away, close my eyes, and remember.

Hearing the flooring creak, I open my eyes. There's a shadow outside my bathroom. It dulls the light creeping in from the space under the door.

"Go away!" I can't see anyone right now. I have to pull myself together and make it look like Sparrow and I never participated in a bloodfest last night.

I get in the shower and wash everything off. I scrub my hair, even loofah the skin of my lips. When I get out, I'm rosy pink all over. I crack the bathroom door and find whoever was knocking got bored and left. Still, there's a chance Noah might show. Not wanting anyone to see the bite marks before they heal, I run to the closet and close myself inside. I grab a pair of tight jeans, a long-sleeved top, and a thin high-collar leather jacket. When I'm dressed, the only skin visible is on my face and my hands. I pull on a pair of tall boots and leave the closet.

Clea is waiting near the window. I sniff. Something smells sweet. Strange, I've never noticed her wearing perfume before.

"Hi," I greet her. "Were you knocking? I just—"

Clea turns and assesses my outfit. An approving smile marks her face. "You don't have to be embarrassed." She crosses the room and takes my hand. "Glad to see Sparrow is coming around. I told you it's not so bad, is it?"

I shake my head.

"Sometimes, Gabriel and I would do it twice—"

"Stop!" I swallow down the bile rising in the back of my throat. "I don't need to know."

Clea shrugs innocently.

"Your girl is causing a ruckus."

My girl? And this is Hell—who cares about a ruckus?

"Nightingale has been collecting the small creatures of the caves. She wants to keep them as pets."

"She doesn't get out much," I reply.

"Those creatures have work to do. They are not puppies or kittens."

"I guess I'll tell her."

Clea glances out the window. "Why are all those birds on your balcony?"

I turn. There's a row of colorful songbirds staring at the window, expectantly.

Crap, when was the last time I put out seed?

"They're hungry." I open the window and locate the bin of birdseed, scoop out a handful, and spread it on the railing. The birds feast with thankful chirps and tweets.

When I turn around, Clea is watching me with fascination.

"What?" I ask innocently. "I was bored, and Noah wouldn't get me a Jeep, and I was too weak from Sparrow feeding to *poof* myself somewhere fun."

Clea smiles before drifting toward my door and leaving.

I decide to hunt down Nightingale.

After jogging down the hall and descending to the next level, I find Nightingale racing down the hallway on her roller skates. She's grasping at a short creature that resembles a raccoon standing upright. The feathers of her now-black wings flutter. Nightingale is whistling. The creature turns to her and hisses before running faster and disappearing into the shadows along the wall.

Noah is standing outside her door. He raises his shoulders in defeat.

"Manservant, you never brought me breakfast."

"I was busy with her!" He points at Nightingale.

Nightingale speeds toward us, twirling in a circle. "Wasn't he the most precious thing you've ever seen?" She comes to a stop, her elbow resting on Noah's shoulder. "I've been chasing him for hours. He's so fluffy!" Nightingale's cheeks are bright red; excitement radiates off her.

"You need to stop," I say. "Lucifer told you to behave. Rounding up the creatures of Hell so you can have your own personal petting zoo is not behaving."

Nightingale's smile vanishes.

I immediately feel guilty for ruining her mood. The poor girl has been living in a cellar most of her life, she should get to have some fun.

Noah thumbs toward the door. "She's got a whole bunch of them holed up in there."

"What?" I move to open her door. Nightingale's hand lands on mine. "Don't touch me," I warn her.

She lifts her hand and shies away. "Sorry."

I push her door open, and a dozen or more creatures scatter out, grunting and hissing, running in different directions down the hall.

Nightingale whistles a gloomy trill, like I stomped on her heart or something.

"You can't do this." I start walking down the hall, motioning for her to follow me. "Come on. I have something to show you."

"If you're going to babysit her, I can get breakfast. What do you want? Pancakes, waffles, fried eggs?" Noah asks.

"Sure." My stomach barely grumbles.

He disappears.

I bring Nightingale to my room and out on the balcony.

"Oooooh," she whispers when she sees all the songbirds.

I grab a handful of birdseed from the bin. "Hold out your hand, like this." I show her.

Nightingale mimics my stance. I pour the seed into her open hand.

"Move closer," I suggest.

She pushes off using the toe of her left foot and glides closer to the railing. A few of the birds hop around her; some flutter away, landing farther down the railing.

Nightingale frowns. She looks sadder than ever.

"Whistle to them," I suggest.

A light trill comes from her lips, melodic and gentle. She calls to the songbirds as though she is their kin. I watch spellbound as, slowly, one by one, songbirds start fluttering up to land on her open hand and extended arm.

Nightingale smiles wide in my direction.

If the only good thing I ever did in my life was make Nightingale smile, it was all worth it.

When the birds eat all the seed, I get more and refill her open palm.

The curtains to my room billow as Noah returns. I smell breakfast.

Leaving Nightingale to socialize with the birds, I walk into my room and sit at the table. There are two plates. Pancakes and waffles on one, the fried eggs on another. I dig in.

"You're not nearly as famished as you usually are after Sparrow feeds." Noah's eyes roam over my clothing, noticing my lack of visible skin. "Did you—"

"Shut up." I don't want to talk about sucking Sparrow's blood with Noah.

His eyes narrow. "Whore."

I point my fork accusingly at him. "And what were you doing last night? Meeting up with your snake-haired mistress, or did you find someone a little sweeter?" I tip my head toward Nightingale.

Noah smirks.

Knew it. I bet he was exploring the darker side of Sparrow's little sister. "Pig."

"Strumpet."

I give up on the name-calling and finish my plate of food.

"Some birds out there that we haven't had before." Noah points to the balcony. "Looks like birdgirl is a regular old Snow White singing in the woodland."

I get up and grab *Birds of the Northeast* off my nightstand and head to my chair on the balcony.

Noah refills Nightingale's hand with seed. I flip through the book, searching for each new species that lands on her hand: grosbeak, fledgling cardinal, shrike, northern mockingbird, tufted titmouse, warbler, towhee, mountain bluebird, red-winged blackbird, common grackle, gray catbird, brown-headed cowbird, and more that I can't identify with this book.

Some aren't native to this area, but it seems the birds in Hell don't follow the same rules as the ones on the earthen plane.

The dead below us moan and shuffle in response to all the noise from the chirping, whistling, and Nightingale's laughter.

I close the book and run my finger over the textured hardcover.

"Is that Sparrow's?" Nightingale is standing in the room, focused on the book in my hand.

I nod.

"He's had those for years. Not going to be happy when he finds out you have it. I was never allowed to touch them."

I remember the way Sparrow took the book from me that day in his living room and placed it back on the shelf.

"Where's the rest?" Nightingale asks.

"His house."

"I wish they were here. I've always wanted to look through

them." She frowns before turning back to the balcony. A tiny chickadee hops on her hand and tweets. Nightingale whistles back to the little bird, and it pecks at the seed in her hand.

I get up and head for the bathroom. After locking myself inside—*poof*—I'm in Sparrow's living room. I head for his bookshelf and grab *Birds of Paradise*, *Birds of the Arctic*, *Birds of the Northern Plains*, *Birds of the Pacific Northwest*, *Birds of the Southern Gulf*, and *Birds of the Eastern Deciduous Forests*. My arms are filled when I hear a noise coming from Sparrow's kitchen.

"Meg?" It's Gabriel's voice.

Crap. I hope Gabriel doesn't have a harsh punishment in his kingdom for burglary. I don't wait to find out—*poof*—I return to my bathroom in Hell.

After unlocking the bathroom door, I carry the books to the table near the window. Noah and Nightingale peek through the glass at me. Noah frowns, stands, and walks into my room.

"Please tell me you didn't just do what I think you did," he says.

"Depends on what you think I did." I crack open *Birds of the Eastern Deciduous Forests*.

Nightingale skates into the room and squeals. "You've got a bunch of them!" She glides over and plops down in the chair next to me. "Sparrow is going to flip when he sees all of these."

"Let's not tell him," I suggest.

Noah sits across from us and picks up *Birds of the Arctic*. Nightingale starts flipping through *Birds of the Northeast*, the book I've had in my possession for weeks now.

Nightingale whistles low, and it sounds like a warning. "He's going to lose it when he sees you creased these pages. Absolutely pop his cap."

"I don't think she understands what that means." Noah grins.

I look warily at them both.

I've already felt Sparrow's wrath, after Noah and I went clubbing and nearly lost our lives. Remembering the way Sparrow growled and threatened to drain me dry makes sweat break out over my skin.

I close my book and stand. Not wanting to see an angry Sparrow-Hellion like that again, I begin moving the books to the inner depths of my walk-in closet.

"Why are you hiding them?" Nightingale sounds disappointed.

Noah chuckles. "She fears the Sparrow Man."

"He's not that bad." Nightingale flips a few more pages. "Unless he sees *this*."

She holds up the book. There's brown sticky syrup stuck between the pages.

Noah laughs. "He is going to beat your ass."

Nightingale nods and makes an agreeing face. "He will."

"Be quiet. Both of you."

"What?" Nightingale turns another page. "I can't lie. He's probably going to beat your ass. He loves these books more than anything. Always has. Ever since we were kids."

Noah makes a face, glancing at Nightingale, then me.

"She can't lie," I say. "She's pureblood Angel."

"I can't." Nightingale's voice is chipper, like it's no big deal that she's in Hell and the only person here who can't tell a lie.

"You lie all the time." Noah's eyes narrow on me.

"Half blood." I raise my hand as though I'm taking an oath. "Tainted with dirt . . . and shit."

Nightingale whistles a doomful sound before holding up *Birds of the Northeast* again. Pizza sauce stains a page.

Oh crap. I run out of the room and up the stairs.

I've never once confessed my sins. Never once with all the bad crap I've done. I may not believe in God, but I believe in Sparrow. Damaging his books has my soul yearning to beg for forgiveness before he's remembered that those hardcovers about birds are even his. I shiver as I make my way up the stairs. Nightingale says he'll beat my ass, but Sparrow has never hit me. He's the only one who's never laid a finger on me with malice, besides Noah—deliberately at least. I don't count him almost sucking me dry; he didn't know any better at the time.

I did some pretty not-nice things to Sparrow when we were two souls lost in Hell. For Pete's sake, I almost shot him in the head, but he never touched me. He respected my wishes until I learned to trust him. That's more than I can say for most people in my life.

Sparrow is the only man who has showed me love and caring and truth, and even if changing into a Hellion has made him forget a few things, he's never hurt me physically. I would never recover from him beating my ass. Deep down I know this. I have to confess to him before he finds out.

I shove open the door to the Hellion's lair. I'm out of breath, and my heart is pumping wild in my chest.

"Sparrow?" I call out.

The place is empty. There's no movement, no sound, nothing. None of them are here.

"Sparrow?" I look around the room and notice the chains dangling from the ceiling. I wish Jim would take that shit down. But I guess when your dad is the vice president of the underworld, you can have crap like that littering your place of work.

Maybe I could wait a bit. I head for the bar, sit on a stool, and wait, tapping my fingers on the glossy countertop.

No one shows.

I wouldn't mind waiting around for a bit longer, but the place is creepy. I give up. Not wanting to make this a wasted trip, I grab four beers out of the fridge before leaving.

When I get back to my room, Noah and Nightingale are gone. They left their books out on my table. I set the beer down, collect the books, and hide them in my closet with the rest. As I'm closing the door, a breeze blows through my room, carrying the faint scent of something familiar with it. I think I see a shadow move in the corner. When I turn, nothing's there.

I return to the table and open a beer. Birds chirp on my balcony. Walking sacks of flesh lament below.

Hell is filled with contrasting sounds.

While listening to this strange orchestra, exhaustion hits me. I shouldn't have traveled between realms, after what I did with Sparrow last night. I sip at the beer as I cross my room, set the bottle down, and crawl across my bed.

Lord I'm tired.

I lie down and stare up at the ceiling for a moment before falling asleep.

...

There's hooting outside my window. It wakes me enough to get up and investigate what's going on.

The elf owl is there, hopping around on the balcony banister. I'm not sure why it keeps visiting. We've never set out food for it. A moth flutters by in the moonlight, and the owl jumps up, grabbing the insect in its beak and swallowing it down. The owl hoots and looks over the forest below, then to the side. I walk closer, follow its gaze, and notice a large shadow flying close to the mountainside. For a moment I think it might be Clea, transformed into the Argentavis, but as the figure gets closer I recognize that it is Sparrow, flying haphazardly.

The owl takes off as Sparrow gets closer. He's covered in red dirt, something black, and wetness. He drops down onto the floor of the balcony in a heap.

"Sparrow?"

He groans. "I need you, Meg."

I run for my blade and grab it off the couch. As I'm running back to him, I strip off my jacket and let it fall to the floor. I drop to my knees, cut my wrist, and hold it out.

Sparrow latches his mouth over the wound and sucks.

Warmth floods me. I try to tamp it down, knowing well that this is not the time, not when he looks like he just flew back from a battle . . . or something.

In the moonlight I notice that all the little bite marks from the night before have healed.

Sparrow stops and licks my arm to seal the wound. He holds my hand over his chest, taking deep, even breaths.

"What happened?" I ask.

Sparrow turns. He says nothing, his eyes vacant.

I take in the dirt on his body, the wetness that looks like tar. Moving, I take his arm and pull him to his feet. I shove my shoulder under his and lead him to the bathroom. Sparrow's breathing heavy, like he's run a marathon.

"Can you get undressed?" I ask.

Sparrow just stares at me, his eyes dark and faded, never moving.

I start unbuttoning his vest. Sparrow growls.

"Shut up," I scold him. "You smell."

I push the vest off his shoulders and bend to start untying his boots. After getting them off his feet, I reach for the zipper of his leather pants. Sparrow closes his eyes. I unbutton, unzip, and pull them down his legs. I try not to stare but—sweet Lord in heaven—he's not wearing underwear.

Sparrow leans against the counter like he's exhausted, like I didn't just let him take a quick sip of my bloodstream out on the balcony to spark him back to life.

I leave him to start the shower. My hands leave muddied prints on the shower knobs. I can't help but think that it's dirt mixed with blood. I adjust the temperature before returning to Sparrow's side.

"Let's go." I shove my shoulder under his and lead him to the shower.

He stinks of death and rich dirt that smells oddly familiar.

There's a memory of me planting flowers at the cabin in Canada that floats to the surface. Jim made me spend a good chunk of my inheritance on the cabin. Nothing good ever came of that place. I ignore it and focus on Sparrow.

I push him into the shower, and he just stands there under the stream of water, leaning against the wall, too exhausted to move.

"Do you need help?" I ask.

He says nothing.

I sigh and begin stripping off my clothes. I leave my underwear on, because, well, it feels wrong to stand naked with him in the shower when he looks like he's half-dead.

I detach one of the handheld showerheads from its holder and begin spraying him down. The bottom of the shower fills with murky water. After replacing the showerhead, I reach for the soap and start washing him down. There are scratches on his arms and small bloody pockmarks.

"Turn around."

Sparrow rolls against the wall of the shower; he flexes his wings, showing me his back. There are deep cuts and scarring across his skin that I don't remember. My stomach feels queasy; something is not right.

"What happened to you?" I ask.

Sparrow doesn't answer.

I do my best to wash the wounds, before scrubbing his hair. I rinse him off, and just as I'm about to turn the water off and get us some towels, Sparrow grabs me. He turns me to face him. Shit, he looks really, really hungry. Like he could eat me whole. I don't think there's enough blood running through my veins to rejuvenate him.

"Sorry," Sparrow whispers, before quickly pushing my head to the side. "I'm sorry for this." He latches on to my neck, and he's not the least bit gentle about it.

My knees give out instantly. I feel warm and tingly; my vision blurs. In seconds, I am nothing but a sack of bones in his arms.

...

Sparrow

Sparrow leaned against the wall of the shower. Meg was washing him, stripped down to her underwear. Every mark of ink on her body was visible. He remembered tasting her the other night, filling her, taking what he wanted. He'd offered himself to her, something that was new to both of them and completely satisfying. Yes, her pain had filled him, but this new taste had been sweeter, deeper—rich and thick in his mouth. When her pulse throbbed in her neck, Sparrow could do nothing more than focus on the steady beat as she cleaned him. What happened after, there was no excuse; he couldn't stop himself.

Meg was a limp rag doll in his arms by the time he finished. Sparrow rolled his thumb over the marks on her neck, rubbing away the blood. He carried her out of the shower stall. Water dripped on the floor, leaving a trail behind him. It was evidence: a trail to what he'd done. Sparrow feared the wrath of Clea. There was plenty Sparrow couldn't remember, but if there was one thing that Sparrow knew for certain, he feared the fury of Lucifer's daughter.

Sparrow settled Meg on the bed, pulled the covers over her, and tucked her in.

He didn't want to leave—knew it was wrong—but that tightness around his throat was so taut it was nearly choking him.

Jim had been draining him, working him ragged. Even though it was the middle of the night, Sparrow was a Hellion, and he did what was commanded of him.

He left Meg alone in the bed, ran to the balcony door, jumped over the railing in one powerful leap, and flew away into the dark night of Hell.

...

Meg

My bed is damp. I move my limbs under the sheets only to be met with the sensation of skin on satin. I'm completely naked, still too tired to move, even after sleeping. The events of last night replay in my head.

Something blows out the spark inside me, the one that's kept me hanging on through all the bad crap I've lived through. I've been waiting to decide what to do about Sparrow. But deep down, he just made the decision for me.

My door opens, and Noah enters. Nightingale glides in behind him.

"Rough night?" Noah wiggles his eyebrows.

"Shut up." I'd throw something at him, but I can't find the energy to move.

"I guess you need something to eat."

I look away from him, emotions warring within me.

Nightingale heads for the balcony and starts setting out seed and singing to the birds. The girl is in her element here. Who knew that a flock of songbirds could make her so happy? I remember a time when Sparrow was like that, the look on his face when he would find a handful of new feathers. It's the same as Nightingale's is now.

Noah returns with a roast beef sandwich and a smile. He sets it on the bed next to me before turning to watch Nightingale. I try to move my arm to get the sandwich, but I can't. I'm too weak.

Noah turns; his worried gaze scans over me. He waits, watching as I struggle to reach for the food. His eyes widen. "What the fuck did he do to you?" Noah's expression darkens to pure hatred.

I shake my head. Tears well behind my eyes. I don't cry. Girls like me don't cry. I take a deep breath and try to swallow it down, my efforts crushed as a tear slides down my cheek.

Something really shitty is going on. I agreed to come here

with Sparrow while he did his time as a Hellion, but this is the second time he's come here covered in dust and half-dead and nearly sucked me dry.

"I'll kill him for this myself," Noah grumbles as he picks up the sandwich.

"Don't." I croak.

"What did he do to you?"

I look away from him for a moment and collect myself. When I turn back to Noah, a troubled expression crosses his face as he holds the sandwich up for me to eat. My humble manservant feeds me bite by bite. I wave him away when I'm done and roll over.

Noah leaves the room. When he returns, he's standing in front of me with a glass of blood in his hand.

"Drink it," he demands.

Shame fills me. "No."

"Now."

Thickness clogs my throat.

"I will hold your mouth open and pour it in," he threatens. "Damn it, Meg. I have never touched you in anger, but you're pushing my buttons right now. Drink the damn blood before you die."

I lean up on my elbow and take the glass, downing the blood in one gulp before handing it back to him.

"Get some rest," Noah orders.

I pull the blankets over my head and shut the world out. Just before I fall asleep, my last thoughts are about how I'm going to rip Jim a new asshole when I finally wake up with enough energy to find him.

...

Nightingale invades my dreams. She's touching my hair and whistling a slow, soulful tune that I've never heard before. I want to tell her not to touch me, but it feels good. I never had a mother to stroke my hair and sing songs to me when I was growing up. I close my eyes and enjoy her soothing touch and song. When she stops, I turn to look at her.

"He needs darkness to rule." Her voice sounds worried. *"He needs darkness to lift the curse."* Her pretty face turns down as she glances over my body. *"He didn't mean to do this."*

I thought if I brought her here she would stay out of my head.

Nightingale vanishes.

I wake to darkness and silence.

My entire body aches.

Glancing at the nightstand, I see that Noah left me a midnight snack: three peanut butter and jelly sandwiches and a carton of milk. As I sit up and reach for the food, I notice Sparrow across the room, sitting on the couch, watching. I pull my arm back and yank the covers higher to shroud me.

Sparrow stands and walks closer.

I blink, trying to remember him before the darkness tainted his soul.

Don't forget me, Meg. Don't forget that I love you more than anything. The things they'll make me do . . .

It's so hard.

Sparrow stops in front of me. His hair is wet; he smells fresh from the shower. Like cake batter and Christmas, soap, and . . . woodsmoke is lingering there, as well. He's starting to smell like Hell.

My stomach churns. "No," I whisper, shrinking away.

I can't feed him. Not after what he did to me last night. I

am reminded of John Lewis and Jim and all the other assholes in Gouverneur who treated me like crap. I don't want to add Sparrow to that list, but he isn't giving me much of a choice. This is killing me. I've lived through a lot of shit in my life, but I'm not sure I'm strong enough to handle this.

I think I should go back to Gabriel's Kingdom until Sparrow is done here.

Sparrow drops to his knees at the side of my bed. He looks wounded, scorned, disgusted with himself. He should be.

"Don't hate me," Sparrow whispers, his voice deep and remorseful.

I swallow down tears.

"Without you I am weak. I am nothing." He touches my leg, and I try my damnedest not to flinch away from him. "I can feel it." He waves his free hand near his ear. "I can feel it on the peripheries of my mind. The memories." His hand moves higher, resting on my stomach. His leathery wings stretch as he exhales.

"Don't leave me," Sparrow begs, as though he already knows I've made up my mind to hit the high road. The darkness in his eyes is there, but so is fear. "I can feel it." He thumps his chest with his free hand. "I can feel it. Somewhere in here."

I've never had a man beg me not to leave. But Sparrow is nothing like the men I've been with in the past. I press my lips together to hold back a pathetic sob.

And then I slap him across the face as hard as I can.

"Don't you ever—"

Sparrow barely flinches before he grabs my wrists, holding my hands down. "Please don't leave me." Sparrow's hand moves to my hip; he drags me across the bed and rests his head on my lap. "I can't do this alone," he whispers. "I just couldn't stop. No matter how hard I tried."

What do I say to that?

My hands hover above him. I'm afraid to touch this giant enigma of a man. I have known him at his most innocent when he was pure and good, his most dark, and now his most fragile. I settle my hands on his head and let silent tears slide down my face.

I decide that I won't flee to my father's Kingdom. I won't even run back to the earthen plane and start a new life. I'll stay with Sparrow, as much as it's killing me. I have to help him; after all, he saved my life in the past. I owe this to him. At least one more chance.

When I am sure Sparrow is asleep on his knees, I move my hands out of his hair.

Sparrow lifts his head. His eyes search my face.

He nods as though he just came to an internal decision. "I will care for you."

"Don't you need to eat?" I ask, afraid that he may have taken one of Jim's Bloodwhores to feed on. The thought of him sucking on some other woman's neck just about breaks my heart in two.

"Blood from the cooler," he assures me.

"But you're strongest when it's fresh."

And after seeing Sparrow so weak, I worry about him. Whatever Jim is up to, I definitely don't want Sparrow weak.

"I'll be fine," Sparrow assures me.

He throws the covers back, not seeming the least enticed by my naked body. The sheets are still damp. I think he put me to bed soaking wet last night. Sparrow bends and lifts me in his arms, carrying me to the bathroom. He sets me on the counter, then turns to start the water running in the bathtub.

I turn and glance at myself in the mirror. There is a bright-pink mark on the side of my neck. I shudder, remembering the way he sucked the blood out of me so fast and so hard that it knocked me out in seconds.

My chin quivers. I swallow it down.

As I'm turning away from the mirror, Sparrow's at my side.

"I can walk," I assure him.

Ignoring me, he lifts me again, then sets me gently in the tub. The water is warm and the tub so deep it goes to my neck. I instantly regret only having used the shower in this bathroom.

Sparrow gets the soap and shampoo from the shower stall and begins washing me. He wets my hair, scrubs it clean, and then rinses. His hands spread soap all over my body. I flinch when he touches the mark on my neck. He cleans my shoulders and arms, and massages soap over the tattoo on my chest. His fingers linger there. I bite the inside of my cheek to keep myself silent. The need to physically harm him dissipates with each passing of his gentle hands.

"Is this me? This sparrow?" he asks.

I nod.

"You marked your body for me?"

"You were there," I remind him.

Sparrow stops washing and pours water over my soapy skin.

"Wait here," he says as he gets up and leaves the room.

I lean my head on the edge of the tub and close my eyes.

Sparrow returns with a large towel. He holds it open and waits for me to stand. I reach for the towel, but he shakes his head, motions for me to step out, then wraps it around me when I finally do. He lifts me off my feet again and carries me to the side of the bed.

"Don't put me in there wet again."

His eyes flash to mine.

Oops, that sounded a little dirty.

Sparrow sets me on my feet and rubs the towel over me until I'm dry. He even dries my hair before tossing the towel aside and pulling the sheets back. They're dry and clean.

I scramble in, and when Sparrow kicks off his shoes and strips off his shirt, I crawl to the other side of the bed to get away from him. I'm not sure what he has planned, but after last night I don't think I can handle much.

Facing me, Sparrow wraps his hand around my hip and tugs me tight against his body.

Sparrow nuzzles my neck. I don't move a muscle.

"You can feed from me," he whispers.

I freeze. Holy awkward. I don't even know what to say or do.

"I'm fine."

He offers his wrist. I push his arm away.

"It's what we are. You don't need to be shy." He nuzzles my neck and splays his large hand over my naked abdomen.

I've never been shy about anything, except this. I don't know why. I am half light and half dark. I was the greatest sinner of all, but this is the hardest thing for me to accept. It makes me feel like a true monster. Even if it's the highest high I've ever felt in my life.

His lips touch my shoulder. I relax only when he simply kisses me. His hands move over my body, a slow seduction. His mouth moves to mine; his tongue toys with my lips until I open for him. Sparrow kisses me deeply, thoroughly, until I forget my name and what day it is. He pulls away, trailing tiny kisses down my neck.

"Do it," he urges.

I can't.

He sucks on the sensitive skin of my neck, never drawing blood but igniting a spark deep within me.

I open my eyes. His neck is on display in front of my face, his pulse calling my name, begging me.

"Do it, Meg."

Oh hell.

I press my teeth into the curve between his neck and shoulder.

Sparrow makes a noise deep in his throat, his fingers move, touching me, bringing me to a high that nearly equals what I felt with him a few nights ago. When I come down, Sparrow pulls me tightly against his body and runs his hands up and down my back until I fall asleep against him.

...

In the early hours of the morning, Sparrow kisses me as he's getting up to leave.

Grabbing his arm, I stop him.

"I have to go," he says.

I move to get up. "I have something to show you first."

He wants to remember; I have an idea that might help.

"Come here." I lead him to the closet. Finding the drawer where I've been hiding all the songbird feathers, I open it. Sparrow looks at me questioningly. I take his hand and press it in the drawer of feathers. His hand flexes, closes, and pulls out a handful.

"Do you remember anything?" I ask.

As he purses his lips, I wait, hoping.

He pulls out the red feather of a cardinal, closes his eyes, and brushes it across his cheek. His eyes flash open.

"I think—"

I hold my hand up, stopping him. I feel like this is a good time to make my confession about the bird books. I move to the back of the closet and pull out *Birds of the Northeast*.

"This is yours." I hold out the book.

Sparrow touches it with his fingertips.

"I stole this from your house." I look away. "And others. Actually . . . I took an entire stack." I flip the book open. "It's damaged." I show him the crease marks and syrup and pizza stains.

Sparrow takes the book out of my hand and flips through it.

I pull some clothes off the nearby hangers and dress quickly. I don't want to be naked in front of him when he realizes I marred his beloved bird books.

Sparrow takes his time, reading a few passages, touching his fingers to some of the colorful images of the birds. Finally, he claps the book closed and hands it back.

"You're not mad?" I ask.

"I'm not sure yet," he says before leaving.

An Echo in Eternity

It has been almost two days since I last saw Sparrow. That means it's been three days since he last fed. That means he is not as strong as he should be. Maybe he's mad about the books. Maybe he's simply busy. I can't wait any longer to find out. I wanted to do this yesterday, but Noah kept me in my room, stuffing me full of food and holding a *Birds of* study group with Nightingale.

Today, I feel strong.

I'm going to confront Jim.

I shower and dress myself in jeans, a blue top, and a fitted jacket. I put on boots, then secure my blade in its holster on my thigh. The thought of using it on Jim causes the blade to hum to life.

Not bothering to knock on the door to the Hellions' lair, I push it open and enter, uninvited. Jim's standing at the bar. He looks annoyed to see me. I cross the room, taking note of the three Hellions at the pool table.

"Meg," Jim sneers.

I want to call Jim by another name instead of the one he was given. A variety of inappropriate terms comes to mind, but instead I say, "Jimboy."

He scowls.

I sit on a stool.

"Where's Sparrow?" I ask.

"As a Hellion, he is under my command, and I appoint him as I see fit."

"He's been gone two days."

"So?" Jim swallows a shot of bourbon.

"House of the Rising Sun" is playing on the stereo. I hate that song for the pure fact that it is Jim's favorite, and it reminds me of the things he did when we were engaged.

I try not to think of my past life with Jim. Instead, I focus on my future with Sparrow, even if it is dwindling.

"Last time you sent him to *wherever*, he came back half-alive."

"Not my fault your little cherub won't snack from the Bloodwhores." Jim laughs. "If he did, maybe he wouldn't feel so guilty about nearly draining you."

"You're running him ragged. What in the name of Lucifer are you making him do?"

Jim takes an intimidating step toward me. Even though there's a countertop separating us, I'm not confident in its ability to keep Jim from me.

"That is none of your trashy business."

I open my mouth to respond with some very unangelic choice words, but I halt when Jim's body stiffens and he sniffs the air. His head snaps toward the open door to the lair.

Nightingale is standing there looking as innocent as a baby deer and dressed like a goddamned playboy bunny in short shorts and a crop top.

"Holy. Shit," Jim growls.

Nightingale's eyes widen.

The Hellions in the room snarl.

Jim rounds the bar, moving toward Nightingale.

I reach out to stop him, but he slaps me away so hard that I go flying across the room and crash into the wall.

"Run!" I yell to Nightingale.

She screams and takes off on her roller skates.

I get up, stumble to my feet, and run after them, making it to the door just in time to see Nightingale exit the burning caves and lift off into the air, her dark wings flapping feverishly.

"Noah!" I shout into the hall. "Clea!"

My mother's figure comes floating down the hall.

"Child?" She looks confused.

I shake off the pain of being tossed across the room, stand, and run for the cave entrance.

"They're going after Nightingale!" I run out of the cave only to be confronted by a horde of walking dead.

Noah finally appears at my side.

"Where were you?" I shout.

Noah holds up a bag. "Getting your breakfast."

Clea gets closer; the dead back off.

"We have to find her."

With grim determination and a wisp of dust, Clea transforms into the Argentavis. "Come." She tips her left wing down, and I climb on her back.

"Come on!" I shout at Noah.

He drops my breakfast on the ground and climbs on. Clea hops twice before launching herself into the air. I scramble to grip her feathers and hold on for dear life.

Clea follows the figures in the distance, which only seem to get smaller and smaller, for miles and miles, until they are only tiny pinpoint dots, and then . . . nothing.

Darkness falls, but Clea keeps flying toward the last spot in the sky—the speck that turned to nothingness.

"We have to go back," Clea finally says.

"We can't. We have to find her."

"It's too dark. We'll never find her at night." Clea glides, tips to the side to turn in a wide arc, and heads home.

My heart sinks. I remember what it's like to be chased by the Hellions. And I remember what it's like to be alone out there in the Kingdom of Hell.

"We'll find her," Noah whispers.

Clea lands at the burning caves. Dust swirls as she turns back into the figure of my mother. She looks pale and a bit drawn, even for a ghost of a soul. A burst of energy pulses around her, nearly tossing me on my ass. Noah catches me as I stumble to regain my balance.

"What was that?" I ask.

"I sent a command to the dead to look for Nightingale."

"But they sleep at night."

"Not if they're told to stay awake." She starts floating toward the opening of the cave. "Come. We must talk with Lucifer."

We follow her down stone hallways and dark stairwells, closer and closer to that ubiquitous gnawing and crying from the center of the stairwell, until she enters a large room.

Lucifer is sitting at a giant desk of polished black stone.

"Father." Clea moves to Lucifer's side. "They've gone after Nightingale."

"Perfect" is Lucifer's bored response.

"And Meg hasn't seen Sparrow in over two days," Clea adds.

I step forward. "Something is wrong."

Lucifer barely glances at me. "I'm sure they're fine."

"This girl—" I turn. Holy crap, I've never seen Jim's father Vine before, but he looks just like Jim, well, before Jim's face half melted off. "She has always brought trouble where it needn't be. My son will find the Angel and return her to the caves."

"Jim is the one who went after her," I point out. "He chased her."

Vine stares me down with an expression so potent I fear I might shrivel up and turn to sand.

"Enough." Lucifer holds up his hand. "The souls are out searching. They'll find them both by morning."

"And if they don't?" I ask.

"We will resume searching in the morning." Lucifer finally looks up from his desk. "Go to bed." He dismisses me.

Clea tips her head toward the door, urging us to leave.

I open my mouth to argue, but one look from Lucifer persuades me otherwise.

I sulk all the way back to my room, feeling worthless and worried. Lucifer is pure darkness, and I don't think he cares much about sins and death. Sparrow and Nightingale probably mean nothing to him. I probably mean nothing to him. The only person I've seen Lucifer care about is my mother.

"See you in the morning." Noah disappears as I'm entering my room.

I shower and change into my regular clothes. Sleeping fully clothed is nothing new. If something happens in the night, I want to be ready to go.

The elf owl has come to visit again, hooting from the railing of my balcony. I move to the window to watch it catch moths in the moonlight. A thousand thoughts cross my mind. I think of Sparrow and Nightingale, before my thoughts turn to Teari. Does she miss us? And then there is Gabriel. I would rather take the punishment from stealing Sparrow's books rather than the one I'm going to get for losing his sister. She's far too innocent to be lost in Hell.

I try to figure out how this all went so wrong. What happened these past few weeks down here? In an effort to cure Sparrow, we dropped ourselves straight into the lion's den. I let myself be holed up and used as dinner. I let Sparrow treat me like crap. I let the birds of the underworld hypnotize me into complacency. I forced Lucifer into hiding an Archangel's daughter in the bowels of Hell.

I focus on the elf owl.

The owl is the bringer of death.

Oh. Shit.

Poof.

I return to the Seven Kingdom's of Heaven and find Gabriel sitting in the dining room of his castle. Like Sparrow, before he became a bloodsucker, the man eats whatever he can get his hands on. Good thing they're giants, or I'd worry about their caloric intake.

Gabriel is sitting at the head of the table, his chin resting on his fist, deep in thought. He is a living Rodin's *Thinker*. Others have warned me that he is losing his mind, but I believe the man is simply a genius. The Angels are always telling each other they are crazy. I'm beginning to think they all are.

"Father," I say, disrupting him.

He lifts his chin from his fist, surprised. "Meg."

"Something is wrong in Hell."

He makes a face. "Usually is."

"No. Something is horribly wrong. Sparrow is missing, and now Nightingale."

Gabriel stands. "For the love of God and all his children. I thought Remiel was jerking my chain when he said his daughter was missing."

"Well, she's been in Hell . . . with me. But Jim went after her with the Hellions. She flew away, and we can't find her."

"Christ." Gabriel starts walking out of the room. He cracks the knuckles on one of his giant fists. "About time someone freed that poor girl from her asshole of a father. Like a pet songbird let out of a cage. Bet she has no sense of direction."

I follow Gabriel through the castle.

"You've been back here, as well, haven't you?" he asks, as I skip to keep up with him.

"Yes. I had to get some books from Sparrow's house."

"Knew it." Gabriel shakes his head. "I was going to warn you something strange was going on down there. Deacons have been chattering. Word made its way up here." He stops and turns. "I tried to visit you. Hid in the shadows of your room but couldn't find the right moment to get your attention. You seemed very distracted down there, and I'm not exactly welcome in that castle."

"I have been," I agree, as I lean forward and sniff him. Gabriel smells sweet, like candy and sugar cane. I never noticed before.

After giving me a curious look, Gabriel resumes walking.

"So what are we going to do?" I ask.

Gabriel stops in front of a metal door. He pushes it open, and we enter a giant room filled with weapons and armor.

"Kick some ass," he replies with a smile.

Gabriel starts to dress in armor that covers every inch of his large body. Lastly he draws a sword, much like Sparrow's but twice as long. The weapon glows in his hand.

"Ready?" he asks.

"Sure."

"Take us." He holds out his hand.

I have been cautious to touch my father in the past; when I finally did I felt nothing but warmth and belonging.

This time I don't hesitate; I take his hand.

Poof.

We are outside the caves of Hell.

It is still night, but none of the dead sleep. I can hear them schlepping it through the forests and the abandoned roads, searching for two lost Angels.

"Still no wings."

It's not a question.

I shake my head.

"Call on your mother."

"Clea," I shout. "Noah!"

Gabriel turns to me. "Who is Noah?"

"A friend from the earthen plane."

"And why is he here?"

"He died."

"And went straight to Hell?" His brows rise.

"Yes."

"Did you have any friends who didn't marinate their souls with the sins of the earthen plane?"

"None that stuck around."

Gabriel makes a face of frustration.

I would argue with him about my upbringing, but Noah and my mother exit the burning caves together. Noah runs. Clea floats, stopping in front of Gabriel. Her image wavers. I am quite sure my father hasn't seen her since she fled Heaven in an effort to give me a better life.

Something passes between them. I feel embarrassed to be watching.

"Will you fly them?" Gabriel asks Clea. "As you know, our daughter lacks wings and faith in God."

Dust whips around us as Clea transforms into the Argentavis. She lowers herself to the ground. I climb on her back; Noah follows.

Clea hops a few times, then launches herself into the air with a powerful thrust that nearly knocks me off her back. Strong wings beat and propel us up and up, above the treetops.

I search for Gabriel and find him to the left, flying with the use of his own giant white wings.

"North." Gabriel points.

Clea flaps her wings. I grip her feathers and feel Noah do the same behind me.

"Why north?" I ask.

"The Deacons say Jim is digging in Canada."

My head snaps in his direction. "Where?"

"Not sure exactly. Deacons are shifty—always out for themselves. We can stop at a Safe House and see if they have more information." Gabriel grips the weapon secured at his hip. "Wouldn't mind putting the fear of God into those punks."

"We owned a cabin in Kingston on the earthen plane," I say. "Had dual citizenship. Just in case."

Jim was always planning for something: taking me on hikes through the wilderness, stockpiling guns and bullets, buying survival gear. That was all before he tried to kill me, before I killed him instead. That was before I found out what he was, and who I was. Thought we were nothing but two small-town kids with a baby on the way.

"In case what?" Gabriel asks.

I shrug. "I don't know. The apocalypse or something. It was Jim's idea."

Gabriel's brow furrows. "Screw the Safe House. Can you locate the cabin from the air?"

"Probably."

Clea flies faster. I have to lie down on my stomach to keep from falling off. Turning my head to the side, I see Gabriel keeping up with the rapid, powerful thrusting from his wings. There's a smile on his face. I look down at my mother, unable to gain much from her beady eyes and beak. I think they're racing.

Daylight breaks.

"The border is below," Gabriel shouts.

I lean to the side. A stretch of water dotted with islands is below us. I recognize Wellesley Island crossing and see the locked gates topped with barbed wire. A man steps out of a guard shack, looking up at us.

Last time I was here, the guard called me a filthy American; he didn't care about my dual citizenship. I guess none of it really mattered. At the time I didn't know that I was actually in Hell—thought I was on Earth—and something really strange was happening. The guard made us cross the border by way of a crumbling dam, cold water flowed over the collapsing cement, and the walking dead milled about just below the water line. If one of us fell, we'd die. Sparrow almost jumped, nearly risking his life for a snowy owl feather.

I screamed at him that day—begged him not to kill himself over a handful of feathers. I promised I'd help him find more. That was the first time I allowed him to touch me. We held each other in the empty road after we made the climb. I think Sparrow was crying over his lost feathers. I was crying because I nearly lost my last friend in the world.

Look at us now, so far from what we started out as. Almost completely different people

"Follow the 401," I shout to my parents.

Clea and Gabriel coast to the left and follow the four-lane highway below us.

There are tiny specks moving along the crumbling asphalt, the walking dead searching for Sparrow and Nightingale. I keep my eye on the road and the signs, remembering the way to the cabin.

We pass exits for Gananoque and Kingston, and just as I see the sign for upcoming Odessa, I shout, "Take a right."

Gabriel and Clea lean to turn, beating their strong wings. I wonder what it must be like to have power like that, rising above the ground and dancing with the wind. Almost makes me wish I had wings like the rest of them.

We soar over treetops, tiny roads, and rivers. I recognize Unity Road as we fly over it.

"It's coming up," I warn them. "There's a cabin next to that lake."

Gabriel nods. "We should descend."

Gabriel hovers in the sky, his body upright, his wings flapping gently as he lowers himself to the ground.

Clea tips to the side, then glides lower and lower in a tight circle before flapping her wings and landing on her feet. She hops a few times and tips to the side so we can slide off, before transforming back to her normal figure.

The walking sacks of flesh are moaning and dragging their feet through the forest, silencing any sound we make. And I thought they were worthless. Gabriel motions for me to lead them. My boots crunch on the gravel road. The dead keep their distance.

"I hope they didn't hurt her," Noah whispers.

"Shh," I scold him.

We turn a corner. I point to the small cabin ahead of us.

Gabriel leads us through the forest and around the back.

There is noise coming from inside: loud thuds, something metallic hitting stone.

A scream rips through the forest.

"Nightingale!" Noah takes off running.

I think we should have planned something, but we didn't. I don't hesitate or wait for direction. I grab my blade from its holster and run after Noah.

Noah kicks the door open like a drug dealer looking for his money. I run in behind him.

Holy crap.

There is a giant arch in the middle of the cabin. Black markings are etched into the gray stone, surrounded by freshly dug dirt. There's a man in the surrounding trench, digging it deeper. The hollow rattle of dried bones echoes with each movement.

I step closer and recognize the wings. It's Sparrow!

He digs into the wall of the trench, covering the bones with dirt. Strange hoses extend from his arms. I follow their path and find that they are draining into a large cask. There are empty glasses next to the cask, coated with blood.

They're draining his blood.

They're draining my blood out of him.

My eyes flash to the stone arch. I have only known portals to be present on hallowed ground. Something is not right about this.

Your blood is rubies and jewels to those who are damned.

The space under the arch wavers and flickers. It looks like heat radiating off the pavement in summer. A shadow begins in the center; it stretches, pulls, and grows. Shimmers with movement. A foot steps through, and then another. Then hands, arms, legs. Forms appear. I recognize Jim and two Hellions.

Jim is talking—doesn't even know what we've found.

Two Hellions step through, each carrying an unconscious woman.

Jim looks up. His face drops. His mouth opens to say something, but I move. Without any thought other than pure rage, I swipe my blade and cut off his head. Fire erupts from Clea's hands, setting Jim's body aflame.

"Bastard won't come back from that," Gabriel says. "Blood from the living makes them even stronger." He shakes his head in disgust.

The Hellions drop the women and charge.

Watching an Archangel fight the warriors of Hell is a sight. Gabriel towers over them, and it is like watching sunlight battle the shadows of evening.

My blade hums in my hand, begging for blood. I don't watch for long before joining in.

A Hellion grabs my free arm. I cut his off and shake his twitching hand away. The beast roars. It seems they don't care that Lucifer forbade them to touch me. Jim has them high on the blood of the living. I duck, spin on the balls of my feet, and slice at the Hellion's leg. The Hellion sways. I jump up on a nearby chair and slice his head off.

Gabriel's laughter fills the cabin. "That's my girl!"

Three more Hellions walk through the portal and join in.

"They will be stronger than normal," Gabriel warns.

I don't care. Leaping through the air, I throw myself at the closest one.

Gabriel shouts orders at Clea and Noah. I can't focus on them, only the wrath building inside me, seeking revenge for what Jim did to Sparrow.

I take on another Hellion. Noah was right: my weapon is way better than the Beretta I used last time I fought them. The Hellion throws a punch and hits me in the shoulder so hard I twist and fall to the ground. He barrels toward me. I kick him in the ankle; the beast doesn't flinch, but he does fall. I raise my blade just before he lands and sink it into the Hellion's gut. The breath is knocked out of me as the beast falls on top of me. Warmth spreads across my stomach as his blood drains out. I lie there, struggling to push the limp body off me. Finally, it's off, and the smiling face of Gabriel greets me.

"Next time, roll." He pulls me to my feet.

I take a deep breath and look down at the blood covering my clothing. The bodies of the Hellions burn, smokeless and silent, igniting nothing other than the figures slumped on the floor. The last of Jim's blond hair singes. He is nothing but scorching bone and cooking flesh.

Nightingale's scream rips through the cabin. It sounds muffled, almost like it's coming from outside.

A Hellion bursts through the back door. He's covered in blood, and black feathers are stuck to his vest.

"That's her blood!" Noah charges, going after the Hellion with only his bare hands. "Where is she?" he shouts.

Noah punches the giant creature in the stomach, but Noah is no match for a beast so dark. The Hellion moves with lightning speed, grabs Noah by his throat, and squeezes.

Noah turns to dust at the Hellions feet.

No! No. No. No. No. No! I run to the Hellion, wield the blade forged for me in the fires of hell, and slice through the Hellion's thick neck.

He crumples to the ground.

Clea sets him on fire.

Noah is gone.

Gabriel moves to the flaming body and plucks the black feather off the ground. "What happened to her feathers?" he asks.

"Lucifer," I answer. "He turned them black. To hide her."

Gabriel's face twists in thought.

The scraping sound catches my attention. I run across the room, jump into the dirt hole, and drag myself through waist-high bones.

"Sparrow," I call.

He stops digging. His shoulders are slumped, his body thin and weak. I reach for him, but he starts digging again.

"Stop." I touch his hands.

Sparrow's vacant gaze falls on me.

"They need a final resting place." His voice echoes of exhaustion. "Can't leave them like this."

My heart breaks. Even in his most dark, Sparrow's light shines through. I take the shovel out of his hand. "We'll bury them," I say.

His tired eyes look into mine. "Promise?"

"Promise."

"A promise is a promise." His shoulders slump, and he leans against the dirt wall of the hole.

"I know."

I pull the tubes out of Sparrow's arms and press my thumbs over the trickling blood to make it stop.

"Council's going to be pissed about this." Gabriel knocks on the stone arch. "Illegal portal." He moves to the bodies of the women on the ground. "Have to take them back to the earthen plane. It's not their time. This is not their place."

Gabriel bends and hefts one of the women into his arms. He turns to Clea. "Will you help me? Have to take them to a portal on consecrated ground. Can't use this abomination." Gabriel waves at the stone arch. "God knows where it leads."

Clea lifts the other woman.

"We will return shortly," Gabriel promises, as he steps out of the cabin.

I help Sparrow out of the trench and to a threadbare couch against the far wall. He drops with a groan. I move his feet up so he's lying down. If I didn't know better, I'd think him one of the walking meat sacks.

Standing up straight, I try to figure out how to best help him. The cask still has a small amount of blood in it. I move to the table and pour the remaining blood into one of the glasses, then bring it to Sparrow. Crouching down, I wrap his hand around the glass, bring it to his dry lips, and help him drink. After he's drained the glass, my gaze falls to the burning Hellion on the floor. We need to get out of here. Just as I stand to move, a loud clap and a bright flash erupt in the room.

"That fucking hurt." Noah appears, rubbing his neck.

"Oh my God." I run to him and throw my arms around his neck. "I thought he killed you."

Noah smiles his lady-killer smile. "I'm already dead, Meg. Can't kill me twice." He twists his neck to the side. "But whatever he did hurt like fucking hell." Concern cloaks his face.

Noah bends and watches the Hellion burn. "They hurt her." His voice is soft, anxious.

I know the pain of the Hellions. They've hurt me once before, but I hope to God that they didn't do those things to Nightingale.

"Gabriel's coming back. We'll find her." I follow his gaze to the piles of ash on the floor. "They're all dead. The only one left is Sparrow."

Noah picks up a small black feather and crosses the room until he's standing next to me.

Sparrow finishes his blood and drops the glass on the floor, showing his fatigue.

"He'll drain you dry if you try to feed him right now," Noah warns.

"I know."

Not knowing what else to do with myself, I turn to the portal and start knocking pieces of stone out of it. One by one they fall to the ground, until there is a hole big enough to lessen its stability. I push on the arch with all my strength until it crumbles to the floor.

Gabriel and Clea walk through the doorway to the cabin as the dust clears.

"Come," Clea beckons Noah.

Gabriel crosses the room and lifts Sparrow from the couch. I follow them outdoors.

Clea turns into the Argentavis. I climb on her back; Noah follows.

Gabriel carries Sparrow. His large wings spread, and he thrusts them both into the air. Clea takes flight and soon we are flying side by side. I don't take my eyes off Sparrow. His arms and legs hang lifeless; the only indications that he is still alive are the occasional moments that he opens his eyes.

I grip Clea's feathers between my fingers and lean down.

Though the wind is loud in my ears, I hear a strange chirping. Noah gives me a curious look. I focus behind him and see a handful of songbirds flying behind us. Their small wings beat frantically, and the pumping of Clea's wings throws some of them off-kilter. It doesn't stop them from following.

We return to the burning caves. Clea lands, then transforms, and the songbirds fly over us. We walk toward the entrance to the cave together.

Gabriel stops at the threshold. "Call on Lucifer. I can go no farther without causing trouble." His eyes fall on Clea. "Your father does not forgive me for taking you from him."

Clea touches his arm. "I went willingly." She turns and calls for her father.

The giant man that is Lucifer appears at the entrance. His gaze falls over us all. "You have violated the treaty," he says to Gabriel, his gaze menacing.

"They're not all dead." Gabriel motions to Sparrow's body in his arms. "This Hellion still breathes."

Clea tells Lucifer about the portal Jim was building and draining Sparrow of my blood.

The king of Hell remains expressionless. "Vine will answer to his son's offenses. I'm sure the Council will be notified of this?" he asks Gabriel.

"Of course."

Lucifer nods. "You may enter. Bring him inside."

Gabriel carries Sparrow to my room and sets him on the bed. His breathing is shallow; cheekbones jut from the skin of his face. He's covered in dirt; blood is smeared on his arms.

"Gabriel?" I ask. "Can you help him?"

Gabriel frowns. "I can only heal pure light. It's too late for

Sparrow." Gabriel's hand settles on my shoulder. "For this, I am sorry."

Lucifer appears in the room next to Sparrow. He reaches out with his fingertip and touches it to Sparrow's forehead. Lucifer's eyes flash open and focus on me. "He will be well."

"Is his time done down here?" I ask. "Is he finally finished?"

"No."

My stomach sinks. "But—"

"The treaty states that one realm is not allowed to fully decimate another realm's patrolling force. Sparrow is the last Hellion. There will be recruits. Vine will take over until Sparrow is well. This is how it must be."

Sparrow stirs.

"I should return," Gabriel says quietly. He leaves the room.

Clea follows him. Before Gabriel is gone from my view, she hands him a large black feather. I am curious to know what Gabriel's feather shows him, especially since he never told me what the first one revealed.

"You are Meg." Sparrow's hand touches my face, redirecting my attention.

I turn and sit on the bed near him. "I thought I lost you."

"Unpossible." Sparrow smiles.

"You can't make up words."

"I can do what I want." He reaches out, his finger landing on the tattoo over my heart. "This is me."

"Yes."

"You are mine, and I am yours." His eyes, though green and bright, look weary.

I nod.

"We'll be invincible together."

"That's what people keep saying." I press my lips together to stop myself from crying.

I drop onto the bed and curl around him.

Sparrow, though weak, rubs my arm and starts to sing "Never Say Goodbye."

There is my old Sparrow Man.

...

"You should visit Elise." Clea is in my room watching Noah as he stands alone on my balcony.

He's been pouring out seed for the birds and staring off into the sky. Guilt throbs deep in my chest. Nightingale has been missing for almost two days. I should have just put up with the dreams and left her safe in Remiel's Kingdom.

"Why?" I ask Clea, afraid to leave Noah and Sparrow right now.

"Take Sparrow with you," she suggests.

"What if I don't want to go? I don't think this is a good time. He just got his strength back. He's just starting to remember."

Clea touches my shoulder. "It's important that you see. As a mother."

My back straightens. The snowy owl is the soul of my dead daughter, Elise. I was never given the chance to meet her in person; this is all I'll ever have of her.

"Okay," I decide. "I'll go. But we need to keep searching for Nightingale."

"I know." Clea smiles sadly. "I'll get you a Jeep."

I turn to collect Sparrow. He's no longer sitting at the table behind me. I check the balcony, then the bathroom. I finally find him in the back of my walk-in closet.

He's crouched near the floor. The dense thud of books being set together echoes in the small place. Sparrow stands, holding the stack of bird books.

Uh-oh.

Sparrow walks around me, through the living space of my room, and sets them on the table. He flips open *Birds of the Northeast*. The sheets make a crackling sound as they're pulled apart. His finger touches a dog-eared page.

My eyes flash to his.

A devilish smile crosses his face.

I back away.

Clea pops in the room. "Jeep's ready. You two better get moving."

Thank sweet baby Jesus. Saved by my mother.

I run out of my room, down the hall, up the stairs, and out of the burning caves. Clea got us a shiny midnight-blue Jeep Wrangler. I jump in the passenger side and buckle in.

My heart thunders in my chest as I watch the entrance for Sparrow. He waltzes out of the caves, his hands tucked in his pockets, his gaze never leaving mine. He rounds the Jeep and gets in the driver's side.

"It's a few hours' drive there," Sparrow says, ignoring the fact that he finally remembered about the books.

"I know." I sound like a scared child.

"You could just *poof* us there," Sparrow suggests.

I couldn't *poof* myself across the room right now. I can't focus. "I'm trying to conserve my energy." I turn to him. "Do you remember how to drive?"

"I got this." Sparrow starts the Jeep, shifts it into gear, and slams his foot down on the gas pedal so hard the wheels screech. All I smell is burning rubber and dust. I scream, and my hands fly to the door and the center console, grabbing whatever I can in a death grip.

Sparrow laughs and starts bellowing out "It's My Life" at the top of his lungs.

I don't care if this is his life; I fear for my life for a few miles, until he finally slows down. "For Christ's sake," I mutter, rubbing my hands together; they ache from holding on for dear life.

"That's for damaging my book." He winks at me.

I exhale, relieved. A near-death experience is more than enough punishment for me. I'll never touch those books again in my life.

Sparrow turns on the radio; "Livin' on a Prayer" is playing. He turns the volume all the way up. He motions for me to move closer. I hesitate for a moment before I scoot over and lean against him as he drives to Route 37. All he needs is a feather in his hair, and he'd be set.

After a few hours on the road, Sparrow comes to a stop in front of a clearing between the trees. Pushed back from the road is the decrepit barn of Route 37.

We wait for "Captain Crash & the Beauty Queen from Mars" to finish. Sparrow's tapping his fingers on the steering wheel and bopping his head to the beat. He flicks the radio off as the song ends.

We get out and make our way through the tall grass, headed for the barn. Sparrow calls to the snowy owl from the shadows: a screeching hoot, a strange dark whistling, a hiss. A white head peeks through a hole in the siding, followed by a neck, brown spotted and smooth.

"She's not coming."

I don't want to admit it, because I'm not as into birds as Sparrow and his sister, but I'm disappointed.

"Put your arms around my neck," Sparrow says.

I reach up, on my tiptoes, and curl my arms around him. Sparrow grips my hips, and his wings spread wide; he bends slightly, then launches us into the night sky. He flies to the hole in the side of the barn.

The snowy owl hoots, softly, sounding like a mother cooing. I reach out to her, but she moves deeper into the darkness of the barn.

"Look." Sparrow points.

Resting my hand on the wood siding, I lean in. There is a nest, scraped together from the wood of the barn, and three eggs.

The snowy owl hoots, then hops nearer.

"Do snowy owls mate for life?" I ask Sparrow.

"No. They are nomadic."

For a moment I stare into the golden pools of the snowy owl's eyes.

Sparrow lowers us to the ground.

"Why is that?" he asks.

Sparrow does not know that this is the lost soul of my unborn daughter. This is Elise. She is two-thirds darkness, one-third light. *"The brightest light in the darkest of places,"* Clea once said.

"Never mind," I say, not wanting to explain. Sparrow's body may be healed, but his brain is still whacked. I have yet to trust him as easily as I did in the past. I'm not sure if I'll ever get back to trusting him after what's happened down here. I'm still trying to decide if I should go my own way.

"I almost forgot." Sparrow reaches into his pocket. "Clea sent this for you."

He holds out a large black feather.

"Clea?" I ask.

He nods.

I hesitate.

He moves it closer. I want to slap it out of his hand and run away. Nothing good has ever come from one of her feathers.

"She said you have to take it," Sparrow urges, pointing it at me.

I reach out, my fingers grasping the quill, just above his fingers. An arc of electricity lights up the feather as we're both touching it. Sparrow's eyes widen; his pupils shrink to pinpoints.

Screaming. There's so much screaming. Hellfire and brimstone. Blood. Pain. Black feathers everywhere. Black owls circle us, faster and faster. The entire time, an eerie trill is being whistled. "Save me!" Nightingale's voice screams.

When it's done, I open my eyes to find both of us on the ground.

"That was strange . . ." Sparrow stands, then reaches down to help me.

"We have to find your sister." I get to my feet.

Sparrow looks away, gritting his teeth.

"What's wrong?" I ask.

"I think . . ." His voice sounds pained as he presses his fingers to his head. "Vine is calling me."

"Vine—"

A pulse rocks the air around us. Suddenly, Sparrow goes flying, as though he's being tugged backward by some unknown force. His hands scrabble, and his wings beat uselessly, as his large frame hurdles across the treetops.

"Meg..." He sounds shocked.

"Sparrow!" I scream.

Poof—I go nowhere. *Poof*—nothing.

My ability to transport isn't working. I run toward the road as the snowy owl hoots from her nest. The Jeep is still parked on the shoulder of the highway, keys still in the ignition. I jump in and start the engine. Shifting the vehicle into gear, I take off for the burning caves.

...

Barreling down the road, I weave around the walking dead who are still searching for Nightingale. A thousand thoughts run through my head. Why can't I *poof* the heck out of here? Why did Vine call Sparrow like that? And where the heck is Nightingale?

I take the back roads. Route 37 to Route 3. Route 24 to Route 11. I make my way south, speeding as fast as I can, praying only that a forest creature doesn't waltz into the road. The speed doesn't scare me. I grew up on these roads in the earthen plane—they're pretty much identical—and drove them going way too fast plenty of times with Noah. Got pulled over enough times that I should've learned my lesson, too. But a raccoon or an idiotic opossum could really fuck up my plans right now.

Just as I turn on Route 26, about to pass through Fort Drum, dark shadows litter the road ahead. A horde of the dead are on the move. I have to slow the Jeep but consider plowing right through them. I don't have time to wait for the walking flesh sacks to schlep across the road. Just before I come to a complete stop, Noah suddenly appears in the passenger seat.

"Jesus," I shriek. "Thanks for scaring the shit out of me." Guess I didn't have to worry about a forest creature.

"Where you been, Meg?" He sounds annoyed.

"Me and Sparrow went on a little trip down Route 37."

"For two days?" Noah asks.

I slam on the brakes. "What?"

"You've been gone *two* days. No one had a clue where you and Sparrow were."

I shake my head. "No."

"Where were you, Meg?"

"We went to the barn on 37."

The walking dead are closing in on us.

"And . . ."

"Clea sent a feather." I recall what I saw: the screaming, the black owls. "It knocked us out but only for a minute or two."

When I look at Noah again, he's shaking his head. "Two days. You've been gone two days. And then all of a sudden, Sparrow shows up at the burning caves without you. Nightingale is still missing, and you . . ." He looks me up and down.

"I can't *poof* anymore. I tried, but I can't."

Noah scowls. "Some shit is going on right now."

I shift the Jeep into gear. "Yeah, I think so."

I press my foot down on the gas and weave around the dead, knocking a few over as I press the pedal down harder. A few heavy thunks, and we're clear of the pack.

Just before I get to Lowville, Noah touches my arm.

"What?" I ask.

"I think we should go look for her," he says.

"Nightingale?"

"They've done nothing to find her. Vine, Lucifer—they never left the caves. No one is looking for her."

"The dead are." I point to an old lady with a half-rotten face, dragging her busted foot down the side of the road.

"Clea sent them. She's the daughter of Lucifer. Do you think she'd really—"

"She's my mother!" I snap. "She's not like the others down here. She torched Jim and the other Hellions to protect us."

Noah's mouth snaps shut for a few minutes. "She's pure darkness," he finally says.

A moment of silence passes. He has a point, even if I don't think Clea would do such a thing.

"We need to look for Nightingale," Noah urges. "I have to find her."

"Where?"

"The cabin."

That is the absolute last place I want to go.

"Sonofabitch." The wheels of the Jeep squeal as I turn on to Route 12 and speed all the way north to Wellesley Island crossing.

...

I slow as I get to the border gates separating the United States and Canada. A guard steps out of his shack and walks toward the Jeep.

"Can't let you filthy Americans in." He settles his hands on his paunch belly and glares at us, real assholelike.

I'm not climbing a dead-infested waterfall again. That was some bullshit Sparrow and I had to do last time we walked here.

"Let us through," I say.

The guard clucks his tongue and shakes his head.

"What if I told you that you are in Hell, and there's no border to protect?" Noah speaks up.

"Dumbest shit I ever heard." The guard tips to the side and examines the windshield. "Where's your inspection sticker?"

"Don't need one." I smile.

"Stupid American kids. You think you can just—"

"Fuck Canada." I shift and stomp on the gas pedal. I plow right through; metal screeches as the gate bends. The chain snaps, and we're in. I don't slow down. Shifting gears, I drive faster, eager to get away and find Nightingale.

When that guard realizes he's dead and he's got no borders to protect, he'll forget about me. In my rearview mirror I see him trying to use his radio. When he realizes it's useless, he chucks it to the ground and glares after us.

"Wow." Noah clicks his seat belt on for the first time since he's been in the Jeep with me.

"Don't like being called stupid."

"You're not stupid. Never were."

This is why I trust Noah. Even when I'm being an asshole, he sticks up for me. That's what real friends do: they spend a summer in juvie by your side; they tie the laces on their shitkicker boots and run through the mud with you; they buy you Christmas presents.

"Flying here was much faster," I mutter.

"It was."

"I bet they'll come looking for us."

"I'm sure we've got time. Took them a few hours to find us in New York City."

I speed down the 401, passing the bus that takes survivors to the Safe House. I turn onto small dirt roads, then rumble over poorly built bridges and narrow trails, until I pull up in front of the cabin we left just a few days ago.

"There's something shitty about this place," I warn Noah, feeling uneasy.

"We're in Hell," he reminds me.

"Yeah." I unbuckle my seat belt and get out. "I know that, but there's something about *this place*."

Noah gets out, too, and we head for the door to the cabin. My hand hovers over the doorknob.

"What's wrong?" Noah asks.

"I'm worried about Sparrow."

"He'll be fine."

"You think? It's like I barely know who he is anymore."

"Did you ever truly know who he was?" Noah asks.

That's a good question. In the short time I've known Sparrow, he's been all over the spectrum—completely insane, lucid and strong, dark and out of control. The problem is, no matter who he is, I'm still drawn to Sparrow. It's those memories of him protecting me when we didn't know who we were—I just can't shake those.

I shove the door open.

The hole in the floor has been filled in with dirt, the bones of the dead effectively buried. There are scorch marks on the flooring where the Hellions and Jim burned. Noah begins wandering around the room. He stops at the back door and touches the frame before tugging the door open and looking around the backyard.

"It was strange, her scream."

"It came from outside," I remind him.

Noah walks toward the pile of rocks, inspecting them. "I think it came from the other side of the portal.

I close my eyes, trying to remember exactly what happened. There was screaming when the portal was in one piece. It sounded like the scream came from the back door, but the Hellion that came through was alone—covered in her blood, but alone. Noah could be right, but . . .

"I destroyed the portal." I glance at the broken rocks.

"So we rebuild it." Noah bends and starts sorting through the debris.

We pile the stones, lining up the black markings like a giant puzzle. An arch begins to take shape.

"We're going to be in deep shit for this." I wipe sweat off the back of my neck, remembering all those nights Sparrow came to me exhausted. "The Council members already hate me. Putting this back together will give them one more reason—"

"To what? Hate you a little more? You've never cared about assholes like that before, Meg. Why start now?"

I shrug, lifting a heavy piece of rock. "I thought once I found out who I really was, life would get easier."

"Life doesn't get easier when you find yourself. It's just new shit for you to doubt." Noah works with drive. "And who cares? If we find Nightingale, it's worth it."

When the arch is finally complete, we stand back.

"What do we do now?" I ask.

"Walk through it?" he suggests.

Unease settles in my gut. "Remind me again why I'm doing this?"

"Because you brought sweet innocent Nightingale to Hell, and now she's missing."

"Dick." I take a step.

Noah grabs my hand, and we leap through the portal.

Realms and realms and ... Goddamned realms

We are on the earthen plane; I recognize the cabin clear as day. It's just like I remember it, just like I decorated it a year ago. That was back when I was pregnant, when I was weaker and too afraid to leave Jim.

I turn to Noah. He's transparent. I reach out to touch his arm, but my fingers go straight through.

"Hey." Noah moves away from me. "That kind of tickles." He glances at my face. "What's wrong?"

"I can see straight through you."

Noah shrugs as though he couldn't care less. "I'm dead, remember?"

Things are different on the earthen plane; I remember that much from the last time I was here with Sparrow. Angel wings can't be seen, the dead are invisible, and Hellions simply resemble really bad convicts.

There's blood on the floor underneath our feet. We look like we're standing in the middle of a horror movie.

"I'm suddenly thinking that this wasn't such a good idea." I lift my foot, leaving behind a nearly perfect impression of my boot print in the sticky blood. I crouch down to inspect it closer. "It's been days. This should be dry. Shouldn't it?"

Noah studies the pool of red for a moment. "Or maybe there was just too much of it to dry up."

I stand straight. I'm not sure how much blood runs through an Angel's body, but I know this is much more than I was drained of the first time Jim tried to kill me.

"We should probably get out of here," Noah suggests.

I walk across the room, trying not to leave any more footprints.

Noah reaches for the door, but the handle slides through his hand each time he tries to grasp it. "Damn."

I grab the knob. "Going to be kinda hard to be a manservant if you can't even open a door here."

As I pull the door open, a black feather flutters down. I catch it in my hand. Small, downy, and soft.

"It's Nightingale's," Noah says.

"I suppose you'd know."

I shove the feather into my pocket and leave the cabin. There's a beat-up old Mustang parked in the gravel driveway. A car I don't remember Jim owning, but there was a lot he was doing without my knowledge.

"Let's take the car."

"You're awful bossy for a dead guy." I walk to the driver's side.

While I'm buckling my seat belt, Noah is trying to paw through the vehicle, looking for the keys. His hands slide through everything he touches.

I flip down the sun visor, and a key drops into my lap.

"Good." Noah looks relieved. "I think we should start in Gouverneur."

"I don't want to go there," I reply.

"I think she's there. I think Nightingale is there."

"What makes you so sure?" I start the engine.

Noah pauses before he says, "We have a connection."

I shift the car into gear and back out onto the road, noticing that the crunch of gravel is softer here—not as sharp of a sound as in Hell.

"What kind of a connection?"

Noah hesitates.

"Just tell me already."

"She can access the astral plane."

"So?"

Noah scoffs. "The place of spirits and dreams. Nightingale can travel into your dreams. She can travel across the astral plane."

I shake my head, not making the connection.

"When you're done with me and my soul goes back to the astral plane, Nightingale can still visit me. I won't be alone. You don't know what it's like there. The loneliness . . . it's exponential."

I grip the steering wheel. I don't want Noah to leave me. Ever.

"So, you're in love with an Angel?" I mock.

"Just like you."

I speed up and ignore him. I was in love with an Angel. Sappy puppy love that twisted into a sick fuckedupness. I'm not sure where Sparrow and I stand anymore. And I can't really think about him right now.

...

It's night by the time we reach the US border. Good thing, too; there's no line.

I don't slow down.

"What are you doing?" Noah asks.

"I left my ID in Hell."

"Shit."

"Yeah."

"Don't do it," Noah warns.

I gun it. Put the pedal to the metal and blast through customs.

"Meg!" Noah's screaming at me. "Don't do it!"

"Shut up, Noah!" I'm screaming back, and the guy in the shack is watching me wide-eyed, picking up a phone to call for help. And I'm sure the cameras are going to show that it looks like I'm screaming at myself.

"Border Patrol is going to be on our asses faster than a fly on cake." Noah is fidgeting, twisting to look behind us.

"Can't you do something?" I ask him. "You're a ghost, for Christ's sake. Don't you have some special ghost power here on Earth?"

"Lucifer altered my astral magic when he tethered our souls." Noah twists the other way and looks out the passenger window. "I can't do much unless it involves you."

"Involves me what?"

"Getting hurt or threatened."

"So, like, if someone tried to arrest me? Forcefully?"

Noah glares. "Yes."

"Good." I press my foot down harder on the gas pedal.

Thelma and Louise got nothin' on Meg and Noah.

I take the back roads, weave along Route 12, turn sharp onto 26, turn again onto another dirt road that will lead me to

37, then South Hammond to 3. I stay on Route 3 for a good long while.

"Surprised the cops haven't caught up with us yet," Noah says.

"Maybe there is a God," I mock as I turn onto Route 10, drive around Yellow Lake, then turn on to 58 and follow it straight to Gouverneur.

"I don't want to be in this town." I slow my speed and come to a stop at the light.

"There's something here. Jim's fake dad on the earthen plane knew about what was going on."

"And?" I'm annoyed. That guy is a jerk. Jim's stand-in father was a Watcher, an escapee from down under who raises a Hell child on Earth.

"We should find the Watcher. He has to know something."

...

I pull up in front of a large old Greek revival. This is the sheriff's house, Jim's fake father, the man who raised him on the earthen plane. Thinking back, I never really liked the guy. The sheriff before him was pleasant enough—seemed to enjoy arresting me as a kid. Thought he was teaching me something. But when that sheriff left and this one came along, things changed; the guy acted like he couldn't stand the sight of me. Made that well known when Jim knocked me up and dragged me back.

I get out of the car and wait for Noah on the sidewalk. He tries the door handle a few times before giving up and sliding through the side of the car.

"Took you long enough to figure it out."

"Hey, this is my first time here as a spirit," Noah says. "Give me a break."

"Like a wee baby learning to crawl."

"Sorry if I'm not living up to your expectations."

I head for the front door and notice the sheriff's cruiser in the driveway. I knock.

"You going to come in with me?" I ask Noah.

"You going to stop talking to a ghost? Pretty soon people are going to think you're crazy, talking to no one." He motions around me. "Invisible man here."

The door's flung open, and the sheriff is standing there, shirt untucked, looking like we woke him from a nap.

"You," he sneers.

"You." I smile.

The sheriff glances at Noah. His hand disappears to the side of the door, like he's reaching for something.

"I think—" Noah starts, but the sheriff throws a handful of white dust at him. A piece hits my bottom lip. Foolishly, I taste it. Salt. Noah disappears in wisps of what he was, till there's nothing.

The sheriff grabs my arm and yanks me into his house. Just as the door closes, I notice the thick line of white around the house. I saw this in a movie before; spirits can't pass the lines of salt.

There goes my manservant.

The sheriff slams the door closed, then pushes me so hard I stumble backward, landing on the couch. The TV is on, and plastered across the screen is my blurry image. Me screaming as I plowed through customs. Next comes an image of the blood-soaked cabin. Didn't take them long to make that connection. Only a few hours. For all the shit I give Canada, they're faster at making connections than the American police. Good for them, bad for me.

"Always knew you'd grow up to be a convict." The sheriff locks the front door, pulls a revolver from a drawer, and aims it at me. "Your kind ain't supposed to be here." He cocks the hammer. "Figured you'd come looking for that leggy brunette. Jim warned me." He kicks a stool away from a rocking chair and sits in front of me. "Girl was dressed like a stripper."

I swallow hard, glancing around to see what I could use to defend myself. The cool metal of the blade strapped to my thigh begs for my touch, but that would be obvious. He'd shoot me in a second. There's a lamp nearby, a heavy book...

"Ah, ah, ah." The sheriff tips his revolver. "Hands up. I remember your sneaky ways. Guy before me warned me about you. Now, what am I going to—"

Someone walks into the room from the kitchen. I turn—recognize the black suit, white Roman collar, the plain face, light-brown hair, and thick eyebrows. If I saw this guy in public, I'd look right past him. Plainer than plain. It's a Deacon.

He stands in the threshold between rooms, staring at me like some creeper. A smile spreads across his thin lips. Looks like a man who just won the lotto. He blesses himself with the sign of the cross, forehead to chest, shoulder to shoulder, his fingertips traveling as he whispers a prayer.

"Where is she?" I ask.

The sheriff smiles.

The Deacon steps farther into the room. "You slither here from Eden? Last we heard, you went back to the heavens to stay with your father."

"Last I heard, your kind were banished to Hell."

"Jim got me out. Said he had a plan."

"Jim's dead, fuckface."

The Deacon frowns. "We've been warned about you."

"Don't care what you heard. I'm just searching for a friend."

The Deacon pauses. "The Angel girl." His thin brows rise with interest.

"Bet you'd get a good bounty off her," I say.

The Deacon seems to contemplate it for a moment.

My blurry picture flashes across the television screen again.

"I can help you find her." The Deacon crosses the room and grabs a jacket off a chair. "Since you can't leave without going to prison, wait for me to return."

I relax against the couch cushions. The sheriff lowers his pistol. I was told to never trust a Deacon, but since I'm stuck on the earthen plane with my ability to travel between realms gone, I'll take all the help I can get.

The Deacon leaves.

"Where's he going?" I ask.

"Bet you'd love to know." The sheriff holsters his weapon.

...

Sparrow

Sparrow stood alone in the Hellion lair, his back bleeding from being raked across the forests of Hell. It was taking too long to heal. Nearly two days had passed, and Sparrow could still feel the blood oozing down his back and legs. Jim had warned Sparrow about this: drinking old blood made him weak. Now, he couldn't even attempt to defend himself against Vine.

Sparrow had been suspended by the chains in the middle of

the room, waiting. The invisible collar tightened around his neck, and Sparrow could barely breathe.

"There will be punishment for the death of my son," Vine promised.

Sparrow couldn't see the Demon, but his voice permeated the room.

"Your mixed-blood abomination is going to pay." Vine made himself visible.

Sparrow remembered the way Jim looked before he and Gabriel had tried to kill him. Fair skinned and blond haired—deceiving for a Demon. Vine was nearly identical.

He smiled at Sparrow. Wicked, sharp teeth appeared.

"Your girl ruined decades of planning. You know how hard it is to work under the thumb of Lucifer? His pesky daughter sticking her snout in everyone's business?" Vine thumbed his nose in disgust. "That portal was our chance for escape." Vine crossed the room and took a whip from the wall of weapons. "That portal was our chance for control."

Vine snapped the whip against the floor. A threat if Sparrow ever saw one.

"You will pay, winged prince. You will hunger until she returns, because we all know she will return. We've moved Heaven and Earth and Hell to keep you apart. Always backfired. This time will be different. When she shows, you're going to drain her dry for good. Put an end to this by your own tongue."

Sparrow licked his lips at the thought of Meg's blood. But the thought of her blood brought thoughts of other things, like the ink on her skin, the brightness of her eyes, the fullness of her ass in leather pants. Sparrow wanted her, wanted her to return, but he feared her reappearance in Hell. Maybe it was better that she was gone. With Vine in charge, Sparrow could barely grasp control.

The whip struck Sparrow's back, sharp and stinging, and the desperate need to feed took over.

When Vine was done, he called on the new recruits. Replacement Hellions appeared, giant lower Demons, more frightening than the Hellions before. Not long after, just as when Sparrow first appeared, the door to the lair opened, and the Bloodwhores entered.

The Hellions fed, emptiness in their eyes.

Sparrow felt the hunger rise from his center, a growing monster, and he knew one thing was for certain: that Demon was always hungry. Sparrow could barely control his Demon. Typically, it controlled him.

Sparrow was relieved that Meg had fled Hell.

...

Meg

Remiel walks through the front door, looking out of place in his flowing robe and golden aura. You'd think the guy would try to disguise himself on the earthen plane. He watches me for a moment before moving closer.

I stand.

"Knew you were trouble." Remiel touches my arm. I move away. He steps closer, invading my personal space. "You infected them both. Ruined them—"

"That was all your doing."

"Shut your filthy mouth." He raises his hand like he's going to slap me, pausing midair. Smiles. "*He* could see that here." Remiel grabs my arm, dragging me out of the room.

"Let go of me." I struggle, but Remiel is much larger and stronger.

"Wish I could. But you're coming with me."

"Where?" I think of dropping to the ground, kicking him in the back of the knee and rolling away. I glance at the Deacon, then Jim's fake father. I'd rather not be left with them any longer.

"Sir," the Deacon speaks up. "The bounty."

"Done." Remiel waves his hand, impatient, dismissive. "Two hundred souls."

I glare at the Deacon. "You lied!"

The Deacon doesn't appear guilty at all. He shrugs. "Nothing's fair between Heaven and Hell."

"And Nightingale?" I ask. "You promised to help me."

Remiel's grip tightens on my arm. "He can't help you," Remiel says. "She's back where she belongs. Been there for a full day now."

"What?"

Remiel crosses the room with me in tow. "She's home. Where she belongs. Recovering from the mess you got her in."

"And how did you know where she was?" I ask.

"She was delivered. Someone smarter than you thought it good to bring her to safety." Remiel's grip on my arm tightens painfully. "After what you did to her"—he shakes his head—"Council will have a field day with it all."

My relief is not as satisfying as I'd thought it would be. With all the bad shit I did in my life, stealing away an Angel has got to be the worst.

Remiel opens the door, and I get my first glimpse of Noah, pacing outside.

"Not today, sinner." Remiel reaches into the bowl near the door and throws a handful of salt at Noah, and he vanishes.

Remiel drags me to the sheriff's cruiser and shoves me in the backseat before sitting in the passenger side. The sheriff gets behind the wheel and starts the car.

Noah appears again. Looking around, he focuses on the cruiser and runs toward it.

The Deacon walks out of the house, rosary in hand. His voice is deep and powerful as he enunciates a prayer in Latin.

Remiel chuckles as I bang my fists on the window. "Leave him alone!"

"Ever see an exorcism?" Remiel asks. "He's going to send your pet ghost back to the astral. Where he belongs."

This time Noah doesn't just disappear in a wisp of fog and smoke. He screams, roars something terrible, mutates, and twists in painful contortions, and then he's gone.

"No!" I slam my fists on the window, but it's over. Noah is gone. The Deacon wipes his hands before spinning and returning to the house.

"Too many supernatural beings where they don't belong," Remiel scoffs. "The need for the Council has never been stronger. To the portal," Remiel orders.

The portal happens to be in an old Catholic cemetery fifteen miles from the sheriff's house. The perfect setting for the transportation of supernatural beings.

An arch of cobbled stone that looks quite unassuming looms before us. After Remiel touches his fingers to the stone and whispers a few words, the space under the arch wavers like a stone tossed in a calm pond. Remiel shoves me through the portal. After a few moments of stomach-churning lightness and feeling like I've been sent through a centrifuge, we exit on the far side of Remiel's Kingdom. His house is off in the distance, which means there will be a long period of being dragged across the expanse of yard that's in front of us.

"Can't you just let me walk?" I ask, wishing he'd get his hands off me.

"I just let you take off with both of my children. Look what that got me? A missing son and daughter. You can't be free. Your filth has tainted them both."

Guess Remiel forgot that he caused the curse, not me.

Magically, we've crossed half of the yard by the time he gets to the next part. "Council's got a surprise for you. Gabriel's not going to be happy, but he's outnumbered. Usually is." Remiel leads me around the back of his castle, to the basement where he kept Nightingale. "Until they're ready, you'll wait here." Remiel shoves open the door, drags me down the hall, past the room where I stayed before, past Nightingale's room, deeper underground, until we come to a barred door. The hinges groan as Remiel opens the door. He shoves me inside, slams the door, and hooks a lock in place.

Remiel looks even more like Sparrow when the shadows touch his face. Makes me miss Sparrow something fierce.

"How long will I be here?" My stomach growls.

As Remiel turns on his heel, walking away, he says, "Until they're ready for you."

...

It turns out "until they're ready for me" happens to be a few days. The hunger I experienced in the bowels of Hell returns, except now I have no castle to search frantically. I have my lonely cell with about ten feet of space to pace. Seems I'm always finding myself behind bars. At least this time it didn't come with a jumpsuit.

I walk in circles, touching the weapon on my thigh; I think about all the ways I could try to escape. This isn't a jail cell in Hell; I doubt escaping would be as easy as before. Maybe I could just wait. My father's Kingdom is not far from this place, and if Remiel is informing the Council, then Gabriel will know I'm here. I've never placed much trust in those around me, but something tells me that my father would do everything in his power to release me. And since he's an Archangel, I'll just wait and see what that is.

My stomach growls, loud and angry.

Shadow darkens the room.

I turn to find Nightingale standing at the door, her hair mussed and greasy. This is the first time I've seen her since she disappeared. I've found the ghost I was searching for.

"Night . . ." I walk across the room toward her.

She still emits that innocence, still bright but . . . broken. I did this to her.

"I'm so sorry," I whisper, reaching through the bars of the door.

She backs away, a candle in her hand lighting the dark hall. "I wanted to leave." Her voice is so soft. "It's my fault. I should have listened to my father."

"What happened to you?" I ask. "There was so much blood."

Nightingale steps into a shadow. "It doesn't matter. Can't go back." Her voice drops. "I know evil. Didn't understand what we fight. Now, I do."

"I never meant for you to get hurt."

"I know." She sniffles. "More than Sparrow connects us now."

I don't ask for details. I can feel the pain radiating off her. "I've been searching for you. Everywhere."

"I know."

The closer I get to the door, the farther she backs away.

"Don't leave," I beg.

A tear slides down Nightingale's cheek before she turns and skates away, her dark hair trailing behind her like a stream.

I drop to the floor and close my eyes.

...

I wake to find Remiel standing over me. He's holding a knife, much like the blade that's strapped to my thigh, but his radiates a white light.

The pains in my stomach are unbearable.

"Move." Remiel kicks at my side.

"Go to Hell." If I had any saliva in my mouth, I'd spit on him.

"Get up." He kicks me again. "Now."

"Let me go."

Remiel laughs. "Oh, we're going to let you go. Going to free your soul and send it where it belongs." He kicks me a third time. "Get up."

The thought of death, of them having power over me, surges straight to my heart. I may not be able to *poof* myself out of here, but I can fight back. I've done this before. The evil of one Archangel is nothing compared to seven Hellions.

I jump to my feet, the motion startling Remiel.

He steps back.

After days of hunger, all I can focus on is the throbbing of the artery in his tense neck. And then, I am nothing but my mother's daughter—an animal, a beast, through and through. Starving and wild, unable to think beyond my hunger, I leap on Remiel and bite down on his neck.

Remiel's hands dig at my back, trying to peel me off him.

The taste of his blood is like nothing I've ever experienced. Pure and warm, powerful. Before I know what I've done, Remiel is nothing but a sack of bones on the ground.

Nightingale's shadow stretches across the doorway. "Killing an Archangel comes with severe punishment." Her voice is low, as though she might actually be worried for me.

"Faced plenty of punishments." I wipe my face and see the smear of blood across my hands. Shame hits me. Shame and . . . power. I've never felt so strong in my life.

"Meg?" Nightingale sounds worried.

"What?"

"You're . . . *something*." She skates backward, farther away from me.

Remiel's blood floods my veins, and I feel my power has returned. There is one thought on my mind. One person. If it's the last thing I ever do, I have to do it now. I can't control the urge.

"I'm going to get Sparrow," I tell Nightingale. "Do you want to come with me?"

She shakes her head, backing away more.

"Okay." I shake my hands, my voice sounding nervous. "I'll bring him back. I'll get him and bring him back here."

I glance at the pile of robes at my feet.

Remiel is dead.

Nightingale is safe.

I am strong.

Poof—I return to the burning caves of Hell.

"Oh, child." Clea is there, her cold arms surrounding me instantly. "You've returned."

I step back, replaying the events of the past days before shit went real bad, trying to figure it all out in my mind.

Nothing is ever as it seems, especially since I woke from that coma months ago, but the one thing I know for certain is that the last thing I touched was Clea's feather.

Clea smiles knowingly. "I won't apologize. It's written in the stars. You will be invincible together."

"What did you do to me?" I ask. "I couldn't travel between realms."

"Just a little curse to keep you in your place. I'm your mother. I can get away with doing things like that." She smiles. "It's lifted. Obviously. Now go find your Hellion."

I run up the stone stairwell to the Hellions' lair, playing the future scene over and over in my head. Actually, it's just a jumble of scenes. There's things I have to tell Sparrow about his family. And then there's the tiny fact that I left him without a good-bye. I've been gone for days.

I push the door open. Sparrow is standing in the middle of the room. Vine is there, as well. A row of new recruits is lined up across the back of the room.

Sparrow doesn't hesitate. As soon as his green eyes lock with mine, he lumbers toward me and grabs my arm. Without a "Hello," a "Hey, girl," or an "I missed you while you were searching for my sister," he takes a bite out of my wrist and feeds. I try to pull away, but Sparrow holds me tight, dragging my body closer to his while he sucks.

Tears burn my eyes. I punch against his chest with my free

hand and consider reaching for the blade strapped to my thigh, but I don't want to hurt him.

The pain in my heart is greater than the sharpness of his bite. The decision becomes apparent at this moment. I must leave him.

Sparrow pauses, only to whisper, "They all warned me that you'd leave me, you'd break my heart, that your kind are like that." There is hurt in his eyes. I guess that's what happens when you try to fix your relationship in the bowels of Hell. Everyone gets a little hurt. So much hurt that not even a drawerful of feathers can fix it. Not even saving an Angel can fix it. Perhaps I saved the wrong Angel . . .

"Give her to me."

Sparrow stops at the sound of a dark voice. He's hesitant, glancing at me before shoving me away and holding me at arm's length.

"Now, boy." Vine is reaching for me, fangs sharp and ready.

"No! No!" I scratch and claw at Sparrow.

He doesn't release me.

Vine moves forward, taking my free arm and jerking me toward him.

I want to tell Sparrow everything that happened. I want to tell him that I found Nightingale, I killed his father, I have Archangel blood running through my veins, that—

Vine jerks me hard and I stumble. Sparrow releases his grip on me; with it goes the last shred of hope I had for us. Vine drags me away, kicking and screaming, and Sparrow just watches.

And just as I'm thinking he's going to stand by and observe whatever terrible fate Vine has planned for me, Sparrow finally roars an ear-deafening "Stop!"

The leather of his wings explodes off his back, a whipping sheet in the wind; it hurdles across the room and wraps around Vine until he is nothing but a mummy. Struggling, stretching against the tight skin, Vine tries to tear his way out. The points of his elbows, the nails of his fingers, the points of his teeth all press against the leather in an effort to escape. It's pointless, though. Vine collapses on the floor. The leather constricts, tighter and tighter, until he becomes still.

"Clea!" I shout.

My mother appears in the room; Lucifer, too. They take in the scene, with me on the floor, Vine a motionless mummy, and Sparrow with bones for wings.

Clea smiles proudly. *"I knew you'd figure it out."* Her voice is in my mind.

Lucifer goes to Sparrow and touches his head; the leather returns to his wings.

My stomach sinks. I bow my head, fighting that familiar feeling of hopelessness.

"Will you let him be done now?" I ask. "Is Sparrow through?"

Lucifer shakes his head. "He's left me without a head Demon." He taps his chin with his index finger. "The only choice I have is for him to take Vine's place." Lucifer smiles.

Clea pales. Didn't think that was possible. The look of shock on her face is surprising. Noah warned me that she might be devious, but now I know that she never was. My grandfather, however, is a very different story. I'll be damned to stand by and put up with this bullshit for one second longer.

"No!" I reach for my blade, ready to *poof* Sparrow out of here like I did in Heaven. We can escape to the earthen plane; I don't care if he's cursed. Dealing with a little crazy is a thousand times better than this.

My grandfather takes one look at the blade in my hand. "You'd dare threaten the king of Hell?" Lucifer spreads his wings, forcing the others away and encircling me. In a second I am surrounded by nothing but blackness. "I gave you a wish." Lucifer's voice drops to a whisper. "I gave you a wish, and you used it on something as petty as *friendship*. There are no differences between friends and enemies. You could have used it for something real. You could have used it for *love*." He spits the word like a curse.

My stomach feels like it's dropped to my feet.

"You could have used it for *Sparrow*." Lucifer's eyes glow. He grins, sharp toothed and wide. I have never seen evil like this before. He's frightening. "You wasted the most valuable gift I have ever given a soul. And you. Chose. Wrong!"

Lucifer's wings whip away from me. Only silence follows.

I make eye contact with Sparrow.

"Do you remember?" I ask.

Sparrow's lips are pressed in a tight line. He doesn't move an inch.

I take that as a no.

Poof.

I return to the earthen plane.

Alone.

Blood and Sin and Freedom

I send myself to a beach, an island in the Bahamas, a place I saw in a magazine once. I can't go home, being a wanted felon and all. I look around the beach I've landed on. Get ready to move, to make a plan. I've got plenty of money. Just have to get a new identity or a really good lawyer to fix the mess I stepped in while I was in Canada. There is no body, but after finding all that blood, I'm sure the Mounties are gunning for me. If there's anything I've learned about law enforcement, they'll never stop until you pay for your crimes.

Poof. Sparrow is standing in front of me.

I step back. "How did you do that?"

Sparrow licks his lips.

Perhaps it was the fresh blood? I'm betting Archangel blood mixed with mine could make a person powerful. Bet it could raise the dead, kill a god. A person could really *do* things with that kind of power.

"You've changed," I say.

"You, too."

I will never forget the sound of Sparrow's voice: deep and smooth.

"This is so far from where we started." I'm not sure I'll ever see the Sparrow I fell in love with again.

"We're not the same. After all that"—Sparrow waves his hand behind him—"who could ever be the same after finding out what we really are?"

I look away. Who could ever be the same after everything we've gone through? The realization doesn't lessen the want.

Sparrow tips his head to the side, quirky and birdlike. "How many times do I have to die for you, Meg?"

"I never asked you to do it. I never asked you to join Lucifer's robot army. That wasn't me. That was you."

"I have to cure my bloodline."

I shake my head. Wishing this had gone another way, into the sunrise instead of the sunset.

"How many times do I have to die?" he asks again.

"I didn't ask you—"

Sparrow smiles, both beautiful and dark. I forget my words.

"That's what makes it worth it every time." His fingers touch my cheek. He is warm, solid, and strong. His finger trails down my jawline, my clavicle, resting over my heart, on the tattoo of the sparrow.

"I am Sparrow. You are mine, and I am yours."

Staring into his green eyes, so much darker than they were before, I know this is true.

"We are broken."

"Unpossible."

"You can't make up words."

"I can do what I want."

Why can't he see that this isn't going to work? Sparrow

rarely gets angry at me. Not when I almost killed him, not when I lied to him, not when—

"I killed your father." I confess.

"Tasted that. Bound to happen one day." He smiles slowly, sadly. "They said we'd be invincible together."

"They never said we'd be ruined for it."

"Some people never go crazy." Sparrow's hand moves to my shoulder; he grips me tightly and pulls me close. "They must be exceptionally bored with themselves." He smiles; his long lashes brush his cheeks as he blinks. "You're a free soul. Soon I will be, too." Sparrow kisses me, desperate and hard and promising.

When his lips leave mine, he starts to hum "Captain Crash & the Beauty Queen from Mars."

"I'll be coming back for you," he promises.

And then—*poof*—Sparrow is gone.

I find myself alone on the beach. Behind me, there's a block of hotels behind a row of palm trees. I trudge across the sand and make my way toward one. I check my pockets for my wallet and pull out a few twenties left over from Christmas with Sparrow. I get a single room, double bed, that's it. Nothing fancy like before.

Sparrow. I ran from all those people in Gouverneur. Ran from a man who I thought was my father. I never thought I'd run from Sparrow.

I open the hotel door to a wicker and pastel room. It's small and damp and smells like beach must. I unstrap my blade and hide it on the top shelf of the closet underneath the extra blankets. If the cleaning lady finds that, she'll definitely report me to the authorities.

I shower, rinse the stench of Hell off my clothes, and hang them in the bathroom to dry. The one luxury here is the bathrobe on the back of the bathroom door. I put it on before crawling into bed.

First order of business in the morning is finding a lawyer. The best money can buy. Maybe I could say I was high on coke when I drove through customs. Go to drug court and do some community service. Worked when I was a kid.

I yawn, listening to the sounds of the beach and the parrots squawking in the trees outside my window. I can never escape them. Birds of a feather.

Somehow I sleep.

"Monsters aren't so bad." Good ol' Nightingale is here, haunting my dreams. *"Most people are scared of them, but I'm not."* She's stretched across my bed, her roller skate wheels spinning, legs slowly scissoring. *"Most people don't know the monsters keep us safe at night."* She flutters her downy-white wings. *"They hide under the bed to scare away evil things. Protect us from the Demons of Hell."* She turns to look at me, suddenly serious. *"He's your monster now, Meg."* Nightingale winks. *"Noah says hello."*

I open my mouth to speak, to tell her I'm sorry, to ask for forgiveness, but nothing comes out.

Seems I've lost control of everything, even my dreams.

About the Author

M. R. Pritchard is a two-time Kindle Scout winning author and her short story "Glitch" has been featured in the 2017 winter edition of THE FIRST LINE literary journal. She holds degrees in Biochemistry and Nursing. She is a northern New Yorker transplanted to the Gulf Coast of Florida who enjoys coffee, cloudy days, and reading on the lanai.

Visit her website MRPritchard.com and join her newsletter to receive a monthly update on new releases, freebies, current projects, and daily shenanigans of an author's life.

Follow on Amazon to get alerts on new releases.

If you enjoyed *The Sparrow Man Series*, please leave a review, tell a friend, or gift to a friend. These small acts keep authors writing. Thank you.

Special Thanks

Thank you so much for reading *Nightingale Girl*! I hope you loved this book as much as I do. If you haven't already, consider reading the first book in this series, *Sparrow Man*, while you're waiting for book three to be published. While *Nightingale Girl* may be read as a stand-alone, there's plenty of awesomeness in book one that you might be missing, like the story behind the snowy owl and when Sparrow remembers who he is—I love that scene.

To all the fans of *Sparrow Man* who have waited so patiently for this second book in the series, thanks so much for hanging on! I sincerely hope you're enjoying the series; I just love getting lost in Meg and Sparrow's world.

Help an author out and consider leaving a review or telling a friend about this series. Reviews help readers like you find great books and help writers like me fund another amazing story.

Other Books by M. R. Pritchard

<u>Science Fiction/post-apocalyptic:</u>

The Phoenix Project Series:

The Phoenix Project

The Reformation

Revelation

Inception

Origins

Resurrection

The Safest City on Earth

The Man Who Fell to Earth

Heartbeat

Asteroid Riders Series

Moon Lord

Collector of Space Junk and Rebellious Dreams

<u>Steampunk:</u>

Tick of a Clockwork Heart

<u>Dark Fantasy:</u>

Sparrow Man Series

<u>Fantasy/Fairy Tale Romance:</u>

Muse

Forgotten Princess Duology

Midsummer Night's Dream: A Game of Thrones

<u>Poetry/Short Stories</u>

Consequence of Gravity

Scarecrow

BY M. R. PRITCHARD

PARADISE BY THE DASHBOARD LIGHT

There is a royal blue feather on my balcony; it's been there for days, stuck in the same place through rain, wind, and sun. It hasn't faded, it hasn't fluttered, it hasn't moved one goddamned millimeter. It's waiting for me to pick it up. A message, a warning, a love letter from a life I'm trying to run from. Been there for thirteen days. I'm not going to touch that fucking thing with a ten-foot pole.

I drink the last of my coffee, set the chipped mug in the sink, then grab my wallet and phone. I glance at the forbidden feather before closing the door to my hotel room.

It's late morning and already sweltering outside, not as hot as Heaven but close. Good thing is, it's not like back in Gouverneur. No one here cares what I wear. Everyone else is wearing bikinis and board shorts. I look perfectly normal.

I make my way across the elevated walkway of the motel, down the stairs, and head for my lawyer's office. Reuben Strong is the first lawyer I ever had that wasn't a public defender. A middle-aged dude with almost a sadder story than mine. He moved down to the islands after some big law firm in New York City bent him over a barrel to show him the fifty states and forgot the lube. Seems New York City is pretty much the same on the earthen plane as it is in Hell. Who knew?

Reuben set up his agency in an old tourist shop. It looks out of place but has a great view of the ocean. I make it there in six minutes and let myself in. He's sitting behind a giant oak desk—reading my file, no doubt. He glances up at me over dark framed glasses. "You got yourself in some deep shit, Meg," is his greeting.

"You're telling me." I pace the spacious office.

"What kind of kid does this crap? You were arrested twenty times in one year for shoplifting."

I shrug. "I was bored." This big city lawyer has got to have seen worse than me. I attempt to change the subject, "What kind of a name is Reuben anyways?"

He groans. "I've told you at least fifty times, it's a family name."

"Never knew anyone called Reuben when I lived upstate. That's a sandwich, not a name."

"Should've checked downstate." He flips through my file. "You should have *been* downstate at a one of those centers where they scare kids straight. Jesus, your juvy record is thirty-seven pages long."

I stop, stand still. 37. There was a time when that meant something to me. Wasn't so long ago...

Route 37.
Old barn.
Snowy owl.

Reuben's eyes flick to me twice. "What's wrong?"

I shake it off. "Nothing."

"Is there anything you didn't do?"

"Thought that was sealed."

"Usually it is, until you do some bullshit like drive through border patrol in a stolen car, higher than a kite with blood on your shoes. What a shit storm."

"Well, I'm paying you a lot of money to clean that mess up."

Reuben leans back in his chair, runs his hands through his hair, focuses on me.

"What?"

"You're going to need a new wardrobe for court."

"What's wrong with my clothes?"

"You're wearing a tube top and those shorts are damn close to underwear."

"It's really hot outside."

"And all your..." he waves his hand instead of using words, "...is visible."

"They're called tattoos, prude."

Reuben shakes his head and mutters, "Girls like you have a name, and it's jailbait."

"Says the walking sandwich."

"It's a family name."

I sit across from him and look out the window. What kind of lawyer gets a beachfront office? It's absurd. The view is amazing; green-blue ocean, white sand, tall palm trees.

"You need something nicer. From a real department store."

"Fine." I cross my arms and glance at Reuben out of the corner of my eye. He's studying my file.

The guy is nice enough, took my case before I even asked

him. All I did was walk in the door. He took one look at my picture on the television, one look at me, and said, "*Hell yes.*"

"Just one question," Reuben leans back and props his feet up on his desk. "How'd you get from Canada to Key West so fast?"

"Magic."

His lips press in a straight line.

"You wouldn't believe me if I told you the truth."

He drops his feet to the floor. "You walked in my door five days after crashing through customs. The entire country was looking for you."

"Must've been a miracle." I raise my palms to the sky; control the urge to mention God. I don't tell Reuben the part where I stopped in the Bahamas before coming to Key West to find a lawyer. That would just involve another round of questions. I don't feel like explaining my life story to this guy. I don't feel like explaining it to myself half the time.

"The judge is going to want to know."

"Can I plead the fifth?" Explaining my ability to *poof* between realms might make his head explode.

"No."

"I'll have to make up some story then."

"Meg, you can't lie to a judge." Reuben is leaning forward now, focused on me, trying to hold in a scolding or something.

I shrug.

"You can't." He throws his hands down on the desk. "You can't just make some shit up. You will be under oath, your hand on the damn Bible. You have to tell the truth."

"The truth." I laugh.

"Yes."

"*You can't handle the truth.*" I include air quotes then

glance out the window again, eager to get out of this office now that it's become the *seventh circle of questioning hell*.

"Try me."

"My name is Meg Clark." I stand. "I killed my mother the day I was born. My father is the Archangel Gabriel. My grandfather is Lucifer. I've done some very bad things. I even own a blade that was forged in the fires of Hell."

"Have you been watching Lord of the Rings?" He doesn't sound impressed at all.

"You wanted the truth."

Reuben's face is slack. I think he's trying to figure out if he'd rather laugh or throw me out of his office. "That's some dark shit."

"Yeah. And it's not even the half of it." I don't even go into the story of Nightingale and how I fucked her life up, or Noah.

Damn, I miss them.

I walk towards the window and stand in the full sun that's shining through. The darkness is strong today and it's gonna take a whole hell of a lot of liquor to quell.

"I should probably go." I head for the door.

"Come back in a few days." Reuben waves. "And stay out of trouble."

...

I sit on the beach until happy hour, trying to ignore the sounds of the tropical parrots and seabirds. I try to remember that I'm in paradise; there will be no bitter winters here, no kerosene fumes, no hostile angels, no terrifying Hellions, no parental units interfering in my life. No... Sparrow. My eyes start to burn which is a clear indication that I must start with my nightly inebriation.

I stand, walk away from the ocean and head for the sidewalk. I control the urge to take off my flip-flops and soak in the heat of the concrete that's been collecting the sun's warmth all day. I almost miss the sweltering heat of Heaven, would nearly put up with it if that meant I could have Nightingale or Noah back in my life.

The walk to the bar that I frequent is short. I pass beach houses painted obnoxious colors, cheap hotels, and shops selling plastic crap from China. I flick the ring on my left hand with my thumb; the one Sparrow gave me for Christmas. It's started turning my finger green. I can't wear it everyday like I used to.

I open the door to Sal's Bar, make my way to the far end of the counter, order the same thing as every night: four shots of Fireball.

I pace myself; take a shot every six minutes. By the fifth one the numbing heat reaches my cheekbones. The burn will takeover my brain in no time. I order four more. The bartender only brings me two.

Read Scarecrow on Kindle

Printed in the USA
CPSIA information can be obtained
at www.ICGtesting.com
JSHW020101081023
49545JS00004B/146